To: Melody Ragan —

MARY BUCKHAM
AWARD WINNING AUTHOR

INVISIBLE RECRUIT SERIES

INVISIBLE POWER
BOOK 2: ALEX NOZIAK

May you always feel visible — unless you want otherwise!

Mary Buckham

INVISIBLE POWER
Copyright © 2013, Mary Arsenault Buckham
First Edition
ISBN 978-1-939210-11-1
All rights reserved.

By payment of required fees, you have been granted the *non*-exclusive, *non*-transferable right to access and read the text of this eBook. No part of this text may be reproduced, transmitted, downloaded, decompiled, reverse engineered, or stored in or introduced into any information storage and retrieval system, in any form or by any means, whether electronic or mechanical, now known or hereinafter invented without the express written permission of copyright owner.

Please Note

This is a work of fiction. Names, characters, places, and incidents either are the product of the author's imagination or are used fictitiously, and any resemblance to actual persons, living or dead, business establishments, events or locales is entirely coincidental.

The reverse engineering, uploading, and/or distributing of this eBook via the internet or via any other means without the permission of the copyright owner is illegal and punishable by law. Please purchase only authorized electronic editions, and do not participate in or encourage electronic piracy of copyrighted materials. Your support of the author's rights is appreciated

Cover and book design by
THE KILLION GROUP
www.thekilliongroupinc.com

DEDICATION

This book is dedicated to my dad who passed away during the writing of the story. He was my earliest storyteller, who made the world a better place for being in it. I'll miss you dad and hope I can live up to your legacy!

ACKNOWLEDGEMENTS

It takes a village to create a book and this book is no acceptation. A huge note of appreciation to the following who helped so much in making sure the story held together: Laurie G Adams, Cari Gunsullas, Debbie Kaufman, Dorothy Callahan and Deborah Anderson. Thanks for being such amazing readers of this story. You guys rock! A special thanks to Mimi Munk for copyediting, you are my Grammar Goddess. Also, a huge hug to Dianna Love for her support and lovely cover quote. And, of course, thank you to my husband who keeps me sane—which is a full time job! Any mistakes or adjustments in detail for the purpose of fiction are entirely my own doing.

CHAPTER 1

"Team report," I spoke the words calmly, coolly even, nothing like my insides felt, jumping a mile a minute. The nerves were part anticipation, part terror.

The next minutes would change everything.

I'm Alex Noziak, a witch/shaman in the temporary employment of the IR Agency. I for invisible, R for recruit, and calling any of my five-member team employed was a load of crock. I was here as an alternative to prison. Long story boiled down to a year's agreement to be a member of a small, highly secret organization meant to combat a rising tide of preternatural agitation against humans. Fancy words for saying five of us stood against who knew how many species that, until lately, were mostly content to stay hidden from human eyes.

So here I was, in the exotic city of Paris, lounging on a street corner, a baby buggy in front of me, dressed like a down-on-her-luck Parisian mother. I had my waist-length braid of hair tucked up under a cheap hat that was itching like crazy and enough makeup on my face to disguise my Native American skin tones. I'd considered using an appearance spell then discarded it. Not that I liked looking like I'd bought every kind of cosmetic Walmart had to offer and used all of it at once, but magic was something I used with extreme caution.

Why? Because it always exacted a price and I was still smarting from my last bout with spell casting. That and a run-in with a demonic African witch doctor.

About two months ago it became apparent that someone, or something, was no longer happy with the status quo of humans being blithely unaware that there were more than themselves populating the planet. Preternaturals had their reasons for flying under the radar, for many of them survival being the biggest reason. Humans tended to kill first and ask questions later when they dealt with anything they perceived as a threat. If you don't believe me consider the poor cockroach. As if a bug that small was really going to do something to them. Non-humans, like most squishy, squirmy bugs, fell squarely under the category of dead must be better.

But someone wanted to change all that and my job, along with my five teammates, was to stop it from happening.

Team leader Vaughn, who was sitting at a nearby café table, sipping espresso and looking more French than the locals, was I assumed fully human. She also was a socialite, pampered money, and stunning looks; more than that though, she was willing to put her life on the line for a cause, protecting those who didn't know they needed protection.

Then there was Kelly, a former kindergarten teacher who was so nice I kept waiting for the catch. Her gift was the ability to turn invisible for short bursts of time. Drawback was, she was still learning how to get a handle on not popping away when stressed or scared. Right now she was playing tourist, complete with a crumpled map, a camera, and a vacuous expression on her face as she looked around the seedy neighborhood. She fit the role so well even I believed she was lost.

She was waiting for my signal to do her thing, become invisible and reconnoiter our target and mission accomplished. A quick get-in-and-get-out-in-one-piece job. Piece of cake.

Jaylene Smart and Mandy Reyes were the two other team members, lounging against a far wall, looking, except for the cast on Mandy's arm like hookers trolling for johns among a few other women doing the same thing. Jaylene, tall, gorgeous, and African American was a psychic, which meant she saw the future. Not always in technicolor or clearly, but that was the challenge with gifts, you had to take the bad with the good.

Hispanic Mandy was a soulless spirit walker; someone who like me, could pass over to the spirit world. Difference was I remained a shaman when I traveled between realms. She might as well have worn a neon sign that flashed corporal-body-ready-to-be-inhabited to any spirit with enough chutzpah to try.

I figured the reason some spirit hadn't succeeded yet was only because they were wary of Mandy's abrasive personality. Smart spirits.

M.T. Stone was our team instructor, and as we had yet to finish our training, was here with us for support. Since he'd nearly died on our last mission, one that was supposed to be easy, I took it as a good sign. He'd barely left a German hospital so his presence was meant for tactical support. He was dressed as a Parisian workman in a one-piece paint-splattered coverall, poking at a chip in a stucco wall. He should have looked harmless but there was nothing harmless about him. One close look and most people's first reaction was to step back, those who hadn't already taken off running.

"Team, report," I repeated, getting antsy, as operational leader. I had the most at stake on this mission. Our primary goal was catching a man named Vaverek and all we had was a faint description: broad shouldered, stocky, dark-haired, who was supposed to be living in the second floor, front right flat in the building across the street, a building so old that if Stone kept picking at it might crumble.

We were to verify the intel that this was his hidey-hole and withdraw, period. no matter how much I wanted us to go in, blast his door open and take him out, after he told me what I wanted to hear. With two of the six of us on the recuperation list we weren't up to doing anything more, even with at least two snipers on nearby rooftops to help us if we needed backup.

Vaverek was the man behind a dangerous synthetic drug used against humans so far that could force them to commit crimes without their knowledge. Two weeks ago we'd stopped two of the women involved in testing the drug on unsuspecting victims. We also managed to seize a sizeable amount of the drug, which should have been a high-five moment for the team, and for me as point on that operation.

The moment lasted a lot less than sixty seconds when a containment spell I'd cast backfired and killed our two chief suspects before they could give us any leads to their power brokers, the individuals who financially backed the scheme, and who might still have enough of the drug, or worse, the formula, to pose a threat.

But there was more. Vaverek was also our only link to the increasingly dangerous agitation among the world's non-human population. We needed to know who Vaverek was working for, as well as free the man Vaverek held hostage.

My brother.

CHAPTER 2

"You sure you got your intel straight?" Mandy snarled into her comm link. "These shoes are killing me."

Poor baby. I didn't appreciate being second-guessed, especially by someone who sat most of the last mission out.

"Can it," I cut her off. "Intel's good."

Or I hoped like hell it was. Given the source was a man who'd threatened to kill me last time we'd met, there was a definite degree of doubt riding me. The same man had been my lover the week before that. Oh, and did I mention, the man whose beloved cousin was one of the two women I'd killed?

It'd been a busy couple of weeks. And that didn't count the side trip to Africa, Stone being almost killed, and my facing a Yoruba witch doctor who was one nasty crazy SOB. Then there was a djinn who belonged in his own category of scary.

"We'll give Kelly another ten minutes to get rid of her new French friends before she moves in." Stone's voice washed over the comm.

Ten? What about five instead? It wasn't his brother being held and tortured by Vaverek. On the other hand, standing around wasn't getting us any closer to our quarry. Stone was right. Time to kick this op into fast-forward.

I straightened my shoulders, stretched to touch the Glock 22mm with silver bullets in a shoulder harness under my nubby sweater. The weapon was a fall back option since Vaverek was a Were, but I didn't expect to use it. Better safe than sorry.

What I really wanted to do was to walk across the cobbles, shoo away the French talking to Kelly or, if that didn't work, march up the stairs I could see from where I stood, and knock on Vaverek's door.

I'd figure out the rest of the plan at that point. Noziaks were more kick down doors and ask forgiveness afterwards types, so I was acting true to my gene pool. And we wouldn't have to keep cooling our heels in this backwater neighborhood.

A quick glance up and down the street revealed about a dozen civilians milling about, in the café with Vaughn, with a few hookers around Jaylene and Mandy. The nice looking elderly couple using hand gestures to explain directions to Kelly were taking their sweet time. I mentally wanted to shout at Kelly to move them along but she was too nice for her own good.

If I crossed quickly, kept Vaverek contained to his own apartment, and called in the team for my backup once I was inside, my frontal assault could contain him. I could pretend I was lost, look clueless and back out. That would also save putting Kelly at risk. She might have volunteered for her role in this op but Stone had done the same thing in Rwanda and look what happened to him.

I was just about to step forward when a hand to my shoulder stopped me.

No Frenchman would be so bold, no team member was close enough, and no bad guy would use this kind of approach. That left one person. Bran. Warlock, former lover, current nemesis.

I snarled as I glanced at him over my shoulder. Tall, dark and dangerous basically summed him up as I ignored the flip-flop of my insides created by just looking at the man. Focus on the job at hand.

"You aren't supposed to be here."

"I have as much at stake as you do."

I understood he was still grieving his cousin Dominique's death, even if she was a sadistic psycho-killer, and that he blamed Vaverek for involving her in the high-stake world of designer drugs and fatalities. But that didn't give him a right to insert himself into this mission.

I kept turned toward Vaverek's apartment building. Never lose sight of the primary target, even if it meant having the biggest threat at my back. "If you kill Vaverek," I said between clenched teeth, "I lose the only lead to my brother."

"If I get a shot at him I'm taking it." I was ready to pull my Glock on Bran, until he added, "But I won't kill him before I get from him what I want. Vaverek's the head of an organization but he's not working alone. I want to know who Vaverek reports to before I eliminate him."

I knew the first part, but not how badly Bran wanted the second part. Leave him to muddle this mission before we ever got started. But we could agree on something. Identify and contain Vaverek.

"Then stay put. I'm going in," I said, not loud enough my team could hear, but loud enough to let Bran know I meant business.

I expected him to release his hold. Instead he gripped tighter.

"You have no idea what you're about to unleash here."

Bran was a warlock with an over-protective streak, one a good mile wide. It was that need to protect that had him shield his cousin far too long, and try to keep me from harm, even though he knew what my job was, and that I was perfectly capable of protecting myself.

What did he know that I didn't?

I glanced at him again over my shoulder. "What the hell are you talking about?" I snarled. "You're the one who told us that the target should be inside that building."

"Your snipers on the roofs have been neutralized."

"What?" It took all my limited training not to spin around and shout at him. That was some bomb he just dropped on me.

His fingers bit so hard into my shoulder they'd leave bruises. "Stop looking with your eyes, witch. Look around you."

I had. I was.

"Close your eyes and look with your inner senses."

My inner senses told me he was playing his own deadly game, but he was also a powerful warlock, strong enough to pull people back from the dead, and he had a lot more experience than I did using magic.

I'd give him sixty seconds. But that was it.

So I closed my eyes, aware of my pounding pulse, the kiss of a breeze picking up bringing the scent of fresh baked beignets, the peal of bells echoing through stone and stucco streets.

"There's nothing—"

And that's when it hit. The wash of otherness seeping through my awareness. Several Weres, strong enough to hide their scent. At least one vamp, maybe two. I couldn't quite identify the others, not from this far away. Fae maybe. A demon, and something else.

My eyes snapped open. Why hadn't I sensed them until now? I glanced at my silver ring, specially crafted to alert me to non-humans. Nothing. No heat, no humming, nothing.

But they were there. Infiltrating the street. Surrounding my teammates.

"Abort. Abort," I spoke into my comm set. "Get the hell out. Now!"

CHAPTER 3

My gaze hopscotched around the street, pinpointing my teammates in arrested movement, even as I lunged forward from my shadowed doorway.

"What the. . . " Mandy's oath dribbled off as the two locals Kelly had been chatting with suddenly showed fangs.

Bad news, all of us, except Stone, were too far away to protect Kelly. Good news, we didn't have to as she winked out of sight. Now I had to hope that vamps couldn't identify her by her smell or the sound of her heartbeat.

I'd assume one safe, three teammates to go, but the area was already in a whir of motion. A Were, who'd shifted so fast he was a blur, was now a fully adult male baboon with tawny fur, a pinkish snout and massive swinging arms. He was circling a very wary Stone. Stone was taller and held his mason's joiner in front of him, but my money was on the baboon that looked a hell of a lot meaner and angrier. And if you'd dealt with Stone on a bad day you knew that was saying something.

Still I'd take the baboon over the Were tiger that was crouching for a leap at Mandy and Jaylene, both fighting tooth and toenail with their fellow whores now revealed as demons. Both demons had shed clothes and morphed forms, now one was naked with skin of checked squares of green and blue, the other was full red with white spots trailing her spine and ribcage. Must be felon demons; quick and nasty types. Still the Were tiger would wipe out everyone it could reach with its teeth or claws.

Vaughn, stationed on the other side of the street, saw the problem but even as she was rising to her feet a Snobble Troll lumbered from inside the café, straight at her. Think ten feet tall, scaly purple rhino hide, two heads, both with slobbering mouths and wicked fast. No way could Vaughn take the troll out; all she could do was hope to avoid it until help arrived.

That was my role. The first target was stopping the Were tiger. But how?

I hadn't come prepared to use magic. Stupid, I know, but I was still adjusting to the use of white magic on a daily basis. Magic and I had this gotta-use-it-even-as-I-hate-it relationship. Right now was a use-it moment, but I had no candles, no herbs, no chalks to write runes. Squat diddley.

What I had was my words. But first I had to chuck my gun. One of the downsides to witchcraft was the inability to be armed when spell casting. Sort of the doctor's oath to do no harm thing. Only it left a witch pretty damned vulnerable when facing a Were or almost any other preternaturals.

But needs must. With one fluid movement I untucked my Glock and slid it along the cobblestone street as I uttered the first words of a containment spell.

"By water and by fire.
By air and by earth.
Be thee bound, as I command.
By thrice and by syce, I thee call. I thee bind.
By new moon, by old moon. Power I thee call.
My will be done.
Earth and air. Shield harm from me and mine.
Power bound, Light revealed.
I command thee. Be sealed."

The Were tiger froze mid-leap as my body jerked forward with the effort to keep the six-hundred pound beast in place. I plowed face first into the rough road, grit and rocks abrading all exposed skin. Only the French would still use cobbled streets, picturesque maybe, but wicked as hell.

"Alex!" It was Vaughn shouting as I rolled to my knees and looked her way. "Save Stone."

Stone?

Out of the corner of my eye I caught the blaze of fur and canvas that was Stone locked into a head-to-head embrace with the howling baboon. Too late I realized that even if smaller than Stone that ape-relative had jaws and teeth that could put a gorilla to shame. And right now the fur beast was aiming for Stone's exposed throat.

I staggered to my feet, most of my energy being used to tether the Were tiger. How much more did I have to help Stone?

Only one way to find out.

Another binding spell? Never heard of being able to bind two different threats in opposite directions at once.

The baboon screamed louder, sending goosebumps racing up my spine.

I wouldn't know for sure if I didn't try.

"Air to wind, earth to dust.
By water and by fire.
Trouble to heed and trouble to find.
Compel. Coerce. Constrain.
I thee call. I thee command.
Threat be gone. Power be bound."

But nothing happened.

CHAPTER 4

Power to the Spirits, what now? Where was Bran and why wasn't he helping me? Not that I expected White Knight stuff, but a little magic help would be nice. There wasn't enough time to look around for him. I needed help now.

Even a squirt gun would be helpful. Then I spied it.

I slipped to one knee, my whole body twanging as my kneecap smashed into centuries old cobbles. But my focus was one hundred percent on my Glock.

Grab it and use it on the baboon without shooting Stone? Odds weren't good. In fact they downright sucked, like hitting a person's shadow at high noon without hitting them. Plus using the weapon would nullify the binding spell on the Were. Suck and suckier.

Too bad Noziaks tend to fight the hardest when the odds are at their worst.

I lunged forward for the gun, face planting once again but my fingers curled around the grip.

A quick roll and pivot, coming to one knee and aiming.

Try to hit fur over Stone, or shoot above them both to scare the baboon?

That's when I saw it. Monkey butt. Or better yet, the telltale red of an adult baboon's backside.

Fur butt it was.

I shot and all hell broke loose. The baboon released a hair-curling screech but it dropped Stone who crumpled to the ground in a Star Trek roll and run he'd have to show me how to do some day. The baboon scampered off to nurse his backside.

Just then the troll smashed both massive fists into the café table Vaughn had been using to ward it off, ripping it like cheap paper. And the Were tiger blasted upwards, catapulted forward as the binding spell evaporated.

Gun wouldn't work on a troll with a hide that made Kevlar look thin. Mandy and Jaylene beat-feet it backwards with the dynamic demon duo crawling over them as the tiger roared, shaking the foundations of the decades old buildings. At least the vampires weren't—wait, I spoke too soon. They were swooping in on Stone.

CHAPTER 5

Like a love match made in hell, I watched the vamp tackle Stone and both roll together, hands locked around each others' necks. The vamp trying to pull Stone closer, Stone stiff-arming it to keep from becoming a blood lunch.

Triage. Who needed the most help the fastest?

Mandy and Jaylene had silver shurikens as weapons so they were on their own, even as I wondered how they'd get enough maneuverability to throw the stars. Not my priority problem yet.

"Alex. Duck!"

I jumped toward Vaughn when I heard the shout behind me even before I registered who had called out. Bran. So he was still around. I'd almost forgotten about him. As if that was ever going to happen. Quick note to self: mayhem and near death help one forget a pulverized heart.

Even if I didn't trust Bran further than I could move him, which wasn't much, I crouched down and just in time. With a piercing scream and killer talons a falconi dove toward my head and missed me by inches. Think of an Utahraptor, a dinosaur killing machine that could weigh as much as a ton and had a single claw, like a medieval broadsword, with the speed of a peregrine falcon and you'll have an idea of what a falconi is. This one was young, so no bigger than a refrigerator, but that meant even faster.

Back at the IR Agency our instructor of bestiary and mythology, Fraulein Fassbinder, would love knowing about all the preternaturals we were rumbling with today. If we survived.

And if we did survive I wanted extra credit for learning enough to recognize preternaturals that less than a month ago I only knew existed in fairytale books.

Right now I was in the open. In the middle of a street. With no cover.

Talk about making it easy for the damn thing to kill me.

I aimed my Glock skyward as it dove and rose, dove and rose, but it was like shooting at a tornado funnel, worse than useless.

So I sprinted, keeping one eye glued to the sky as I crouched and ran, hoping I didn't break my neck on the cobblestones.

The café awning had been demolished by the Snobble troll. No cowering there. There wasn't even a vehicle in sight to dive under. Where was a doorway when I needed one?

Then it hit me. An idea. Chancy but I didn't have a lot of options.

I rocketed as fast as I could toward Vaughn who was holding off the troll with the metal leg of a café chair, everything else around her—tables, dishware, chairs—pulverized.

With only a fleeting thought of survival I raced past Vaughn and leaped toward the troll, hitting its rough hide, and, like a dozen aunties hugging at a funeral, I latched on to the troll's side beneath his stinky armpit, with one hand wrapped around his neck and clung for dear life.

I'd had stupider ideas but right then couldn't think of one.

CHAPTER 6

Like a flea clinging to the backside of a rabid dog, I hoped I didn't have to hold on for long. The troll had turned its attention from Vaughn and was now swinging its massive club-sized arms in my direction, which hurt like hell when it could connect, but at least it was focused on me and not the shadow I brought with me.

One thing that could be said about falconis was they might be lethal and wicked fast, but they also possessed bird-sized brains in spite of their girth. Right on time my air nemesis dove, and hit the troll instead of me.

As I released my grip I rolled into a boneless heap, avoiding the feet of a pissed off troll who had no idea what just hit him but was now mad enough to go on the offensive, and away from me, anyway.

Vaughn grabbed my arm and hauled me upright but she wasn't focused on me, she was looking at Stone drooping beneath his attacking vamp. I was impressed he'd lasted this long, but that was going to change quick unless we helped him. I had dropped my Glock to grab troll hide so I was looking around for a potential stake or wedge of broken glass big enough to decapitate a wrestling vamp.

As if.

I glanced at Vaughn as she pushed past me, not toward Stone, but away from him, which shocked the hell out of me. They were cuddle buddies, so why wasn't she running to him . . .ah, I saw what she was doing. Looking for her purse, which meant her gun and silver bullets.

With a very unladylike shout of success she dove for a small hand clutch that I couldn't have stuffed a used Kleenex into, but she pulled out a lethal looking Mossberg Brownie 22-cal derringer. That should take care of the vamp.

Great. Let her save Stone. Other team members needed help. My help.

As I raised my head to scan the other side of the street my heart stuttered.

Where before Mandy and Jaylene had faced two demons and a Were tiger, now I could barely see them in the midst of a preternatural onslaught that made a biker gang rumble look like tea with the queen.

With four pops of Vaughn's gun saving Stone's hide behind me I stumbled forward to help Mandy and Jaylene.

Between them and us, the Were tiger crouched in a defensive huddle, blood streaming down one useless paw, but he didn't seem to need it as he swiped and batted with his other good one at a pole poking at him. Like a lion tamer's thrust, the pole, which looked like it previously held up the café's awning, now wove and jabbed, with no one holding it.

Kelly. Must be her. Unless we had spirits working on our side, which wasn't likely.

Behind her were the real problems. The original felony demons had been joined by at least three fae, each one uglier and meaner looking than the last, the other vamp who'd previously been talking with Kelly before everything went to hell, and what looked like an Amphivena. At least I thought it was based on Fraulein Fassbinder's lectures. Could this day get any worse?

An Amphivena was a snake as long as a boa constrictor, with glowing orange eyes and a head at each end, which meant it could attack in either direction and do so in the space of a heartbeat. And that wasn't the worst part. It also possessed venom, which if injected into a human, even in a minute amount, created a wound that never healed, meaning a long, slow, painful death.

Aren't we having fun.

Hands on knees, chugging air for all I was worth I paused, trying to see where I could help and not hinder. That's when I caught sight of Jaylene clicking her empty gun and tossing it to bounce off the head of the white and red felony demon. Mandy was using her cast as a billy club, which meant she had no silver or any other bullets left. If they fell, the rest of us weren't far behind.

What the hell was I going to do? Another containment spell? Not with a group this size. I needed to freeze them, but I didn't know that spell.

Like a wallop alongside the head it came to me. I might not know the spell but I knew a bad-ass warlock who did.

CHAPTER 7

"Bran!" I shouted at the top of my lungs, not knowing where he was or if he'd even answer.

"You called?"

Damn him, he was right behind me. Leave it to a warlock to scare the pants off me in the middle of a smack down with a dozen preternaturals. I straightened and glanced at him over my shoulder.

"I need your help."

He arched one arrogant brow that made me want to slug him. But I didn't have time. Now.

"I need to link."

"Because?"

Oh for the love of the Goddess could he be more difficult?

"They're going to die." I waved my hand toward my teammates. "Unless we can do a freeze spell."

"We?"

"Yes, you and me."

"Last time we did you killed my cousin."

Only a warlock would bring that up at a time like this. A quick look forward told me Jaylene was down on one knee and Mandy wasn't far behind.

"Fine. I'll do it myself." Which I couldn't and we both knew it. For one thing I didn't have the spell to the freeze time part, only the containment part. And no way did I have enough power alone to stop so many people. I hadn't even been able to hold a Were tiger and a baboon at the same time.

But if I did nothing they'd die.

Turning my back on Bran I stepped forward, narrowing my eyes and sucking in a deep breath to calm my racing heart.

"Seriously, Alex, you're going to try this alone?"

I ignored him. It wasn't like there were a dozen powerful magical creatures lining up behind me to help.

Balance. Focus. Intention.

Skip the time element and go for the containment spell even if it failed last time.

Exhaling slowly I started the chant, *"Continere. Continere. Continere."*

"You'll kill yourself," he mumbled behind me, his words ice cold.

"Save you the trouble," I shot back, my tone telling him to back off. I meant it.

Only days ago he'd promised to kill me if I didn't track down and apprehend Vaverek. Well I couldn't do that without my team. But more than that these women had become my friends. Okay, not all of them, but some of them and as long as I could breathe I wouldn't let them die. With or without the help of one arrogant, stick-up-his-butt warlock.

Even as I inhaled to continue the chant I heard him. "Alright."

I exhaled, relief flooding me.

Then he added, "But only because I still need you to track down Vaverek."

"Of course." I said it in a smarmy voice, but he'd earned that. But he just stood there. I shot him a what-are-you-waiting-for glance. "We don't have a lot of time. Could you get started?"

He tightened his jaw then nudged me aside to focus his Celtic blue gaze on the mess before us.

"Hemma, hanna, druia." He chanted, a low, deep baritone, the words so ancient I didn't know their origin, but I could feel their punch. Right in the solar plexus. *"Hemma, druia, sanctum."*

That was it. If he manipulated time just a smidge I could do the rest.

I pushed forward until my shoulder brushed his and joined my voice with his, *"Continere. Continere. Continere."*

Like a wind tunnel beginning its process of morphing into a killer tornado I could feel the power tugging, building, but it wasn't enough, not near enough.

I willed Bran to try harder, work faster, do something more and then I felt it, the sweet siren song of power calling my name.

Like a childhood rhyme the words thrummed within me, taunting me. I didn't have to rely on Bran. I had everything within me and more.

No. My father's voice echoed through me. Never, Alex. Remember your promise.

But here? With good people's lives on the line, he'd understand. He'd have to understand.

He's not here. This wasn't my dad but another voice whispering around me. A calming voice. Feminine. Nurturing.

Mom?

It's okay Alex. You were given the gift to use it, not hide from it.

But?

Do not be afraid. I'm with you.

And just like that I knew what I would do. What I had to do.

Swallowing deeply I stood taller and started pulling from Bran's magic. Making it my own.

Adeo. Adeo. Agero. Adepto.

Come. Come. Increase. Acquire.

"Don't, Alex," Bran whispered at my side. "It's too dangerous."

What did he know? He didn't care about me. He just wanted to use me.

Listen to yourself. I'm here with you. You're not alone. The woman's voice again. It had to be Mom. Who else could it be?

I steeled my own voice as I continued.

Suscipio. Solvo.

Receive. Break free.

I pulled words I didn't know I knew. Was my mother really here? Helping me?

Singluaris. Praesentia presencia.

Free the power.

Bran glanced at me, a frown knitted between his brows, but neither of us could speak. It was taking everything we had to weave the magic.

A heady rush washed against me so that I braced myself so I wasn't pulled, not only from Bran but all the other non-human abilities around us. And there were a lot of preternaturals in the street.

I stood statue-still in the nexus of a power vortex as I reveled in the potency roaring through me. Dangerous to everyone around. But not me.

This is what you're meant to do.

The woman's voice. I nodded, accepting.

Biting my lip till I drew blood, I tasted the copper taint and zeroed in. Thrice called, thrice to contain.

"As thou be, so now change. Thought to image. Image to bind. Bind to blood let."

I raised my hands skyward, aware of the swirl of grit and particles from the destroyed outdoor café whirling around us. One of the demons and two of the fae paused in their forward assault to look around them.

But they wouldn't be in time, because like a psychic vampire I tapped into their power too.

"*Continere. Continere. Continere,*" I shouted, feeling free, truly free.

A crack of thunder roared across the sunny day. A flash of white-gold light. Everyone on the street froze, then dropped, unconscious.

Even as my arms flopped to my side, drained, I caught a quick movement out of the corner of my eye. From the second story window the twitch of a lace curtain fluttered and fell into stillness.

Vaverek's apartment.

I sank to my knees and knew the worst. Whoever, whatever he was, he now knew my secret. He knew how powerful I could be, harnessing others, willingly or not. He knew there are only two things to do with a weapon like me.

Use me or destroy me.

CHAPTER 8

"I don't know what you did, or how you did it," Mandy groused less than an hour later, cradling her still healing arm with her good one. "But next time do it without the splitting headache aftermath."

"You're welcome," I mumbled, still too exhausted to even fight verbally with her. It wasn't the weariness weighing my bones though that was bothering me, it was the fear roiling through my stomach. What had I done? My arms trembled and I wiped sweat from my face as the Spring day chilled my skin.

As if echoing my thoughts, Stone limped up, glaring down at me. "You want to explain what the hell just happened?"

"We won?" I couldn't raise my gaze to his. My father had warned me about this, exposing my freakish ability. The first time my dad had seen me lose my temper and manipulate others' abilities he walloped me a good one then found me a witch mentor. I was barely fifteen, and that lasted about three months.

Second time I forgot and let my fear drive my actions, I'd ended up in prison. And today?

Today the team knew I was a loose cannon.

Why the hell I couldn't have just waited, seen if Bran could have stopped time long enough to extract my teammates and get the hell out of Dodge, or Paris?

Now even he had vamoosed, no doubt as wary of me as my teammates were. By the Spirits, they were smart to be.

I had to be the savior and throw caution to the wind. As if. And who was the woman speaking to me?

Too many questions, not enough answers.

"Talk to me, Noziak," Stone demanded, his voice ratcheted back to a low throttle. He looked wrung out, but then fighting a vampire at full form was not easy and he was far from full form. "Tell me what you did here?"

What he was really asking was what kind of scary freak are you and should we cut our losses now and send you back to prison? I could read between the lines.

I'd taken their power from them. What was the price going to be for that? There would be a price and I wouldn't be able to hide from it.

Stone had been the one who'd rounded up the dead preternaturals and disposed of them. But why did they all die? Had my sucking their power killed them? A question that I could tell was bothering Stone, and me. Connecting what I'd done to those deaths meant I was going to be out of the agency so fast I'd get whiplash. But that was better than what could happen to me if the Council of Seven learned I was what I was.

Talk about being between the rock and a hard place.

The Council was ruled by seven beings who'd earned a seat for life and who held ultimate power among all the preternaturals, non-humans and magic-endowed people like me. The Council's sole function was to keep the knowledge of non-humans from humans and sometimes that took draconian measures.

Not that I was losing any grief over the Weres, demons, fae and other assorted beasties that we'd just contained. It had been a near call that we were the victors and not being carted off in body bags, what pieces of us that would have been left.

At least that's what I told myself. I was glad to be alive and glad my team was alive too, but I wanted to spew out everything in my stomach just thinking about the ramifications of my actions. I was still shaking from the use of so much strong magic. Or was it from the lure of holding such power over others; too much power, seductive and still calling to me. This made black magic look like child's play.

I hunched over on a curb near the demolished café. How did I undo what had just happened? Hope only Stone was aware of the ramifications? Pray to the Great Spirits that the others had been too busy fighting to know exactly what went down? Sneak away now before Jaylene and Vaughn joined us?

Kelly was already sitting to my left. She couldn't see the destruction around us, because as a side effect of her ability to turn literally invisible, for every minute of transparency she experienced, she was blind for double the time once she popped back into corporal form. She might accept what I'd done but I doubted the others would.

Vaughn and Jaylene had just checked Vaverek's apartment, which had been sanitized, but they were standing far enough away with their backs to me that I could make a dash, if my legs could hold me.

"Thought your intel was supposed to be good," Mandy continued to grumble at my side. But at least she was shifting the conversation away from my magic spell casting. Stone's look said he wasn't finished with me yet, so I'd better enjoy my reprieve.

Trust me, Mandy couldn't kick me any harder than I was kicking myself. "Technically Vaverek *was* in that apartment."

"So you say." Mandy shot me one of her patented WTF looks. "But your informant didn't share he was there as bait. I thought your warlock wanted to track down Vaverek."

"He does." I ignored Mandy's first statement. I doubted that she wanted to hear that Bran had warned us, only it was almost too late. And he didn't want Vaverek except as a means to another end. And Vaverek was dead once Bran had the intel he wanted.

Keep talking about Bran, not about what I'd done.

"Lay off her, Mandy," Stone said. "Some ops go belly up."

I glanced at him, not sure I'd heard him right. The kick-ass and take-no-prisoners instructor was giving me a break? Or a small, additional reprieve before he struck?

My shoulders sagged as I fought to keep my stomach contents down.

Mandy eyed him too, but before she could verbally launch into him he surveyed the street and spoke as if to himself. "Vaverek must have damn good intel to know who we are and that we were coming."

"Could he have used a seer?" I asked, not wanting to look at the other possibilities, especially ones involving warlocks betraying us. One warlock in particular.

Or maybe it was Bran who had set us up to see if I could do what I just did?

By the Mother Goddess that made things worse.

Stone glanced away, examining the street as if seeking insights there. "Vaverek had enough lead time to empty the street of humans and bring in reinforcements. These weren't bodyguards, but a group specifically assembled to stop us. To test us in several ways. Which is why they had us surrounded before we even tumbled to them."

I glanced at the silver ring on my finger, designed to alert us to the presence of preternaturals. Sort of an early warning device. "Why didn't the rings work?" I asked, not really expecting an answer.

"I'm going to make sure I find out," Stone promised with a tone that said when he did it wasn't going to be pretty.

"Find out what?" Vaughn asked as she and Jaylene walked up and joined us. All of us looked pretty worse for wear, except her. I swear the woman had to be non-human to look that put together after battling preternaturals. I willed her not to bring up what happened at the end.

Bless her heart, she didn't, though she gave me a smooth look that said we'll-be-talking-later.

Not if I could help it.

"The set up this morning was too good, too orchestrated and too smooth to be reactive," Stone replied, rubbing one hand along the back of his neck. "Vaverek, whoever the hell he is, has some good inside connections."

"Didn't we already know that?" Kelly was the only one amongst us, other than Vaughn, who might call Stone on something and not regret it for the rest of her life. "Alex brought the intel from her last assignment that suggested Vaverek was involved with something called the Seekers."

"Something or someone," I mumbled. "All we know after nearly getting killed is that Vaverek is a stronger adversary than we thought, has more resources available than we assumed, and is willing to risk a dozen preternaturals to find out our strengths and weaknesses."

"Nice summation." Jaylene nodded, arms crossed. "I'd say Vaverek one, the IR Agency zero. Even with whatever Alex just pulled off."

I shook my head, regret making it hard to even spin back a response.

"So what now?" Kelly looked around as if trying to read our expressions behind her still-blind eyes.

No one answered right away. Though I noted everyone kept their gazes averted from mine.

I stood to shake off my lethargy. Noziaks don't mope. Well, not for long. All I managed to accomplish though was to set off the bongo drums in my head.

I squared my shoulders before I spoke. "Jaylene's wrong."

"About what?" Mandy stepped forward to defend her ally. I had to give her credit for being willing to mess with me after what she'd seen me do.

"It's Vaverek two, IR Agency zip." I let my gaze rest on each of them individually, even sightless Kelly before I spoke again. "Vaverek is still holding my brother hostage and Van's time is running out."

"If he's still alive."

Leave it to Chiquita-girl to stick the blade in and twist.

"Yeah, if he's alive." Like it or not I had to agree. Every hour that Van remained a prisoner meant that whatever torture he was going through would be successful. And once that intel was extracted, Van was no longer needed.

Think about him. Not me and my screw up.

My brother knew a heap-lot about the preternaturals who worked with humans, particularly in Europe, even if those humans didn't know who, or what, were rubbing shoulders with them. Expose those non-humans and all hell would break out; pogroms, witch-hunts, mass stakings of anyone assumed to be a preternatural. The Council of Seven would no longer be able to hide the existence of non-humans and neighbor would be eyeing neighbor worldwide.

"You look like you have a plan." Vaughn's voice shook me from my dark thoughts. "It'd better include all of us."

Not what I wanted right then. What I had in mind was better accomplished witch-to-warlock. Alone. "Yeah, I do."

"Going to share?" Jaylene nudged.

"Vaverek may have won this round." I scuffed my beat up shoe against the sidewalk, wondering how I was going to get what I wanted, a free hand, only make it seem like someone else's idea. "But there are five of us, six including Stone."

"Don't forget Ling Mai." Kelly came to her feet.

Jaylene snorted. "Yeah, she's a nuke all on her own."

Ling Mai was the head of our agency and Jaylene was right. Our secret weapon working behind the scenes.

"So we have seven to one." I was just warming up. "Surely between us we can find and nail this bastard."

Mandy played devil's advocate. "Paris is a big city."

"But we've already destroyed a city block and the morning's still young." Use humor to deflect them from looking too closely at what I wanted to do, which was a solo mission.

Stone stepped into the mix. "You're saying let's get a move on it."

"Yeah." I nodded. "Play to our strengths. Ferret out where this guy's hiding. How he connects with the troop he sent after us. Rattle some people."

Stone shrugged, then shot a lightning fast, and sexy grin at Vaughn. "Princess, you should have some contacts here from your days as an ambassador's daughter."

"Damn right I do," she purred back. "Bet I get a lead on Vaverek before you do."

"You're on." Stone had to have some Irish in him to rise to the bait that easily. Either that or there was an unstated sub-bet going on, not that I needed the details.

But at least two of them were heading out on their own. Three left to take care of.

"I don't know a lot of French but I do know the underbelly of a city." Jaylene stepped forward. "I'm sure I can shake loose something."

"I can help," Mandy said, looking resigned. "I speak French."

We all glanced at her. Chiquita had hidden depths. Who knew?

"What about me?" Kelly piped up. "Once I get my sight back I should be able to do something."

"We need a coordinator. Someone we can all report to who will also be able to track all of us so no one runs into another Vaverek ambush."

"Playground monitor?" she replied with a small smile.

"Call it what you want, we still need you." Leave it to Vaughn to make a crap job sound like the lynchpin position. "We're stronger as a team. Less risky for all of us."

"I agree," Stone added, looking straight at me. "Now's the time to use what we have together. No individual heroics."

He looked at me in particular but waited until each of us nodded in assent. My nod must have been the least impressive, and Stone's frown indicated he'd noticed. But he said nothing.

"I'll go back to the Campanile then." Kelly's tone saying she'd make the best of being stuck at the cheap hotel we were staying at while the rest of us went hunting.

Stone threw a kibosh into my plans by clearly announcing, "Alex, you head out with Mandy and Jaylene. There's safety in numbers."

Yeah, right, as if I didn't know what he really wanted—them to keep an eye on me. I guess I should have been grateful that he didn't pull me off the team right then and there. On the other hand, knowing Stone as I'd come to know him over the last few weeks, I bet he was giving me just enough rope to hang myself.

Then he added, "Just in case your warlock was the one who set us up here, I want zero contact with him. By anyone."

Now Stone was a mind-reader? I plastered a yeah-okay smile on my face that didn't mean squat because I didn't trust my voice to sound like I was really going to do what he just ordered me to do.

It hadn't been that long since I'd become an IR team member and I was actually finding that I liked having these strong, focused women at my side. So ditching them now wasn't an easy step, but I felt it was a necessary step toward getting what I needed. And getting that meant going through Bran.

If I didn't take this chance to follow up on the one lead I had, who knew if I'd get another opportunity to head out on my own. Not that Mandy and Jaylene knew that was my plan, but they would.

First step, shake their company. Second step, find Bran and force him to see me. Third step, save my brother by doing the first two steps.

I could make this work.

I had to.

CHAPTER 9

Delmore Vaverek stood at his balcony window in the *7th arrondissement* glancing at the slate roofs across the street, the glaring white stone walls brightened by the high noon sun, listening to the childish shouts from the gardens of Champs de Mars nearby. But his attention was totally on what he'd just seen.

Was this the reason he'd been sent to acquire this witch? He'd heard she was powerful but *merde*, what he'd seen was not supposed to be able to happen. Or was what occurred outside his *pied-à-terre* the result of something else? What did the Americans call it? A sleight of hand. A scam.

Could this be what he'd been waiting to appear at last?

His cell phone rang and while he was inclined to ignore it, one look at the number had him answering before the end of the second ring.

"Vaverek speaking."

"So you survived your little fray?" The Druid on the other end of the line laughed his nasty, rasping laugh. "You may thank me now."

"I survived but so did all the members of this upstart agency. The same individuals you said would be easy to eliminate."

The sudden silence on the other end told Vaverek he'd earned the druid's attention. "And your people?"

"I would have thought you'd have heard by now." Vaverek wanted to share his own laugh but this man was dangerous, too dangerous to taunt lightly. "They are dead."

"All of them?"

"*Oui.*"

"*Merde.*"

Vaverek allowed himself a smile, knowing the Other could not see him. "Which means you must clean up the details on your end."

"How did you fail?" came the whiplash response.

"Oh, I did not fail." Vaverek lowered his voice though there was no one in his salon to overhear him as it'd been swept that morning for listening devices. Still one could not be too careful. "In fact, I learned more than I expected from this morning's fiasco."

"About the witch?"

"Yes." Vaverek stepped closer to rest one finger along the wavy panes of the two hundred year old window, aware how fragile so much of this world could be. His smile ratcheted up. "You did not share with me all of her amazing abilities."

"Explain."

"When we meet later. Not over the phone."

Vaverek heard the druid catch his breath. Anger? Or anticipation? Either way Vaverek was now the one with the upper hand and they both knew it.

"Fine. Until this evening."

"You won't be disappointed."

"I'd better not be." If Vaverek thought he'd gotten off lightly he was wrong as the other added, "And speaking of disappointments, how is our guest doing?"

Vaverek tightened his grip on the phone. "He still breathes." What did the other expect? One minute Vaverek's orders had been to use any means necessary to extract the information wanted, the next the prisoner was needed alive. It'd been a near miss but the orders were rescinded in time.

That rasping laugh again. "Will he be breathing as you conduct the next experiment?"

"I'll make sure he is."

"Good." Vavervek could almost see the druid nodding. "Still on for tomorrow?"

"No. I think it would be better to push it back to Wednesday."

"Because?"

"One day will not make a difference and I have decided to make some alterations to the original plans."

"Such as?"

"I think it would be more effective if his sister were present."

"You are forgetting she is mine. It's part of our agreement."

"I don't plan to sacrifice her. One Noziak's death is all we need."

"And if she is hurt, our agreement is finished. You understand?"

There was no mistaking the threat beneath the druid's tone. "A Were never forgets," Vaverek said.

What he didn't share was the presence of the other at the morning's event. His presence made the stakes higher, the risks greater, but without either the rewards would not be as sweet. How to capitalize on this new piece of knowledge was the key. A game changer as the Americans would say.

"You still there, my friend?" the voice jabbed at Vaverek.

"I am." But not for long. There were pieces to be put in place on the chessboard of life.

"Nothing else to report?"

"No." Not yet. Maybe not until it was too late for the other.

"I shall see you later then?"

"Until tonight."

Vaverek hung up before the druid could say more. No doubt there'd be a penalty for that small show of disrespect but he was willing to pay it to retain the upper hand. Vaverek was not just any Were, but of the *Erdő* clan, the mountain deep Weres that came out of Transylvania before mists were born. The ancient ones. Some said the original Weres.

Soon the druid would be currying Vaverek's favor and not the other way around. Vaverek now had the key.

Alex Noziak.

CHAPTER 10

"Forgive me, old friend, for this call but it's necessary."

Jebediah "Jeb" Noziak set his mug of thick coffee down on the porch rail of his ramshackle farm, knowing that when Philippe Cheverill called it was not to share good news. "You have learned something of my son?"

"No, but I am still seeking information."

Jeb released a sigh he did not realize he'd held. No news meant no body. Yet. Van was strong, and resourceful, and Jeb's visions had not shown his oldest son's corpse. So Jeb would hold on to that knowledge. There was little that he could do on the physical plane, as Idaho was thousands of miles from Paris. But working with the spirits, he could and had been doing much.

So had one of his oldest friends, Philippe, though druids did not usually go out of their way to be of service to others.

"Is this Council business then?" Jeb asked as silence lengthened on the other end of the line.

"Yes and no."

Philippe was a cautious man, not an obtuse one, so Jeb waited, leaning against the front porch post, watching the first rays of dawn kiss Antelope Butte in the distance. This had always been his favorite part of the day, early when the sun slowly revealed herself and all was fresh and new. Jeb did not think of himself as a romantic man nor a verbose one. Aideen, the woman he loved so wildly, so dangerously, had always said he never shared enough with her. Then one day it was too late.

He had tried since then to be both mother and father to his four sons and one daughter. Tried to fill the void left by their mother's abandonment. Tried to raise his offspring, each with their own abilities and talents, to be good people.

And they were. Even Alex, who had killed a man and was still paying the price. Just as Van was paying the price for being the type of man who took his responsibility as a soldier, as a citizen, so seriously.

Jeb wasn't sure why Van had disappeared, but the minute Van did, Jeb had started searching, seeking the truth, holding the knowledge from his other children so they would not feel the empty, gaping wound that Jeb felt every waking hour. Even as he watched dawn give way to morning.

"Jebediah, we must speak."

Was that not what they were doing? Or did Philippe wish to connect in the supernatural realm, though they both were aware there were listeners there, too. Dangerous ones.

Jeb found his tongue reluctant to voice what his soul knew. Even powerful shamans could break if bent under the burden of too much knowledge, too much pain. Yet his tone held no waver as he asked, "You are worried?"

"*Oui.*"

If there was one thing Jeb had tried to instill in his children it was responsibility, whether it was accepting punishment for a childish prank or facing the consequences for choices made. Jeb could do no less. "Tell me what it is you wish from me."

"Come to Paris."

The answer felt like a body blow. Jeb walked the earth of his forefathers, gained strength from his physical connection to the high desert country of his home. He rarely traveled beyond his self-imposed boundaries, unless called by the Council of Seven.

But Philippe was not the Council. One of its oldest members, yes, and that meant something as druids were known to be long lived, even older than many of the others on the Council. So why Paris? And why now?

Instead of asking, though, Jeb did what he knew his friend would do for him. "I shall find the next flight available."

"*Bon.*" Jeb could hear the relief in his friend's voice, which worried Jeb even more.

"I will contact you once I arrive." Jeb took a deep swallow of cooling coffee.

"I shall open my home to you," Philippe replied, then added. "but I ask a small request."

"Yes?"

"Tell no one you are coming."

"No others on the Council?"

"Especially them."

Now Jeb knew the situation was dire. Philippe took his position as senior Council member very seriously, often acting as the lone voice of reason between the various interests and factions. Since the Council included fae, shifters, vampires, witches and demons as well as shamans and druids, reason often butted heads with warring needs and ancient feuds. These seven members spoke not only for themselves but for the peoples and the beings not represented on the board, and there were many.

Juggling the needs of preternaturals made raising five children on his own seem smooth sailing in comparison. So why the sudden secrecy?

"I will speak to no one," he said, to allay his friend's concerns. "Until I speak with you."

"You are a true friend, *mon frère*."

Jeb knew Philippe used his word choices intentionally and being included as a brother meant a lot to both of them.

"I shall send Pádraig to meet you at Orly."

Pádraig was Philippe's newest protégé and Jeb had heard a lot about him, though they had never met. "I look forward to meeting this young man at last," he said. "And we shall see if he lives up to his name's birthright."

Philippe gave a soft chuckle, maybe surprised that Jeb would know the meaning of the Irish name. But then Aideen had been Irish through and through, her Celtic witch roots running deep.

Philippe's words broke Jeb's dark memories as the Frenchman spoke of his protégé's name. "To be born noble you mean? I think you will be as impressed by him as he will be by you. There's nothing greater I can give him than to share our friendship."

Jeb was truly touched. Yet Philippe wasn't finished. He cleared his throat.

"One more thing," he murmured, his voice suddenly lowered as if someone new had entered the room. "The request I just made to you..."

"To speak to no one of my coming?"

"*Oui*." A pregnant pause. "I ask that you extend that request to your own family."

This was asking a lot, as Jeb did not like to keep secrets from his children. Adult grown though they were, to him they were still his responsibility.

Before Jeb could reply, or even know his answer, Philippe added, "It will not be the first time," his voice solemn.

Jeb straightened, knowing what Philippe spoke about though neither had mentioned that event, or its cost. So why now?

"Before I placed the needs of the Council above my needs as a father," Jeb said, each word striking his heart. "And I have paid the price of that decision every day since."

"I am aware of this my friend."

But was he? Was he really?

The case the Council had reviewed was complex. The use of magic to stop a rogue Were from killing a shifter who was in the middle of his change and thus vulnerable to attack. One sibling trying to protect another. In a different situation a jury could hear all the details and the accused would have not only been hailed a hero, but allowed to go scot-free. But not in a world where humans must never learn of the presence of non-humans. And if the human jury could never learn of the extenuating circumstances then the verdict was a given before the trial ever started.

Jeb had been told to be happy that the death sentence had not been decreed. Scant condolence when he saw his youngest child, and his only daughter, leave the courtroom for a life sentence.

It wasn't Philippe's deciding vote cast that day on the Council last spring. The vote that sent Jeb's only daughter to prison.

It was Jeb's.

CHAPTER 11

I marched up to the very modern and very imposing glass building near the Neuilly Bridge, and stopped. Shaking Mandy and Jaylene had been easier than I'd expected. A quick detour to a public toilet to change out of my dowdy disguise, leaving my cell phone so it couldn't be tracked, and a simple cloaking spell. Yes, using the spell for personal gain was going to bite me, since all magic use came at a price. But today I was willing to pay it to get some answers and confronting Bran with my two shadow guards was not the way to pull info out of him.

Besides, I'd already earned so many black marks today between using powerful dark magic and killing preternaturals, I figured how much worse could the backlash get? And if my team asked me what happened to my phone I could say I'd lost it leaning over one of the many bridges crisscrossing Paris.

So here I was, ignoring the clouds whisking across the sun, leaving me wishing I'd brought along something warmer than my black hoodie, even as I shook myself to focus on the task at hand.

Leave it to Bran to house his Paris offices in not only the tallest building in the city, but one that, because of its alignment with the Louvre and *l"Arc de Triomphe*, thumbed its nose at the older, stubbier landmarks around it.

The three wings created a whirling, spinning wheel effect, reflecting the mid-morning light in all directions. It was enough to make me dizzy.

But if that's where Bran was, that's where I had to go.

As I shouldered past dark-suited men and women who looked down their noses at my jeans and sweatshirt garb, I wondered how they survived in this cold stone and steel city. The only trees around were lined up soldier-straight along the boulevards or regimented in contained parks. You couldn't even hear bird song over the surging traffic everywhere. The only wildlife were pigeons, and even they seemed to blend into the grays, whites and pale stone colors everywhere.

As I swung through the revolving door into a marble and glass foyer I admitted a wobbly smile. I was mentally bitching at the city when my real target was Bran. He belonged here and I didn't. It was as simple as that.

Taking me away from my Mud Lake, Idaho roots was one thing. But facing a man as powerful and arrogant as Bran in a place that suited him to a T, only threw up our differences more, made my stomach knot and my hands grow clammy.

Sure he'd said I was a stronger a witch than I believed was, but that had been at a time we were still on speaking terms. Before I'd managed to get his cousin killed. Besides, strong witches could control their abilities. My gifts were hit or miss and that wasn't good.

"Crap," I mumbled under my breath, wondering how the hell I found the CEO of Bran Inc. in a place this large with only enough French phrases to order breakfast and find a bathroom. And I had trouble with that.

Looking around I spied a half-moon desk with several young, snooty looking types behind it, acting busy and important, but at least they answed the questions of people who approached them. Either that or telling everyone to go to hell with tight smiles.

But I'd been born a Noziak, which meant being willing to face danger head on instead of crawling away, no matter how much the latter sounded like a great idea. What could a few suits do to me?

Using hand gestures that made me look like a windmill run amok I spoke to the first woman who was free behind the desk. *"Ou is Senor ..."* Damn that wasn't right. "Bran." I made a tall height gesture with my hands. "You know? Big mucky muck. Clothes?" This time I used both hands to indicate an hourglass figure, which caught the attention and earned humma-humma smiles from the nearest males on both sides of the desk.

Get real.

I could feel my face heating. "Bran?" I raised my voice, feeling like every stereotype of a stupid tourist who used volume over language skills. *"Monseigneur Bran. Dove?"* That was the French word for *where,* wasn't it?

Behind the desk the woman's nose pinched tighter, her smile so thin-lipped she was going to cut herself.

Hell, if I couldn't even find him how was I going to ream him a good one? Extra for putting me through this exercise in patience. Not my strong suit.

Blowing out a puff of air, I glanced around before trying a different approach. "Does anyone here speak English?" I asked, throwing up my arms.

"Of course," came the snippy reply from the woman whose look said so much more, and none of it flattering.

Bite me.

I was tempted to reach across the counter and curl my hands along the woman's precise navy-colored suit lapels and shake her a good one. Probably not the best move for American-French relations. So uncurling my fingers one at a time and pasting on a smile that said WTF loud and clear in several languages I asked, "Then how do I find him?"

"Fiftieth floor," came the snippy response.

Of course. Not the penthouse but damn near. Why hadn't I thought of that. A quick look around had me pausing again, turning back to the woman, already ignoring me like her life depended on it.

"Excuse me?" The woman didn't look up.

I cleared my throat. "Excuse me, Miss?"

Nada. The guy next to her cast us both a wary glance then went back to talking to a balding woman in front of him.

Okay, I'd tried to play nice. Now I'd play it the Noziak way. So I leaned forward and lowered my voice to a syrupy sweetness. "Hey bitch?"

That had the French woman's head snapping up.

"Yes, you," I continued, leaning even closer. "Where are the elevators?"

The woman waved to the west.

"*Merci.* And have a good day," I chirped, feeling so much better about bearding a warlock in his den.

CHAPTER 12

By the time I reached the fiftieth floor my optimism was flagging. Or maybe it was the uncomfortable carnival-ride feeling my stomach got every time I rode an elevator. Mud Lake didn't have enough buildings in it to need elevators past the third floor and most of them were so old I could run up the stairs and beat them to my destination.

That free-floating feeling got worse as I spoke to Bran's receptionist who looked like the twin of the woman downstairs.

"*Si non possible*," the receptionist shrugged and shook her head at the same time, which helped me get the message. Why didn't Bran have a bilingual receptionist? But who was I to complain, my only other language was sarcasm.

"*Pourquoi?*" I asked, glad of the one word I had down pat. Why?

The woman rolled off a spat of French that sounded nice but meant nothing to me. So I used the universal shrug and raised hand response I was learning to perfect.

"*Un* meeting. Very, very important." Why hadn't I thought about that? Of course Bran would be up to his sexy eyeballs in meetings. But it wasn't like I could make an appointment with him either. He'd probably like that, but I wouldn't and he'd no doubt blow me off.

So what now?

I glanced at the closed office door. Stay and wait like a good girl or barge in on this very important meeting?

Flashing a quick he-won't-blame-you-I-hope smile at the receptionist whose shoulders relaxed, I ambled over to a series of frou-frou chairs around a glass table. Trailing fingers along the magazines resting there, as if I read these all the time, not. I waited until the receptionist turned away before I marched to the door.

I was going in!

"*Mais, mademoiselle!*" the receptionist squawked. But it was too late, I was already bumping the door closed behind me on the incensed woman.

"It's not her fault," I said as I stepped deeper into the room just in case the receptionist decided to ram the door. Then I stopped, looking around at the space that made my dad's farmhouse look like a shanty in comparison. The floor to ceiling windows along one wall were enough to bling me blind even if they had that special glare-coating stuff on them. Feeling as disjointed as Kelly was after doing her disappearing act, I blinked to get oriented and then wished I hadn't.

I don't know what I expected. Maybe a lot of stuffed shirts with double chins sitting around a massive table. Wrong.

There were only two people in the room. One a stunning blond with mile-long legs lounging in a chair on my side of a massive desk, and Bran, glaring from the other side.

I was used to Bran's thunder frowns. He tended to use them a lot around me, but I wasn't used to facing women who belonged on magazine covers or in the Miss Universe contest. A new dress model for Bran's tours? Or someone else?

Refusing to feel the quick stab of jealousy that last thought created, I notched my chin up, steeled my voice and looked only at Bran. "We need to talk."

Bran opened his mouth as if to say something then thought better of it as he ran one hand through his devil-dark hair and shook his head. "Miss Worthington," he said, smiling at the sexpot in the chair with a look he used to give me. "May I introduce Miss Alex Noziak."

"*Bonjour*," the other woman purred as if I could be appeased by a come-hither French accent.

Okay, maybe Bran's but that was different. And in the past.

I inclined my head toward the other woman, not trusting my voice. Not yet at least.

"Miss Worthington and I are in a meeting," Bran spoke between clenched teeth.

I gave him a stink-eye look. "So I was told."

"And your discussion couldn't wait?"

"No."

I swore he rolled his eyes before turning back to Miss Bonjour. "Would you mind waiting for me in the other office, Miss Worthington? I'm sure this will only take a moment."

Think again big guy, I wanted to say, but two could play the we're-all-civilized-people-here game even if we weren't. He couldn't be civilized. He was a warlock for cripe's sake. He might wear the veneer but that was all. Scratch the surface and his warlock tendencies tended to erupt.

I offered the sex kitten an aren't-you-sweet smile as the other woman brushed past me in a cloud of perfume that no doubt cost a thousand dollars an ounce, and felt my ring heat up indicating the Worthington woman was non-human.

Interesting. I wondered if Bran knew then ditched the thought. Of course he did. It was only one of the traits that pissed me off about him. I might identify Weres, warlocks and vamps pretty easily but was still getting used to all the other preternaturals roaming around. Mostly because before joining the IR Agency I didn't have a lot of exposure to non-humans. More than my teammates, but less than Bran, far less.

The plus side to my naiveté was that I was more wary around what I didn't know whereas Bran assumed he was the bigger, badder threat. Most times he was, but not always. The one session with his cousin who turned out to be a nasty, and rare, Grimple, didn't seem to have taught him otherwise.

Arrogant or not, I still needed him, so I waited until the door clicked shut before crossing to the middle of the room and taking the vacated seat. "Your latest bimbo?" I asked Bran as I settled into the plush cushions, hoping the lingering perfume wouldn't gag me.

Bran continued to stand, hands flattened against his desk, his knuckles white, the pulse point along his temple beating hard. "Is that what you came to discuss, Alex?"

Damn. Just the way he said my name made my skin heat and my pulse kick into high gear. Which explained why my voice was a little tighter than I intended as I snapped, "Of course not. I expected no less of you."

He smiled, a real smile that crinkled the edges of those dark blue eyes and made him less arrogant warlock and more approachable lover.

He so didn't play fair.

"So you have thought of me with other women already, Alex? You betray yourself."

"Don't be an idiot." I wanted to jump to my feet to dispel some of the tension rocketing through me but that would put a lie to my next words. "I have more important things to focus on than you and your conquests."

He eased into his seat, his smile now mocking me. Warlocks learned arrogance in the cradle and Bran was no exception. Damn his hide, and his patience as he steepled his fingers before him, tapping his forefinger against his lips, waiting for me to speak first.

As if I'd give him the satisfaction. On the other hand I could only stare at his fingers tapping against that sexy lower lip of his, again and again, and not turn into a needy puddle begging to taste him.

Good thing Noziaks never surrendered.

Instead I cleared my throat, leaned back in my chair as if I had all day and glanced at the windows before finding enough spine to meet Bran's too-penetrating gaze. Only then did I demand, "How did you know Vaverek was ambushing us this morning? And why didn't you tell us sooner?"

"The option was always a possibility. It's what I might have done myself. So I came to see for myself and informed you as soon as I was aware of the preternaturals surrounding you."

Believe him? Or not? Oh, the part about him being underhanded and devious was a given. It was the I-was-there-to-help-you part I had a hard time swallowing. Threatening to kill me last time we crossed paths tended to make me a bit more wary than usual.

"And now?" I pushed.

"Now?"

"Now I want to know everything you know about Vaverek." I didn't mean to growl but it sure sounded that way as I gave up my pretense of calmness and jumped to my feet. I hated this strain between the two of us. Not that ours had ever been an easy relationship but now it felt like ice rain pelting me.

"There's something more at play here with Vaverek, but I don't have all the details yet."

"Such as?"

He paused, then continued, "Have you heard about the family in the 8th *arrondissement?*"

"What family?" If he was trying to confuse me he was doing a great job.

"Mother, father, two boys and an infant daughter appeared to have been attacked by a wild dog." He looked at me as if waiting for something.

"And this means what? That Paris needs more dog catchers?"

"Don't be flippant." He jammed his hands in his pockets. "They all died."

I unfurled my hands that I hadn't realized I'd clenched. "I don't know what you're trying to tell me."

"Think, Alex," he almost growled the words. "What's the likelihood of a whole family being savaged by a dog?"

I paused, chewing over what he said. "Are you talking about a Were?"

"Or shifter. . ."

That had my back snapping straight. "Are you saying my brother Van?"

"No." Before I could inhale a breath, he pushed ahead. "My contacts indicate a shifter was used to attack the family, but he then killed himself, his human body being found a few blocks away. Only those who knew him connected his suicide back to the killing of the family."

"What does this have to do with Van?"

"It has to do with Vaverek. It looks like he's testing his drugs on preternaturals."

I swore I could hear the toll of death knells. If Van was held by Vaverek, how soon would it be before he was forced to do something that he could never recover from?

I faced Bran head on, not caring if he heard the pleading in my voice. "I'm running out of time to save my brother. Why won't you help?"

"I *am* helping." His words slapped like a wet towel against my bare skin. "But I won't run head on into another ambush as you're suggesting."

"I made no such suggestion."

He stood, barely holding in the pressure I could see building behind his rigid stance. "Vaverek is dangerous, but he's nothing compared to the individuals behind him."

"I know that."

"I don't think you do." He lowered his voice until it stroked my awareness like heat lightening before a summer storm. "You're acting like one of your American gunslingers, rushing in unprepared, and only by sheer luck do you come out without dying."

I walked up to the edge of his fancy huge desk, this time planting my hands on it, to give me support and to keep me from crawling across it to shake some sense into him. "Have you forgotten my brother's life is at stake? I don't have the luxury of sitting around, twiddling my thumbs, and—" I waved my hands at the door where Miss Bonjour had just exited, "doing casting calls. Van is going to die if I don't help him."

Bran leaned forward and I swore I could see steam rolling out of him. "Is that what you were doing this morning? When you used me? Tapped into my abilities?"

So that was it. That's what all this emotion hid. He was angry because I'd pulled power from him. To save the lives of my teammates. To save my life. And his too because he was there. Mister I'm-in-charge didn't like not being the one in control.

I straightened, brushing my palms against my jeans, corralling my own emotions so they wouldn't betray me. Up until this moment, in spite of his threat to kill me, in spite of our differences, and in spite of everything I knew about him, knew about his kind, I had hoped a tiny kernel of hope that he would help me. That he, who valued family so much, would know why I was willing to risk everything to save Van.

"What? No pithy comeback?" he said, his jaw so tight I was surprised it didn't fracture. "No justification as to why you put all of us at risk to pull that stunt?"

Stunt?

"That wasn't any stunt, Mister High-and-Mighty," I snarled, stepping away to give myself breathing room. "What I did I'd do again to save lives."

"And if it had backfired? What then? You'd have left all of us vulnerable to attack with no abilities, no powers. You blindsided all of us, Alex. Can't you see that?"

"Yes." The single word shot from me. As if I was so clueless. So uncaring. "But if I hadn't acted you, and my teammates, would have been killed. So it was a risk I was willing to take."

He shook his head, his eyes darkening in color, his shoulders tensing. "Your risk. Your decision. I don't know how you can call yourself a team member when you don't have any idea what the word means."

Where was this coming from? I *was* a teammate. I was part of the IR Agency. And who the hell cared anyway?

Not him obviously. He was just nursing a bruised ego.

I didn't have time for this crap. Or for him. I'd have to hunt for Van on my own without his contacts and assistance. I had to believe my team and I could find and nail Vaverek.

But just as I was turning to storm out, his desk phone rang.

For a second our gazes clashed. His unreadable. Mine no doubt looking as I felt—betrayed.

As he reached for the phone I started walking across the expanse of his office, until his words stopped me. "She's right here."

He thrust the handset toward me as if daring me to ignore it, and him.

But who would call me here? No one knew where I was.

I swallowed, a nervous betrayal of emotions and something I hoped he couldn't see.

Walking back to take that phone from him was as hard as facing down a raging rogue Were who was trying to kill my brother.

And look where that had got me—a life sentence in prison.

"Hello?" I had to speak over the fist-sized lump in my throat. "Alex Noziak here. Who's this?"

"Ling Mai."

CHAPTER 13

Bran jammed his hands in his pants pockets to keep from reaching for Alex. He had no idea who the hell was on the other end of the phone. He knew it was a woman but he didn't know who or why they'd tracked Alex down here.

All he knew was her skin had paled and the fiery emotions behind her eyes winked out and he wanted to grab her, pull her close, and protect her from whoever was on the other end of that line.

No doubt he'd get his head bitten off for the gesture.

Alex was the prickliest, most infuriating, most pig-headed woman he'd ever met and she continued to have him tied into knots even as he debated whether eliminating her might be the best approach to protecting her and everyone around her.

Did she have any idea what she'd done this morning? Fairytales and ancient manuscripts spoke of the ability to steal and amplify others' abilities, but he'd thought it was the stuff of legends.

Now he knew better. He knew and feared. For her and because of her.

Sacre bleu, the woman was going to be the death of him. But that's not what had him awakening in the middle of the night in cold sweats, nor what was driving him to shout at her like a fishmonger's wife. He feared she would be the death of herself. And that would be a loss he'd never recover from.

"No."

"But I–"

"If you'll let me explain."

Each of her chopped words sounded softer and less acerbic and he doubted it was because he was in the room. From her body language he might have been another chair, an inanimate object that could be ignored. Witches could be like that—use you and then discard you. He knew that going into a relationship with her and yet it still blindsided him when she had manipulated him to get what she needed. Her and her team. The 'greater' good.

He caught his hands curling and released them, out of sight of her. Not that she would notice. Alex Noziak was the most focused person he'd ever met, outside of himself. He had been a fool to get involved with her once. He was a bigger fool to still care now.

"Yes, I'll be there." She spoke the words with the somber cadence of death bells ringing and replaced the phone in its cradle without looking at him.

"Who was it?" he demanded, aware how close he was to losing his control.

"Doesn't matter."

This wasn't the spitfire, in-his-face Alex of a moment ago. The one who crashed his meeting like a heat-seeking missile and latched on to Guinevere Worthington as the target. An action that gave him the most hope in weeks that he wasn't the only one hurting since their breakup.

No, this Alex was pulled in, which wasn't her way at all. Hurt or preparing herself for battle? Knowing Alex, it was probably the latter.

As she reached for the closed door he stepped toward her. "Then tell me what they wanted? What they said."

She glanced at him then, the light behind her eyes only a pale flicker. "Not your business." Her voice so low he rocked forward on the balls of his shoes to hear her.

"Your brother?"

It had to be. He knew that gutted feeling too well, with his cousin Dominique's death still raw within him, even understanding at last that so much of their relationship was built on lies and manipulations.

But Alex only shook her head.

"Then what?" At this point he didn't care if she heard his concern. She was shredding him.

She continued to open the door as if he'd said nothing, pausing only long enough to glance over her shoulder. "Nothing to worry about. My problem, not yours. I'll be out of your hair from now on."

What did she mean by that?

He couldn't ask, though, as she closed the door behind her. Not a slam, but a near-silent click.

Something was wrong. Very wrong. And as usual, Alex was at the heart of it.

CHAPTER 14

Wedging himself through the disgruntled and vocal crowds packing Orly Ouest arrival terminal was only one of the reasons Jeb Noziak detested flying. As an arriving passenger, and one with platinum status based on his connections with the Council of Seven, he'd not had to stagnate in the long lines waiting to pass security or to move almost anywhere within the terminal. A square-shouldered older male shifter had met him upon disembarking, grabbing Jeb's carry-on luggage and acting as a battering ram, which helped Jeb move through the terminal as fast as possible to the town car waiting outside. Yet Jeb still felt the need to shower, and they hadn't even braved the morning Paris traffic.

The roar of arriving and departing jets, Frenchmen who had a love of leaning on their car horns, and the jerk of the motorway traffic had him leaning against the seatback cushion and closing his eyes, travel fatigue but mostly concern draining his energy.

Astral traveling on the spirit plane took a lot less wear on his body and usually sufficed when communicating with Philippe. So what was different this time? And why had his friend sounded so worried over the phone?

Though maybe Jeb was reading his own concerns and fears into Philippe's voice. Somewhere beyond the tinted vehicle windows Van was being held hostage in this city. That was the last information Jeb had received, two, or was it three days ago now? With that realization Jeb jerked forward, his earlier exhaustion giving way to anger, an anger that had no release.

Van had known what he was getting into working with the hush-hush NATO organization on behalf of an equally hush-hush US agency. His son was smart, resourceful, and strong. But damnit, that didn't mean that Jeb still didn't worry. Worry and feel next to useless. While he was here he would find the time to nose around, use the resources given him as a shaman to ferret out some news. Any news had to be better than this useless waiting.

Now he must be circumspect. But once his son was found. . . after that . . . those who did this to Van would pay.

As the town car glided up to Philippe's *pied-à-terre*, located in an old stone building close to the *Trocadero* and with a bird's eye view of the Eiffel Tower, Jeb wondered, not for the first time, why Philippe didn't resign his position on the Council and retire to his much larger, and much older estate in Provence.

Jeb loved the 16th century country chateau, not for its age or elegance, but for the fact it was surrounded by land, something he valued over a pretentious address. The private but tiny garden located in the town apartment was the difference between having a cat box and having sixty acres.

He sighed as he exited the car, stretching his legs in the process. He, more than most, understood that once a Council member always a Council member, unless sidelined by serious health issues. Since all the members possessed preternatural abilities, including longevity and superb health, the last member who'd voluntarily resigned had been sometime in the 1500's and then the reason was madness, a side effect of age in some vampires and druids.

But Philippe was still in the prime of his life, being a little less than three hundred years old.

No, Jeb's friend would never give up his seat on the Council, no matter how much bickering and infighting he had to referee.

A butler who looked part fae with perhaps an element of selkie, opened the main door and waved Jeb and his shifter driver now valet inside to the hushed foyer. Not large but filled with exquisite antique furniture several generations older than the eighteenth century building.

"Would *Monsieur* wish to freshen up in his room before meeting with the Master?"

The man's accent sounded middle eastern, which surprised Jeb as Philippe was a Francophile through and through.

"Where is your Master? Is he on the premises?" he asked, aware the shifter waited in the doorway leading to the single guest bedroom. Philippe valued his privacy as much as he valued his antiques. It was only in the last year or two that he had allowed one of the side rooms to be converted into a room for the butler. Otherwise the smallness of the apartment gave Philippe the excuse he often needed to not host more-out-of-town Council guests or casual dinner meetings. The fact Jeb was always welcome had actually been a sore point with some of the other Council members who felt slighted. Their problem, and Philippe's, not Jeb's.

The butler nodded toward the living room and the French doors open beyond it. "*Monsieur* waits for you in the garden."

His friend must truly be distressed to be at his home during the day instead of the suite of rooms used by the Council as their primary offices. Their main headquarters were a best-kept secret in the foothills of Rockport, Missouri, but most major cities held at least one place to assemble in case the group, or even members of the group, needed to gather. A minimum of three Council members were required to be present to handle small issues, so if the issue was regional, the member who lived on the continent where the transgression occurred would host any other two members available to sit in on the session. All seven needed to be in attendance on issues that impacted preternaturals worldwide, and for the yearly summit which was held in Rockport.

Jeb nodded at the shifter. "Drop off my bag in my room." He thought he saw something pass across the man's expression but it could have been a trick of the light. Turning to the butler he added, "I'll be joining *Monsieur* Philippe outside."

The butler nodded and moved forward to show Jeb the way, though he could have found his own way, the garden being one of the few places in Paris he enjoyed. He could have even predicted the linden tree Philippe would have been standing under, but not that the Frenchmen would be with another, and with a pose of tension and discord marring his patrician features.

It was the other, a younger male, who arrested Jeb's attention. The man could not have looked more different than Philippe, with an open expression, laugh lines bracketing his eyes, a smile resting lightly on his face, and a build that was shorter and stockier than the Frenchman's. An athlete's stockiness, with wide shoulders and muscles that looked as if he used them. A Gene Kelly build versus a Fred Astaire look.

When the young man turned toward Jeb his smile deepened as if greeting an old friend. Something about him seemed familiar but Jeb couldn't place it. The impression disappeared as Philippe raised his leonine, artistic head and stepped forward, both hands outstretched.

He greeted Jeb in the French way, grasping both Jeb's hands while leaning forward to kiss his cheeks. The action was sincere and heartfelt but not from Jeb's background so he still braced himself. It wasn't the male-to-male kiss that bothered him as some might suspect, but the feeling of entrapment the closeness created. If anyone other than Philippe forced the action Jeb would have no problem putting him in his place.

Pádraig, for that must be who the young man was, appeared to understand intrinsically, or Philippe had coached his protégé, as the Irishman extended his hand for a friendly, without competition shake. No proving who was stronger or higher in the pecking order. Just a quick strong motion and then a step back, allowing plenty of space to remain between them.

"Jeb, this is the young rascal I've told you so much about." Philippe's smile took years off his face as he glanced between Jeb and the younger man. "Pádraig, you can ask for no finer friend or better ally than Jebediah. Remember that."

There were undercurrents here that were as obscure as the first time Jeb traveled from the physical realm to the spiritual many years ago. Jeb knew Pádraig was a druid as was Philippe, but there were different levels of druidism and even regional variants as to druid practice, which set the true druids apart from the neo-druidism that served as a reference point for many contemporary humans.

Neo-druidism was to druidism like Wiccan practices were to true-born witches such as his daughter Alex or his wife Aideen. Philippe was not only Druid born but an arch druid, which one could only obtain after decades of intense study including shamanistic knowledge. It was one of the reasons Jeb and Philippe were drawn together. They were the only two on the Council, and among the few non-humans, who could easily traverse to the spirit world, travel and return to their corporeal form.

Jeb didn't know where Pádraig was on the druid hierarchy. His physical appearance indicated a younger age but the shell was often only that, an external manifestation that hid the true soul. How strong a druid he was, or what sort of druid he was, remained to be learned.

Jeb kept his expression neutral as he nodded to the Irishman. "Please, call me Jeb."

The man's smile ratcheted up. "A pleasure and one I've looked forward to for some time." A quick glance back at his mentor before he lowered his voice and replaced warmth with wariness. "I just wish it wasn't under these circumstances."

Van? Had something happened to his son while Jeb was in transit?

He had not earned his position on the Council by hasty thought or action and now was no exception. He cast a quick look at his friend. No need to ask outright what was happening and how it involved the three of them, but he held his tongue, and his temper.

Instead of answering directly, the Frenchmen waved them toward a weathered table and sturdy chairs that looked at home in the sculpted garden in spite of their wear.

"*S'il vous plait*," Philippe murmured, steering first Jeb and then Pádraig to their seats before he took the third chair.

Jeb could tell his friend's unease by the lapse into his native language, a sure sign of distress.

"Would you care for something to drink? Or eat after your flight. I could. . ." Philippe turned to wave over the butler hovering in the doorway when Jeb laid a hand on the Frenchman's sleeve and lowered his arm.

"Tell me what I have come over five thousand miles to hear. All else can wait."

The Frenchman sighed as Pádraig cast an anxious glance at Jeb as if saying, see the state he's in.

When Philippe held his tongue Jeb prompted, "There is nothing you can not tell me, old friend." Shooting a look at Pádraig to include him, Jeb continued. "What are friends for if not to lessen one's worries?"

Philippe leaned forward, his hands clasped tightly together. "I have no words to tell you this." He raised his head enough for his gaze to latch on to Jeb's before he glanced at his protégé. "You brought the news. Will you share?"

"Certainly." The younger man scooted forward in his chair, concern creasing his forehead, his gaze turned inward until it snapped to Jeb's. "I have learned some disturbing news."

As if a rubber band pulled to breaking point Jeb wanted to clip the young pup along the head as he would his own sons if they dawdled over telling an unwelcome tale. Avoidance only prolonged the tension, making everyone suffer.

But this was Philippe's home, his friend, so Jeb schooled his features to betray nothing except a willingness to listen.

Pádraig leaned further forward and lowered his voice. "It's about your clan."

Jeb glanced at Philippe. "Your family. Your offspring." Jeb knew what the younger man meant but bought himself some time as his heart stuttered and he struggled to keep his pain under leash. "Van?"

Pádraig cast a quick glance at Philippe who was the one shaking his head. "No."

Jeb considered himself a man of reason. A man who held to his code, no matter the cost, of temperate response unless action was needed and then he would execute that action swiftly and surely. No gray areas for him. But such restraint cost and his voice roughened as he faced Philippe. "Tell me. Now."

The Frenchman nodded. "It's about your daughter."

"Alex?" Jeb spoke as if far away, braced for one blow but reeling under a different one. "Is she hurt?"

By the Great Spirits don't let her be dead. Anything but that.

"Not hurt. Not yet."

Like a wounded animal ready to lunge Jeb latched onto the hard edges of the chair, his skin biting into the wood. "Tell me."

"She's in Paris," Pádraig answered, his gaze not meeting Jeb's. "And there's a price on her head."

"For what?"

"Someone wants her alive. No questions asked. Collateral damage acceptable. The sooner the better."

CHAPTER 15

Van Noziak lifted his head, spying the late afternoon light filtering through a shuttered window high over his head. He couldn't see the gap shackled as he was against the wall, but he tracked the wedge of light spilling on the packed dirt floor, memorizing its movement as if doing so would create sense of what was happening to him.

The ten-by-ten-foot stone-walled room smelled of damp, old straw, sewage, and despair. Wherever he was it had been used as a cell of last resort before. For many years would be Van's guess.

His tongue felt swollen and fuzzy. Dehydration? Or drugs? Or a combination of the two? His head pounded as if the bells of Notre Dame rang insistently within it.

No idea how long he'd been here. The first days had been the worst, then his captors, all wearing hoods to disguise their faces, backed off on the interrogation, and the torture.

Obviously he was now worth more to them alive than dead, but no idea how long that would last.

They clearly knew he was a shifter, which explained the silver wrist and ankle cuffs burning into his skin, as well as the collar around his throat, but they seemed to ignore the fact that cloaked as they were he could still identify them by their stench. Either they ignored that fact or didn't give a damn as they assumed he wouldn't live to ferret them out. Only one of their mistakes.

He'd memorized each and every one of them. Revenge was the only thing keeping him going now. That and the knowledge others would be looking for him. Not his NATO allies but his family. Daily, whenever he was aware enough to do so, he reached out with his thoughts, searching for his dad, who would not be stopped by the underground location or the thickness of the stone surrounding him.

If he could just hold on a little longer. Hell, he had no choice, he was a Noziak and no matter how rough the going got he'd never give up. But that didn't mean he couldn't die.

He was coming to terms with that. Not in an abstract but as a distinct and very real possibility. Whoever these people were, and so far only one or two carried the scent of humans, they wanted something from him. And it was no longer the intel they had tried to extract the first week.

Down a far hallway he heard the squeal of metal against metal. A door opening. Another detail he'd memorized, too far away to see it, but his shifter hearing knew when someone was coming to check on him long before they appeared.

The silver bands holding him kept him in his human form but the second he was given the chance he'd shift. Then they'd have to kill him for sure, either that or be killed.

Three distinct sets of footsteps drew closer. The thick-soled one was human, and a regular visitor. He was the one who brought Van tepid water and surprisingly good food, though lately Van accepted that the French cuisine hid drugs that made him groggy and sluggish. He ate the meals anyway, knowing that when the time came he could fight through whatever he was being fed. Some kind of Dextromethorphan was his best guess, which explained the dizziness, blurred vision and fast heartbeat. Once he shifted he could burn the effects out of his system. At least he hoped he could.

The second shuffle belonged to someone Van mentally called the Doc, a Were by his scent. He possessed some kind of medical background by the questions he always asked. Not that Van gave him straight answers. Why make anything easy for his captors?

The third steps were new. Someone who walked with precision and force, each step tattooing authority as they marched across the cement floor. Not a lackey doing a job. One of the power operators?

If so things could be about to change.

Van braced himself even if he might still appear to be weak and not dangerous.

The steps stopped beyond the bars covering one side of the square cell. Three men. The human stoop-shouldered and avoiding eye contact, even beneath his Ku Klux Klan cowl. The doctor leaning forward as if near-sighted. And the third. Something different? Not human. Something Van didn't cross often and without a reference point he had to guess what type of preternatural he was dealing with. A warlock? Possibly. There was that power stance they usually held. But what would a warlock want with him?

"Mr. Noziak. So nice to see you." The voice sounded cultured, educated, and supercilious, which also fit a warlock's description. But there was something else about him. A stillness masking emotion. Excitement?

Van raised his head an inch or two, as if responding to the summons, but more to see if he could identify this third individual.

"I hope you have been treated well during your stay with us."

Van didn't bother with a response. The a-hole was goading him, seeing if he could spark a rise, but it'd take more than verbal prodding to get Van to dance to these people's tune.

The new man glanced at the Doc and nodded. The Doc then moved deeper into the cell.

"How much have you given him?" the newcomer asked, treating Van as invisible.

"Enough to keep him calm. No more."

"I want nothing to interfere with the trial tomorrow. Cease administration."

The Doc turned his back to Van who kept his smile to himself. They were growing complacent, which he could work to his advantage.

The Doc stuttered as he spoke. "W-without the drugs he can become violent. Hard to manage."

They had no idea how hard to manage he would be.

"He might even break free."

That was the plan.

"Then you must find another way." Newcomer ordered, adding, "With no risk, there is no reward." He stepped forward, close enough to raise Van's head and stare with calculating brown eyes into Van's own. But he spoke to the Doc as he said, "The trial must be flawless."

He dropped Van's head then brushed his palms together as if removing the taint of Van from his cultivated hands.

It took everything Van had not to snarl and betray that seventy percent of his weakness was being faked. He needed to lull them into a false sense of control.

Newcomer pivoted and strolled to the cell door, speaking over his shoulder to the Doc who remained near Van, fear and anger sweating from his skin.

"Till tomorrow Jean-Claude. No mistakes."

Then he was gone. Jean-Claude, the Doc, shook his head and shuffled after the first man, only stopping long enough to growl at the human. "Do as he says."

"But-"

"Those are direct orders."

"And if he breaks free?"

"Either way we'll die."

The cell door clanged shut and the footsteps receded.

Van didn't have any idea what they'd meant by a trial but he'd be ready. A quick glance at the path of the light trail on the floor. It couldn't move fast enough.

CHAPTER 16

I walked into the Hotel Le Meurice and knew I was in deeper trouble than even I could imagine. And at times I could have a very active imagination.

It wasn't Mandy and Jaylene silently flanking me like I was on the way to the gallows but they didn't help. They'd been waiting for me outside Bran's office building and "escorted" me into a waiting cab, neither saying a word. Jaylene gave me a headshake but it was Mandy's smug look that was getting to me. I wanted to tell them that I hadn't ditched them to slight them, but only because I needed to make sure myself, that Bran had not set us up back in the street. It wasn't something I didn't want my team aware of immediately if he had. Plus I needed to see if he knew anything else about Vaverek that he wasn't sharing and thought he might be more open to telling me alone.

That was a big fat no. The telling part at least.

Now, walking through the lobby of a hotel that made frou-frou look pedestrian, I was actually glad for their presence. At least I wasn't the only one glancing around me, expecting royalty or some VIP to brush past.

So this was how the other half, and Ling Mai, lived.

Sheesh!

By the time we arrived outside her door and knocked my throat was bone-dry and my heart rate double-timing it.

Jaylene must have heard Ling Mai say something from inside as Jaylene opened the door and nodded for me to step in. Alone.

Chicken-hearts.

Then she closed the door behind me.

I was gobsmacked. Silks and brocades, that fancy French furniture with curly-cued legs and gold detailing, and a white with black veined marble fireplace along one wall. A real one.

I wasn't in a hotel room, I was in a palace. Even the bouquets in big glass vases were real and larger than life.

This had to be the fanciest place I'd ever been in and, given I'd traveled with Bran for almost two weeks from one luxury spot to another, that was saying something.

An intimidation factor? No doubt. Or was this just the way Ling Mai traveled? Yeah, with her timeless Amerasian looks and elegance that dripped from her fingertips, I could see where she'd feel comfortable here.

Not me.

But then that could be a good thing as I straightened my shoulders and braced myself to take her best shot. I had no doubt she planned to use her big guns. Let her try.

I wasn't the scared little witch that I had been when I'd first come to the Agency. I still wasn't proficient with my spells and skills, but I was a damn site better than I had been. Her returning me to prison wasn't the same threat it had been when I first arrived at the Agency. Now if I was sent back it'd cost me time in finding my brother that I couldn't afford. So I'd do what I had to do to stay in Paris. I'd miss the team if I was booted, but Ling Mai had better know I was not the same witch/shaman she'd hired on only weeks ago.

I looked around the room, not seeing the agency director right away until she walked from a side room to the main room, her footsteps silent as she crossed the patterned silver rug. She was shorter than I was but it took only about two seconds to realize that size didn't matter around her. She was in charge and everyone knew it.

"Would you like a seat Ms. Noziak?" It wasn't really a question as she gestured toward the nearest chair. Good grief the room was big enough to contain half a dozen chairs and not look crowded.

I shook my head. Best to face the firing squad standing upright.

Ling Mai eyed me, watching me from those calm, impenetrable eyes. Ever since first meeting her I felt she was nonhuman, but the silver ring I wore to identify preternaturals never heated around her. On the other hand, the rings all of the team had worn this morning hadn't worked either, so I'd go with my gut and walk wary around the director. No telling what she could morph into to lop my head off.

She said nothing as she took one of the two chairs facing one another across a coffee table that mirrored the afternoon light off its pristine white surface. I waited, expecting the worst.

Immediate transportation back to the Women's Correctional facility in Pocatello, Idaho? A strong possibility. Or, now that Ling Mai was aware that I possessed a wildcard magical ability, for I was sure Stone had told her what had happened earlier, there could be other fallout. The Council of Seven didn't have a holding cell for nonhumans deemed too dangerous to let them remain amongst the human population. They simply killed the offender for the greater good. Could Ling Mai do the same?

Damn, I should have read the fine print on my one-year contract with the agency, but I was jumping so fast at the chance of leaving prison that I would have signed away my soul. Maybe I had.

"You abandoned your team, Miss Noziak." she paused, then continued, digging my grave deeper. "Plus you ignored a directive from your senior instructor to remain away from the warlock." Her tone dared me to justify or refute.

There was no need. She was in the right. But she wasn't finished either.

"You are undisciplined and put others at risk." I could hear the coffin nails pounding. "You have great talent and abilities and yet you choose to squander them."

Wasn't I the one who saved the others this morning?

"Leaving your team behind was dangerous for you and your team, even if such behavior from you is not unexpected."

Which must be why she knew exactly where to find me. Leave it to her to be three steps ahead of me when I'd only made the decision as a way to salvage the morning's disaster.

"Unfortunately we still need your help." She was throwing

me off kilter. No "You're off the team as of now". Leave it to her to take the knots inside my stomach and tighten them.

But her words made no sense. I worked for the woman, wasn't I already helping the agency? If that's what she meant by "we".

I raised my brows and waited. My family would have been in shock as I tended to be the most jump-first-and-learn-how-to-swim-later one of the bunch. But I was learning.

However Ling Mai was a pro and I was just a newbie in the patience game.

After a moment that I swore lasted several hours I shrugged my shoulders, released a deep sigh, and scooted to the nearest chair and sat in it. "What do you want and why me?" I didn't ask why she should trust me given her low opinion of me. That I could answer for myself. She didn't trust me and that was my fault. Good intentions didn't count as my father would say.

"We're involved in a very dangerous mission, Miss Noziak, with stakes you don't even recognize."

Like I didn't know that? I'd been at the ambush that morning.

My look must have betrayed me as she offered a half smile and leaned forward, the we're-all-on-the-same-side ploy. Which I didn't trust for a nanosecond.

"Vaverek is a thread in a much larger tapestry," she said.

"Figured that."

"I assumed you did. But what you don't know is that so far he's been our only link to a much larger, and much deadlier threat than his use of synthetic drugs."

"Drugs that caused innocents to steal for him."

"As well as not-so-innocents to murder."

We both knew she meant Dominique, Bran's cousin, and her assistant. What a kerfuffle that mission had been.

"So what do you want from me?" I asked again, curling my fingers over the chair arm as if that would keep me from pushing her harder.

"Our mission in Paris has changed."

I froze before I found enough spit to speak. "You trying to tell me we're not going after my brother?" The words dripped with venom. "After your promise?"

She leaned back, looking all calm and collected, but at least she shook her head. "We are still seeking the whereabouts of your brother."

My heart restarted. "Then what's changed?"

"Our original mandate was to find your brother and in doing that find and apprehend Vaverek."

She wasn't telling me anything that I didn't already know, but seemed to be circling around something else. But what?

I bit my inner lip until I could taste blood pool in my mouth. "I'm not good about beating around the bush. Tell me what's going on?"

"It involves your . . . contact. Bran."

Another loop de loop, even as I was impressed at how she tap-danced around exactly what Bran and I were to each other. "What about him?"

"He's being brought forward to the Council of Seven."

"What?" Talk about a blow to the gut. The Council was bad news. I had been lucky that they had allowed me to only be imprisoned for life. Being brought to them in person always meant a lot more than a slap on the wrist. Usually they chopped the wrist off. Then the head. But Bran was a celebrity figure, not a peon like myself. His disappearance could cause waves, depending on why they wanted him and what they did with him as a result. "Why was he called?"

Instead of answering me directly, which wasn't Ling Mai's way, she tilted her head, scanning me like a bird to a worm. "Do you remember the Librarian?"

I racked my brains before the light bulb went off. "Yeah, isn't she the person who keeps track of who married who, to figure out if their offspring are human or non-human?"

"That's one of her mandates. Her other is to gather information."

Ling Mai's point? Then the nickel dropped. "You mean secrets."

"Yes, among other data."

"And then what? She sell it to the highest bidder?"

"She is not adverse to making a profit. Though I think she views herself as providing a necessary commodity to the marketplace."

"What does this have to do with Bran?" Or me for that matter, but one issue at a time.

"The Librarian has come across information that indicates the Council believes Bran is withholding information once held by his cousin."

"Dominique," I whispered the word. Like a bad nightmare that psychopath was continuing to haunt me though she was dead. "What kind of information?"

"It appears that she had more than one drug formula in her possession. A compound targeted specifically at non-humans."

The drug we'd traced back to Dominique on our last mission gave her temporary control over individuals, the kind of control that acted as an autosuggestion to do whatever she wanted them to do and then forget they'd taken any action. As far as anyone had known the drug only impacted humans, in spite of the fact it'd been administered to Dominique the day she died. Could that have been a different drug? There wasn't enough of her body left to find out. Could these be the raised stakes Ling Mai meant?

There was a quantum leap from unsuspecting humans committing crimes for gain and programming a preternatural to commit crimes against humans.

"Oh, crap." My stomach plummeted as I swallowed deeply. "Is that true?"

"If the Council believes the information is accurate then we too must believe it has a solid basis in fact."

"Does Bran know?"

"He's been issued the summons."

I'd just been there. Did he know then? Is that what had been bothering him?

I shook my head, then asked the question thrumming through me the loudest. "So what's this have to do with me?"

"You are our strongest link to Bran. And the Council. Bran is our best option in finding Vaverek . We need him to remain involved in finding Vaverek before the Council clips his wings because Vaverek is our best option in finding who is agitating the non-humans world-wide and we need him alive."

Holey double-crap. Clip his wings might mean a warning or

the death sentence. I'd deal with the fact Bran very clearly wanted Vaverek dead later.

"So you think I can protect Bran from the Council?"

"We want you to motivate Bran to help you find Vaverek before the Council takes action."

Yeah, like I had any sway with the warlock. Especially since I just promised him I would get and stay out of his hair.

"How much time are we talking about?"

"Forty-eight hours."

And here I thought it was going to be hard.

I stood, feeling in a fog but if the clock was ticking I couldn't sit around like a pampered princess.

As I turned to the door Ling Mai's voice stopped me. "I've requested special assistance for your mission."

"What kind of assistance?" I eyed her.

"Someone who knows Bran well and who might be willing to help."

"A friend of Bran's?"

"A connection."

That didn't help. The Bran I knew had few friends, except for his cousin and I'd helped kill her.

So I shrugged and walked to the door. But leave it to Ling Mai to throw a few daggers before I escaped. "Mandy and Jaylene will be working with you at all times."

I got the message. No more escaping on my own. No more off the reservation as Stone would say. Now I had guards.

Better than being sent back to prison.

"Oh and Miss Noziak." At this rate I'd be down to twelve hours and counting.

She waited till I looked at her before continuing.

"Remember there is no "I" in "team"."

My smile was tensile tight as I nodded, wondering if they had a t-shirt with that logo on it. Then she added, "This is your last chance."

Somehow, though she hadn't mentioned my freaky ability, I knew she knew. Which meant she was no longer threatening me with prison as an alternative to being an IR agent. She was threatening me with the Council.

CHAPTER 17

As if a jet had slammed into him, Jeb scrambled to understand what Pádraig was saying. Alex never mentioned she was coming to Paris. Last he'd spoken to her she was in a work release program in Maryland.

He speared Philippe with a look. "I don't understand."

Philippe nodded at his protégé who leaned so far forward Jeb was sure the young man was about to topple from chair to grass.

"I have stumbled across conflicting reports but it appears your daughter is wanted by certain people."

"Why?"

Pádraig shrugged. "I haven't been able to determine this. As soon as I uncovered what I had I brought the intel to Philippe."

"Who wants her?"

A head shake as Pádraig added, "I don't know that either."

"Then tell me exactly what you do know," Jeb demanded, aware his voice had risen.

Pádraig sat back as if slapped. But his voice was calm as he said, "Your daughter is in Paris. She's a target with a sizable bounty on her head, but only if alive."

"How much?"

"A million euros."

Jeb glanced at Philippe. "Roughly a million two hundred and eighty thousand US dollars."

"For Alex?" This time the words escaped as air from a deflated balloon. "This doesn't make sense."

"I was concerned," Philippe kept his tone even, "that this attempt on her might be tied into your son's disappearance."

Jeb shook his head. Not because his friend's words didn't hold a possible explanation, but because he was still grappling with the ramifications. He eyed Philippe. "But why Van and Alex? What's to gain? I'm not a wealthy man."

Philippe released a long slow breath. "You are an influential man, Jebediah. That may be the key."

"You mean the Council?"

Philippe nodded before glancing at Pádraig. "It is the only thing that makes sense to us."

Jeb stood, no longer able to sit. Not with a father's fear roaring through him. "Do you know where Alex is? Right now? She should be under protection."

Pádraig crooked his neck as if to relieve strain even though it was Jeb who was avalanched by the weight that had just come down on him.

"I'm sorry, Mr. Noziak." Pádraig rose to his feet too as if in commiseration. "I had a lead on her earlier today but then I lost her."

"Where?"

"She was visiting a notable dress designer who has offices here in Paris. At the *Tour FIRST* building."

"Alex?" His daughter wore jeans and t-shirts. What in the world was she doing with a dress designer?"

But before he could ask more questions Philippe gestured to the seat Jeb had just vacated. "I'm afraid there's more, my old friend. It involves Council business."

Jeb sank back upon the weathered surface of the chair, wondering how much more he could handle.

"Pádraig, would you check with Zeid about some refreshments? I know I am famished."

The young man cast a quick look between Jeb and Philippe before offering a curt nod and leaving.

"Zeid?" Jeb asked, latching on to the mundane while he grappled with the explosion.

"Tunisian butler," Philippe mentioned, leaning forward, more serious than Jeb had ever seen the druid. "There's more going on here than I can tell you in a few moments, but I will share this. The Council is under attack."

No words came to Jeb so he listened.

"The threat against your children must be part of this larger threat. You're the only Council member with offspring, which makes you vulnerable."

He could see the logic behind Philippe's words. "But who is attacking? And why?"

"I'm attempting to get to the bottom of that." He glanced toward the house. "Pádraig has been invaluable as my eyes and ears. You can trust him if you need to do so."

That had Jeb more alert. "Do you fear for your life?"

"There have already been two near-death occurrences. I don't know if I shall survive another."

"But . . . you didn't tell me. And why isn't the Council up in arms?"

"They—or I should say some on the Council—may be behind the agitation."

This was more than serious, this was catastrophic. The Council was the only law between non-humans and humans and had been for centuries. If the Council fell the mostly peaceful co-existence also fell. There had always been beings within the preternatural community who resented keeping their identities hidden. The Weres were always agitating for more recognition as they held no Council seat. Could they be behind these new disturbances? But what would they hope to get out of Jeb?

"Who on the Council are working against you?" Jeb asked, knowing their time was limited as Pádraig was already crossing from house to garden.

"We'll talk later. There's a gathering this evening that I'm afraid I must attend. Pádraig is going with me." Philippe smiled as the young man set a tray of cheese and bread down on the table before them. "Why don't you join us, Jebediah? As my guest. We can talk after."

Jeb shook his head. Last thing he wanted to do was bide his time when his children were under attack. "Jet lag," he murmured. "I'm afraid I'd be poor company."

"I understand." Philippe leaned back in his chair, once more the convivial host. "Then instead of talking to me, I think Pádraig should show you what we've gathered. In the library."

Jeb rose to his feet before the older man finished speaking. "I'd like that. Regarding Van?"

"Regarding both your children," came Pádraig's response.

"Then let's have a look." Jeb started to walk away then stopped, turning to Philippe. "This dress designer. He have a name?"

"Bran."

"Only the one name?"

"*Oui.*" Philippe glanced at his protégé. "Pádraig has a thick file on him."

Good. Finally something was going right.

CHAPTER 18

I was chomping at the bit as I tapped my fingers on the metal top of an outdoor bistro table. It was late afternoon and my time frame was winging past; last thing I wanted to be doing was biding my time waiting for my new contact to appear.

"Where the hell is this guy?" I snarled at Jaylene loud enough to earn a few head turns from other bistro patrons. I was tempted to bare my teeth at them. That would show them that not everyone spent their days lounging around sipping *café au lait* and reading *Le Figaro* or *Le Monde*. Didn't these people ever work?

"He's coming," Jaylene murmured, her attention on some hoity-toity French magazine. Bran probably read it too.

"Why can't we approach Bran without him? Meet this guy later?" My voice intentionally nudging my handlers into action.

"Ling Mai said meet him first. Approach Bran second," Mandy replied around a sip of some chocolate drink with whipped cream on it.

"Never saw you as a bootlicker." I raised my brows, waiting for the explosion.

Jaylene reached a hand out and stopped Mandy from lunging across the table without ever raising her gaze from her magazine. "She's just pissed that she screwed up."

"Again," Mandy snipped.

This time I was the one standing, my fists curled, my temper on a short and getting shorter fuse.

"Dahling, you don't have to rise on my account," a familiar voice brushed against me.

Male. Cocky. British.

No way.

"*Oui*, it is *moi*, François Dupris, at your service."

I turned, my whole body stiff, except for my shaking head. "Tell me you're a figment of my worst nightmare."

The man before me, looking radically different than when I knew him on my last mission, was too familiar. Before he'd been effete, mincing and a royal PITA. The last part still applied but now he looked more like Gabriel Aubry, tousled blonde hair, stubbly chin, smoldering sexy golden-brown eyes. I felt like I'd tumbled down the rabbit hole.

"You like the look? *Oui?*" he prodded in the voice I associated with Franco, a majordomo in Bran's fashion events. But this wasn't Franco.

Obviously enjoying my discomfort he lifted first Jaylene's and then Mandy's hands for a kiss as he murmured in a sultry deep accent, "*Enchanté, Mademoiselles.* I have met the delectable Jaylene before but you, ma <u>bichette,</u> I have not had the pleasure."

"Did he just call you a bitch?" I asked, wondering why Mandy let him linger over her palm instead of scratching his eyes out.

"He called me his little doe." Mandy didn't even look at me but kept her focus on François or whatever he was calling himself now. And she was smiling. A sappy ooh-la-la smile.

I wanted to gag.

Jaylene whistled. "François," she purred his name. "You're looking good. Like what you've done with the hair, the clothes, the whole you."

He flashed her a dazzling smile.

At this rate I really was really going to gag, or shoot myself.

Instead I resumed my seat and leaned forward, knowing that whatever his name, or look, or accent he was still an undercover agent for a new branch of MI-6, an elite group tasked to keep an eye on preternatural activity just like the IR Agency. He was also a shifter. I couldn't out him in public for being a fake, but I could remind my fellow teammates not to fall for his acting abilities. Or one teammate in particular.

And Ling Mai didn't think I could be a team player.

"Look," I snarled, but quietly, "Enough of the reunion. What are you doing here?"

"*Mais, ma minette,*" he said, earning a snort from Mandy. "I have been called in to be of assistance."

I didn't know what he just called me, but I'd find out. Right after I wrung Ling Mai's elegant neck for foisting another handler on me. One not of my choosing and one I didn't quite trust. Heck, I didn't even know if I could remember to call him François so I didn't blow his current cover.

Yes, he turned out to be one of the good guys on the last mission but Frank here . . . François, call him François . . . always had his own agenda.

"What are you getting out of this?" I asked, almost nose-to-nose with him, which given the way he looked now was disconcerting.

He gave a Gallic shrug, released Mandy's hand but not after one more come-hither glance from his eyes that I didn't remember were an amber color. Almost wolf-like. He pulled a chair to the table, giving me a few seconds to catch my breath and adjust to the new Franco or François. Which I wasn't doing so well. "I'm here because Bran is my friend and he needs me. So do you."

"Your friend?"

"*Oui*, didn't I tell you we were at Balliol College Oxford together?" He arched an elegant brow and for a second I could see him with Bran in their school days—arrogant, at ease, killer looks—even though I had to wonder if either had ever attended Oxford. Bran was too secretive about his past and François here made lying as easy as breathing.

But I didn't care about the past. I cared about the now that was slipping away from me. "You can get Bran to see me?" I asked, all business. I didn't share that I'd tried to text Bran several times while waiting for François to arrive. Not in front of Mandy or Jaylene but under the table and he hadn't responded.

Each non-answer making me more afraid for him. But that was neither here nor there.

"I'm meeting with Bran in about twenty minutes," came François' blasé response.

At last, something breaking open. "Then let's get going." I rose from my seat.

"Not looking like that," came François' quick and almost horrified retort. A little more tone in his voice and I would have sworn he'd switched back to Franco.

I eased down, bracing myself to pulling out word by word what François meant. But it was Mandy who beat me to the punch. "We need to change?"

"*Oui.*" He flashed a dazzling smile. "I have arranged to have us all present at an very exclusive soiree." He raised his hands, palms out. "You may thank me later."

Yeah, like right after I took him out. Or cast a rash-inducing spell. Not that I would, magic had too much backlash. Just like my now having to work with Franco/François here, probably as a direct result of the amplifying stunt I'd pulled this morning.

I ignored the voice deep inside me that whispered, *you wish.* I hadn't been able to forget that twitching lace curtain, or who had been behind it.

"Alex?" I glanced over at François who actually looked worried. "Are you alright?" And he sounded concerned. Damn he should have gone onto the stage.

"She's prepping herself to do battle over dressing for this soiree," Mandy sniped. "How formal is it?"

"More than jeans and your wind-cheater," François said.

"He means hoodie." I glanced at François, waiting for what he wasn't saying.

"Cocktail dresses. Evening theater. Casual, by Parisian standards, not . . ." He eyed me and I stuck my tongue out at him.

Oh yeah, working together again was going to be loads of fun.

"Bran's going to be at this event though?" my words sounded even as my gaze drilled François. The you-screw-with-me-and-you'll-pay look both of us understood.

He nodded.

We were on the same page. Not for the same reasons and finding out what François wanted was on my to-do list. Right after getting Bran to help me, before he was arrested, and right after freeing my brother. If he was still alive.

"Where are you going?" Mandy asked.

"To get dressed. We don't have that much time."

Mandy's stunned expression was worth having to try a dress on. But only one.

No shoes though. I didn't do the frou-frou shoes.

"I have just the shoes for you," François murmured, looking straight at me as if he'd read my thoughts.

Oh, yeah. One big happy team.

Not.

CHAPTER 19

He had not expected much to happen at the soiree. A lot of useless chatter, a few pointed expressions, one or two sycophants angling for more connection but he could ignore them. All of them.

The pieces were in place. The game had commenced and whatever else one might say about him, he was a player without peer.

Standing on the open second floor landing of the *Nissim de Camondo* Museum, he sipped champagne from a fluted glass, watching the arriving guests below. Tonight one of them would not leave and the game would begin in earnest.

With a smile he hid with another sip, he noted five of the Council of Seven members, blending seamlessly with the bankers, power brokers, politicians and society elite of Paris. Philippe Cheverill was half-listening to Mme. Bonheaur who was a bore of a woman but very well-connected. The dress designer Bran had just arrived, looking impatient and not happy to be here. Wouldn't he be surprised at what was in store for him?

The Council members had been invited as individuals, each not necessarily knowing the others would be in attendance. Nor did they all know they were in Paris at the same time. That took some maneuvering but not as much as one would expect. Preternaturals were nothing if not predictable, once one knew which strings to pull, which inducements to use. Jebediah Noziak was the most unpredictable, but even he had been brought to town via his Achilles Heel; his loyalty and trust.

The fool.

Noziak did not need to be at the soiree though it would have been enjoyable to see his expression when the events unfolded.

Patience. The game always went to the one who dared and the one who was resolute enough to see it through till the end.

He was just turning away from the gilded wrought iron railing when a commotion at the front door arrested his attention. Three women and a man. Two of the women he dismissed as attractive and preternatural, at another time and place he would have been interested, but it was the third woman that intrigued him now.

She had come. Here? But why?

Then he caught her looking around, seeking someone and not impressed by the private residence-turned-a-frozen-monument to the *Belle Epoche* décor. A shame because it was quite good. Most were only able to enjoy the place as a museum with grubby-fingered urchins whining as their parents trudged them through the expansive mansion or Japanese tourists snapping photos at every turn, as if one only succeeded by the sheer volume of images taken while abroad. How pedestrian.

But there was nothing pedestrian about the woman standing in the black and white hallway below. He leaned a little closer to the rail, following her line of sight but only paying attention when her expression shifted from restive to engaged.

Ah, of course, *Monsieur* Bran.

He had stepped in to help her earlier but without a clear motivation. Though one look at her now and the motivation might be simple.

She was stunning, in a gold strapless gown that glowed against her caramel skin, in part because of the revealing slit that opened thigh length as she shifted. Her hair was pulled away from a sculpted face but when she leaned over to speak to the blonde man at her side a rope of thick dark hair was visible down her back.

He'd been told she was attractive but that paled in seeing her in person. The banked vibrancy, the raw energy simmering within her. She was a woman dressed to capture the eye, particularly the male eye, but in spite of the several very interested looks cast her way, her focus was only on one man.

A complication or a bonus?

Tightening his fingers around his empty glass, he weighed the probability factors, the pros and cons of tweaking his original plan, and only when sure he could still accomplish his goals did he set his glass aside.

The game had just become more stimulating.

CHAPTER 20

"I see him," I whispered to François who was hovering at my side like a parental hawk. "I'll be back."

But leave it to François to have his own agenda as he placed my arm over his, a gesture that looked refined but made a very effective deterrent to my walking away. Not without tugging him along like a reluctant barge.

And he wasn't budging.

I flipped my hair which I'd tied in a braid over my shoulder and leaned in close to him, a smile plastered on my face, my whisper for his ears alone. "You want to tell me what you're doing? We're here to talk with Bran."

"Patience *mon chou*," he murmured, nodding his head at a couple strolling past us. "It will be better if he comes to us."

But he wouldn't. Not after this morning. Bran was nothing if not stubborn and difficult.

I eyed François, the first part of his words seeping into my awareness. This time I didn't keep my voice low. "What did you just call me?"

It was Mandy who answered. "He called you a cabbage."

She was still chuckling as she walked away, until stopped by a very attractive man introducing himself to her. An older man but familiar looking, though there should be no reason I'd know anyone in France. Except Bran who had his back to me across the room. A very tense back.

Another man was approaching François. A younger one who looked like he belonged on an American magazine cover, such as *Success* or *Entrepreneur*. Fit, assured, almost cocky.

Not Frank kind of cocky but that same the-world-is-my-oyster-look.

Not what I wanted to be doing, chit chatting with a bunch of strangers. But the other man did act as a distraction as Frank slipped into his role as François Dupris, urbane, charming, and cultured.

The second François turned his head to talk to the newcomer, I kissed him on the cheek, surprising him enough to loosen his grip. "I'll be right back, *Cherie*," I murmured. Two could play the false endearment game as I flashed a smile at the other man. It must have been one hell of a grin as he looked as taken off guard as Frank.

I didn't hang around but pulled away and crossed the crowded room, reaching Bran just about the time he turned around and spied me. Thunderstorms looked more warm and friendly.

"What are you doing here?" he snarled, grabbing my upper arm and tugging me toward an oasis of quiet in the curve of the circular stairway leading to an open second floor. Tara had nothing on this place. "Don't you realize how dangerous this is?"

What was he talking about?

With my back against a marble wall he had me effectively caged, not that I was planning to escape; I'd worked too hard to get to him.

"Do you mean the Council?" I whispered, looking around to make sure no one else could hear us. Of course they couldn't, they were too caught up in their own chatter to pay attention to us. Except for Frank and the other man who still seemed off kilter. As if no one had walked away from them before. And any vampires in the room. Or Weres. Come to think about it there could be a lot of eavesdroppers.

Bran towered over me, all pent up emotion, dark looks and flashing eyes. Which as the old Franco would have said was a very good look for the warlock. Very hot. "What do you know about the Council?"

Shaking my head to get back on task I was pleased my voice didn't betray my distractions. "They summoned you. Didn't they?"

Unless Ling Mai made up a threat against Bran to make me jump higher and faster.

"How do you know?"

I shrugged. I doubted Ling Mai wanted me to blab agency secrets. "What does it matter? You're in danger if you go."

The sound he uttered was a cross between a snort and a choked laugh. "I have no choice."

That word again. But he was right. One didn't ignore a Council summons without dire consequences.

Suddenly I wanted to soothe the deep lines along his brow, the weariness around his eyes. He was seriously worried and, if my guess was right, on the razor's edge of losing his warlock control.

"When do you have to appear?" I asked, no longer just on my mission.

"Tomorrow at one."

"Why?"

"You don't know?"

The way he said it you would have thought I'd been the one to turn him in, not his cousin's actions. Damn her anyway. But that was the way it'd always been between us. He'd protect psycho Dominique till his dying breath even if she'd already bit the dust. What would it be like to have that kind of loyalty?

Didn't matter.

"I heard that there might be another synthetic drug still out there." It was petty of me to add, "One Dominique knew about."

I watched him take the blow and flinch. Not noticeable except to someone looking for the response.

He said nothing for a moment but he averted his gaze as I felt the beat of my heart slow. He was pulling in and away.

Wasn't this what I'd asked him to do earlier? Have nothing to do with me?

Be careful of your wishes, little one, my father had told me more than once. Wishes create intentions and intentions create actions, and actions create your results. So what did I want now?

My brother's safety of course. Could I achieve that without harming Bran more? I didn't know. But maybe he did.

"Bran?" His gaze rose to mine and I forgot my next words as I felt the free fall created just by looking at him. His eyes were open, vulnerable, unsure. Not the arrogant warlock I knew too well but a man at war with himself.

I raised one hand to brush it against his cheek, just one touch like the ones we'd shared before.

As if he read my desire, his eyes darkened, became opaque and unreadable, as his own hand caught and banded around my wrist.

"What do you want, Alex?"

And that fast I fell to earth. Splat.

I shook my head to make sure there was no stardust in my own gaze, no remnants of hope. It was to be business, and only business between us. Fine. The boundaries were drawn as clearly as any Berlin Wall.

"I need to know what you know to find my brother." I was proud how controlled and smooth my words were, given the disappointment racing through me.

"Always the mission," he said and I swore I could hear the echo of regret in his tone. Or maybe that was wishful thinking.

"Yes." I looked around, shaking his hold off of me, seeking a few seconds to gather my shredded what-might-have-beens. That's when I noticed the silver-haired man who'd been speaking to Mandy earlier. He was standing across the room from me but we could see one another easily. Before I'd noticed his good looks, now I noticed his paleness as he stared at me. As if he'd seen a ghost.

He raised one hand to his throat as the other hand gestured to me. A one-finger admonishment as if shouting no, no, though he was making no noise. No noise at all.

Until he fell to the floor and the room erupted into movement.

A fit? A stroke? What did it matter; I only knew that I had to get to him, against the tide of people shuffling away from him.

I didn't say a word to Bran, just pushed against the people, not caring who I knocked against though I was aware there were a fair number of preternaturals in the room. Not an unusual amount given the wealthy and powerful at this gathering. Give yourself a few centuries to get your act together and many preternaturals, those who gravitated toward possessiveness, tended to acquire enough material wealth to reach the higher rungs of a material society.

But that's not what I was thinking about right then. I was focused on reaching this stranger's side. Which I did, my breath short as I knelt beside him, a man I took to be a doctor on the other side, searching for a pulse.

I didn't expect him to find one until the man who'd collapsed flashed his eyes open. He clawed at my hand. "Alex?"

How did he know my name? Who was he?

I leaned closer, aware of his need to tell me something. "Yes?"

"Seekers," he whispered, his words more breath than substance. "Beware." He coughed and his lids fluttered closed.

I grabbed his palm, feeling its coolness between my hands as I glanced at the doctor who was shouting directions in French. I doubt he knew the answers to the questions I had roaring through me.

"Don't die," I murmured over the man, "Please don't die."

He knew information I needed. Desperately.

His eyes quivered open. Hope tap-danced through me. "Help is coming. Just hold on."

A sad smile touched his lips as if his pale blue eyes could already see more than I could. He crooked one finger, gesturing me closer.

I leaned near enough it looked like I was about to kiss him. But he was fading so fast I had to hear what he fought to tell me.

Just as I was ready to pull back, let others with more experience at saving lives help, he muttered in a low chant. "Beware. Beware . . . beware."

"Yes, I know to be careful." I was aware of how hard he was struggling to say the pitiful amount he was. "But beware of what? Or who?"

He smiled then, a real smile that showed me the attractive man I'd noticed earlier.

Then he coughed out a single word. "Jebediah."

My father? Someone else?
But it was too late. He was gone.

CHAPTER 21

I was gobsmacked. How many Jebediah's could there be in the world? Surely more than my father. Please, let there be lots more. So why did I know, deep inside me, that this stranger meant my dad?

Maybe because he knew my name? Fought so hard to speak to me even as he was dying?

The younger man who'd helped me escape François earlier suddenly appeared at my side.

"Philippe?" The single word sounded like a cry from the heart. "You can't. Philippe." He raised his head, spearing first me, and then the doctor across from us with a look demanding answers. "You have to save him."

Thank the Spirits the doctor answered because I still couldn't find my tongue.

"I'm sorry young man, there's nothing we can do. Did he have a heart condition? Health issues?"

"No. None."

That's when it hit me. I glanced at my ring, not trusting the heat I felt from it. But it glowed almost pink against my skin. The dead man was a preternatural of some kind. So were others nearby. Very close.

I shot a glance at the young man who was shaking his head in grief, an anguish so deep it made it hard to look at him. "I'm sorry," I said, speaking to his pain. An automatic gesture. "The paramedics or whatever they're called here have been summoned."

His gray eyes seemed to focus then, latched on to my face as if searching for something.

"You're not French?"

I shook my head. "No."

I understood this response to shock. The tendency to grab on to whatever one could, the more mundane the easier until you could shore up too volatile emotions.

The man cocked his head at me as if really seeing me for the first time. "Did you know him?"

Another head shake. "No." Then before a lot of messy questions could be asked I said, "It's obvious you did. A friend? Relative?"

"The best friend I ever had or could hope to have." He turned back to the dead man.

The words startled me for their stark simplicity and raw pain. Could one wish for a better epitaph. Then I realized what I was doing. Ignoring the man's final words.

I stumbled to my feet, needing some air. "Excuse me. I must go." I smiled at the man still crouched at his friend's side. Until he rose beside me.

"I'm sorry, who are you?"

"Alexis Noziak." I extended one hand. "Though everyone calls me Alex."

His handshake was half-hearted, as if going through the motions, but he didn't release my hand as he said, "Thank you for being with him. At the end."

What could I say to that? "Not a problem."

"Did he say anything? Any last words?"

Nothing that needed to be bandied about came my gut response. So I shook my head again, adding a, "Sorry, no."

There was something off here, apart from the whole stranger knowing my name and dying in my arms bit. But I couldn't put my finger on it.

"Foolish of me to ask." The younger man quirked a wobbly smile as he glanced at his friend. "I just hoped for some last something. To hold onto."

Made sense. Might not be my way but who was I to begrudge this guy what he needed.

I wanted to leave but it seemed rude to just jerk my hand out of his so I gave him a shaky smile. "You didn't mention your name."

"I didn't?" he looked like he was stumbling around in a fog. "Forgive me. Pádraig Byrne."

"Nice to meet you." I could have kicked myself for sounding so banal given the situation but thankfully I was saved by the arrival of two men and a woman all dressed in black with orange vests. Must be the French emergency response service, which gave me the excuse I needed to tug my hand away from Byrne's and step back. I don't know if he even heard my mumbled excuses.

Didn't matter. I still needed that air and space to think. But leave it up to Bran not to give me either.

He must have been right behind me as he snaked a hand around my waist and propelled me toward the rear of the house, not as noisy, and less in an uproar. I wasn't sure if he was treating me like a wilting flower because he thought having a total stranger die while I was holding him was going to undo me, or if the act was for show. Either way the second we entered what looked like an empty kitchen I pulled away from him, practically swatting his hands away.

Not that I didn't like being pressed up against his hard body. I did. Too much and that was the problem. I had too many things to deal with already tonight; I didn't need one more.

"Enough," I said, stepping back to put space between us. "I won't faint."

"Never thought you would," came his quick response, but one without heat. "You want to tell me what you were doing rushing to Philippe Cheverill's side like a long, lost friend?"

"He called me," I said before I realized the words were going to escape. Bran's arched brow gave me some backbone as I clarified. "Not call as in speak but he seemed to summon me. With his hands."

"Why?"

"I have no idea. I'd never met the man before." Bran gave me a perplexed look I didn't understand. So I added, "He appeared in distress, from across the room, and then when he fell it seemed like everyone was moving away from him, just when he needed help."

That I could relate to, especially in my complicated relationship with Bran. But now wasn't the time to point fingers or create more antagonism between us. We had enough painful memories for a lifetime. Instead I shrugged. "He needed help and I thought I could help."

"In what way?"

Why was he being so difficult? "I don't know. You might have been able to do something."

"Meaning?"

I looked around though we were the only ones in the room. I lowered my voice anyway. "That whole bring-someone-back-from-the-dead-thing you can do."

He stared at me for a moment until he jammed one hand through his hair, then shook his head. "Just for your information I don't go around reversing death every chance I can. That's as unnatural and dangerous as what you did this morning with your power-amplification act."

That hurt. In the space of one sentence he turned my good deed, to help a stranger, and twisted it around to make me an abomination. On the other hand the fact he once returned me to life after I'd died made me feel better about what he was willing to do for me. That was then though, this was now.

But he wasn't finished. "Death is as much a part of life as birth. Reversing that has consequences."

"I know that." What did he think I was? A total idiot? I understood the cost of magic, better than most, so he didn't need to rub it in my face. "So I'm a freak. You're not. I get it."

"Not what I said."

We were way off the reason I'd tracked him down tonight. "Can we get back to the finding Vaverek and locating my brother discussion?" I asked, knowing even as the words left my mouth he was going to take offense. So I offered a carrot. "Won't finding Vaverek help you if you have to go before the Council?"

He looked at me as if I was talking Swahili. "You really don't know do you?"

"Know what?"

"Who Philippe Cheverill is . . . or was."

I raised my palms to him in an I-give-up universal gesture. I wanted Vaverek. Bran wanted to beat a dead horse, neither of us particularly happy with the other one right then.

Just as Bran opened his mouth, and I assumed was going to tell me who the dead stranger was, Frank or François bustled into the room.

"There you are," he said with a buzz of urgency beneath his voice and a minimization of his French accent. "I'd get out of here. Now. Before a world of hurt comes smashing down on you."

I glanced at Bran who actually looked like he knew what François was babbling about.

Instead of cluing me in, he spoke to François. "She says she doesn't know who Philippe Cheverill was."

"I didn't. I don't." I wanted to shake them both. "Why should I?"

Frank tsked, tsked as if dealing with a cranky toddler. He looked at Bran. "Leave it to her to get in the middle."

Bran nodded, which made me want to kick them both. Not the best of moves when dealing with a powerful warlock and a temperamental shifter.

"Will someone please tell me what's going on?" I growled.

Bran gave Frank a nod. But Mandy came bursting through the kitchen door before he said a word. Did no one have anything to do except run into the kitchen in hysterics?

"Go! Go! Go!" she shouted at me. "Now!"

Was this a trick? Have her scare me off only to turn around to Ling Mai to tell her I'd vamoosed? End of my short stay as an IR agent. "Alone?"

"I'll come with you," Bran said, shocking me more than everyone else yelling at me to run.

"Won't that put you in more trouble with the Council?"

François grabbed my elbow. "Can't get into much more trouble. I'm coming too."

I knew I looked like an idiot standing there with my mouth open, wondering what all the hullabaloo was about.

Mandy was flapping her hands at me like I was a chicken escaped from the henhouse. François was dragging me toward the back door. Bran's expression was so intense he scared me. And no one made sense, until Jaylene came slamming through the hallway door.

"Did you really kill him?" She looked only at me. "The head of the Council."

"The Council of Seven?" I croaked, my whole body going numb.

"Of course, how many Councils do you know about?"

Four gazes lasered in on me as I stood there, a frozen wreck in the middle of a dark kitchen. "You mean the old man?"

It was François who answered with a nod. "*Oui, ma cocotte,* Philippe Cheverill was an arch druid. And the head of the Council."

CHAPTER 22

The next hour was a blur. François gabbed one of my arms, Bran the other and hustled me out the back door into the brisk air of a spring night. The roar that was Paris echoed around us as a waxing moon peeked from behind scattered clouds. The old child's rhyme came to me:
If you see the moon at the end of the day
A bright full moon is on its way
If you see the moon in the early dawn
Look real quick, it will soon be gone.
Latching onto the mundane, just as I had earlier. No way could the dead man be the head of the Council. That was like saying I'd held the President's hand as he lay dying. Or the Pope's.

So how did he know my name? Maybe he remembered it from the vote that sent me straight to prison when the Council decided revealing there were extenuating circumstances—of the supernatural kind—to the murder I was accused of last year, would create more harm to the larger preternatural community. I got it then, I was a small cog in a very large wheel of worldwide preternaturals trying to just get along.

Okay, maybe I was a little bitter, a little resentful of the Council's decision. If they had a few more balls, and created their own policing force that kept lowlifes like the rogue Were in check, then they wouldn't screw with the poor peon who was just trying to protect herself. Me being that peon.

But that was water under the bridge.

Since I'd never appeared in person in front of the Council I was surprised that the head of the group could remember my name from a file and maybe a mug shot. It had been a year ago and surely he'd had bigger issues to handle since then. Such as this whole Vaverek mess. And the Seekers. Though the old man had mentioned them.

But why in the world should anyone think I killed him? I'd only held his hand.

Unless someone had put who I was together with my past and found an easy scapegoat. But how likely was that? Nothing made sense.

I careened to a halt, making François and Bran pull up short.

We were in a bricked alleyway, the smell of boxwood hedges and ivy strong in the space barely wide enough to have the three of us abreast. The moon almost obscured by clouds so maybe we'd been running longer than I thought we had.

"I didn't kill him," I said, wanting to scream it from rooftops. My breath was chugging but my skin felt cold and clammy. If going through the human judicial system was scary it was nothing to facing the Council's wrath if they really believed I'd killed one of their own. "Someone is setting me up."

"Why, duckie?" François' teeth gleamed in the near dark. "As much trouble as you create I could see someone wanting you out of the way, but what are the chances of that particular person being at this particular event?"

Damn, when he said it like that he made perfect sense. I dug my heels into the cobbled path, which wasn't easy given I was still in stilettos. "But I didn't do it. I'm innocent."

Bran snorted, but for once I didn't feel like kicking him. I was running way low on allies as well as being too double-whammied by tonight's events. And that didn't include why the head of the Council warned me about my father, if that's who he was talking about.

"Get a move on it," came Bran's terse response. No warm and fuzzies from him. "I can't hold a cloaking spell out here for much longer."

"You can do that? While we're on the move?" I was impressed. I could barely do that when hiding in the shadows. Not that my rusty magic abilities were important right now. At least the simple spells. The suck-everyone's-powers-around-me thing I could do, but not the simple stuff. I was so messed up, plus I was doing that focus-on-the-everyday-detail thing again.

"Come on." François took my hand this time, handling me gently as if I were fragile. He was right. Inside I was splintering.

But Noziaks didn't shatter. Implode maybe, but not until we fought back and I hadn't even begun to fight back.

Ignoring François' hand and Bran's impatience shimmering through the night I bent to peel off one of my shoes.

"What are you doing?" Bran growled, as if I was intentionally being perverse.

"You try running in stilettos."

"Do you have any idea how much those cost?" François moaned. "Those are Borgezie stilettos."

I smiled, a real smile, the first one all night as I removed the second shoe and handed them to him. "Then you wear them."

I thought I heard Bran choke back a laugh but it could have been a cat knocking over a garbage can lid. Either way I had started to run and it didn't take long for Bran to catch up with me. I tightened my hand around my clutch, not wanting to lose my phone in it.

"Any idea where you're going?" he said, as he jogged beside me.

"Nope."

"Why should I not be surprised."

I didn't bother responding; my focus one hundred percent on pounding the ground, hoping there were few rocks or shards of broken glass around, and wondering what I was going to do next.

CHAPTER 23

It was after midnight when the three men returned to Van's cell. Another change of routine that had him curious as to what was up and why.

All he could do was wait. Not one of his favorite pastimes.

The footsteps sounded faster now. Impatient. Two of the men were breathing heavily as if they'd raced a long way. The human's hands were clumsy as he fiddled with the cell door lock. Van could smell his fear from across the room.

"I want to know his status. Now!" The one Van thought of as the power broker snapped. It sounded like he was finishing an ongoing conversation.

The doctor, Jean-Luc was it? No, Jean Claude, scuffled across the room, his nerves obvious by the pounding of his heart, the increase of his sweat, the shallowness of his breathing. Something was scaring these two. Something or someone.

The doctor was rough as he jerked Van's head up, shining a penlight into his eyes.

"What the hell?" Van snarled, not having to work too hard to sound pissed.

"Ah, Mister Noziak, you do know how to speak," the power broker murmured and yes, he was the same man from earlier. "Shall I share with you a little secret?"

Torment came in many forms. This man's specialty, so far, seemed to be verbal torture. But if he felt chatty, and let something spill that Van could use, who was Van to let the opportunity pass.

He grunted an assent, knowing the other didn't expect much more from him.

He was right, as the power broker nodded. "*Bonne*. I think you will like what I have to say."

But the a-hole didn't continue. Instead he waited.

The prick.

Van nudged him along with a taunt. "What makes you think I care about anything you have to say?"

It worked like a charm as the other cleared his throat. "Even if the news I have concerns your sister?"

The growl ripped from Van this time was not feigned as he tugged at his restraints.

The doctor jumped back. "Do not aggravate him, I implore you," he said, clicking his teeth. "Not if you wish the experiment to go as planned."

So the trial was now an experiment. But what did that have to do with Alex? Did they really know something or was this just more torture?

"*C'est la vie*." The power broker's tone showed he'd learned what he'd wanted from Van.

When Van broke free he'd make sure this guy didn't die quick or easy. It was his turn to taunt. "Big man, aren't you," he said, his voice husky and low. "Only a coward goes after a man's family. But then I wouldn't expect anything less from you."

"That is a shame, Mister Noziak," came the quick reply. "That you think I am only, how do you say, poking at you. For I just saw your sister a few hours ago."

Van held himself very still. No way was Alex in Paris. She was in prison. It sucked, but at least she was safe there. So why was this creep saying otherwise?

"Like I would believe anything you said," Van spat out, ignoring the doctor as the man slipped a blood pressure cuff around his arm.

"A suspicious man, I see. Would you believe me if I told you her hair is still waist length?"

"A photo could tell you as much."

"True."

The blood pressure cuff tightened.

"This is not good." The doctor shook his head, before glancing at the other over his shoulder. "I must insist that you cease."

The power broker released a sigh, as if he was finished anyway. "The shifter will discover in due time whether I speak the truth or not." He stepped toward the door, waving the human forward. "Don't forget the photo."

Blinded by a flash of light, Van could do little more than scrunch his eyes closed to rid them of the dancing motes. "What the hell—"

"For your sister." The power broker laughed. "A momento."

For real? Or another way to undermine Van?

"Till tomorrow." The man touched a hand to the brim of his hood before walking out of the cell, followed closely by the doctor and the human.

Van tugged at his restraints, knowing it was useless, and only earning the stench and pain of them burning deeper into his skin.

Whatever was going on he'd find out tomorrow. And if these people had involved Alex they'd rue the day they were created.

CHAPTER 24

Jeb Noziak was awakened by an insistent knock on the door. Philippe? With news of Van or Alex?

He threw off his bed clothes though it'd been less than an hour since he'd gone to bed. His attempts to reach either of his children on the astral level had failed. Something was blocking them from his awareness. Not a simple cloaking spell that any hedge witch could produce but more like a jammer. He'd never encountered anything like it before, which didn't make him a happy man. Especially after what he'd learned from Pádraig's files earlier.

Alex had a lot to explain to him once he found her. A whole lot.

The knocking became louder. More frantic.

"I'm coming," he called out, grabbing a bathrobe and tightening the belt around him. He didn't bother with turning on a light as he could see as well in the dark and the room was familiar enough.

"What is it?" he asked, his voice a near snarl as he recognized Pádraig standing in the hallway, his hair mussed, strain bracketing his face. "Where's Philippe?"

"He's dead," came the abrupt reply. "The Tunisian has run off."

What? Shock roared through Jeb. Not possible. Then he remembered Philippe's earlier words, about the previous attempts on his life. But why?

The Tunisian? Oh, yes, the butler. But what did the butler have to do with Pádraig's news?

"What happened?" he demanded, stepping into the hallway. "An accident?"

The younger man shook his head, his face looking pale beneath the glare of lighting. Every lamp in the house must be switched on as if to scare away the night threats. But if what Pádraig had said was true, the worst had already happened.

When Pádraig didn't respond, Jeb steered him toward the library, and once he'd been seated, slumping forward in the chair, his head in his hands, Jeb grabbed a bottle of Jameson's and splashed a liberal amount in a crystal glass.

"Drink this," he urged Pádraig. "Then we'll talk."

It took the younger man two gulps to down the whole glass. Jeb kept his surprise to himself. Shock did different things to different people.

"Tell me what happened?" he repeated, the minute Pádraig appeared stable.

"They think he was poisoned." Pádraig's eyes showed far too much white, like a spooked horse, but Jeb couldn't wait.

"By who?"

The Pádraig shook his head, holding out his empty glass. Jeb rose to pour him some more, frustrated at the delay.

Only when Pádraig swallowed the next full glass did he continue. "There are names swirling around. Innuendos. Accusations. It's a bloody arseways cockup." His Irish accent as well as slang had increased. A sure sign of distress. He glanced up as if noticing Jeb for the first time. "They're on their way here. The *Guards*."

At Jeb's frown he added, "*Un policier*. The coppers."

Jeb got the message, but still he pushed for details. "Now?"

"*Oui*."

"But why?"

"Philippe was well connected, within the Council and outside of it." Pádraig ran a shaky hand through his hair. "He made a lot of enemies. Now everyone is a suspect."

The man was distraught, speaking wildly. Surely the French police would have to search Philippe's home, ask questions of his friends, but Pádraig was indicating more was at stake.

Jeb leaned forward to ask for more details when the front door knocker boomed through the house.

"They are here." Pádraig jerked upright as if Nazi jackboots were beating down the entrance, looking for him.

"What are you afraid of?" Jeb wanted to shake him, seeing the flash of blue light cleaving the night outside the window. "Tell me now."

"For all our sakes, say nothing about your daughter," came the stunning response.

"What about Alex?"

The young man shook off Jeb's hand and straightened his suit.

"Tell me about Alex." Jeb pressed harder. "Now."

"She's the chief suspect."

"For what?"

"Killing Philippe. That's what."

CHAPTER 25

I wasn't sure where we were but Bran seemed to know what he was doing as he punched a key code into a discreet panel near a metal door. It looked like we were in an industrial area, or maybe a former industrial area, with rows of low brick buildings looking boxy against the skyline.

François pushed open the well-oiled door. A scent of cement floors and damp wafted toward me but it didn't smell old as much as empty.

When he went to reach for a light switch, Bran stopped him. "Wait till we're all inside."

I guess that meant I wasn't moving fast enough.

Bite me.

My feet were shredded from who knew how many miles we'd trekked. I was freezing as the dress François had picked out for me—which worked fine in a packed crowd—was paper-thin against a Paris April night, and I had to wrap my arms around my upper body to keep from shivering.

Still I shuffled in after François, trying not to smack into him in the darkness that was worse than outside even as Bran left the door open. A small shaft of moonlight leaked into the room but it wasn't enough to show me anything.

"Where are we?" I whispered. "If this is your place, won't they be looking for us here?"

I knew which "they" I was most concerned about. The take-no-prisoners Council.

"Owned by a friend," he mumbled as he trod past me. Leave it to a warlock to be able to see in the dark. And then his words struck me. A friend. As in blonde with mile long legs and a French accent?

Why I should care right then was beyond me, not with the other crap I was dealing with. Still it pricked. "She won't be back soon will she?" I asked.

"Who said it was a she?" he said somewhere deep inside the stygian space. I could have sworn there was a smile beneath his words.

So I kept my mouth shut.

François leaned closer to me, brushing my shoulder as he whispered, "Betrayed yourself that time, didn't you luv?"

His accent was pure British right then. And all snark.

I didn't have time to tell him where he could stuff it though as a whiff of something came my way. Familiar.

François tensed beside me. This time I was the one leaning in close to him. "Were."

There wasn't time for more as a large shape came hurtling from the shadowed doorway and slammed into François and I like a bowling ball set on stun.

We both sprawled forward, in opposite directions.

Two things saved us. The first was the Were remained in human form, in spite of his preternatural scent. I was lucky as I could smell both Weres and shifters, even in their human forms. The second, he seemed to pause, as if he was hesitating. Or waiting for something.

Either way, as long as he remained human we might survive.

If Bran joined us we might stand a chance, but even as I was saying my thank yous for having a warlock along, a second shadow spend past me and toward the kitchen.

Now I know why the first one waited. Backup.

"Were," I shouted, giving Bran as much advance warning as possible, which wasn't much as I heard a hard wham, the sound of two solid masses colliding.

Not going to be a lot of help from that direction.

François was a shifter, which could usually take on a Were of equal size and weight. But François in shifter form was a poodle. Not the kind bred in World War II as attack dogs, but the frou-frou kind, look-at-me-aren't-I-something kind.

Which left me and my scant training as a fighting agent. Since we were barely into our second month of Krav Maga at the Agency that wasn't saying much. But I held one advantage; being raised with four brothers who thought street fighting was a basic form of communication.

They were right.

I rolled to my side then paused, as if hurt. I was winded, but only a fool gave up before the real fight ever began. My eyes adjusting to the darkness, could see the Were's shape come after me again.

A quick twist and sweep of my lower body tripped him. This time he was the one splatting across the floor. I was on my feet again before he scrambled to his knees. Unlike him I wasn't going to give him the chance of getting close enough to do serious damage.

I rocked from foot to foot, wishing I'd had my anathema dagger, my ritual knife with me, but the cocktail dress I was wearing didn't have a scrap of fabric to hide it. Go figure.

Behind me I could hear François shifting. Changing body shapes was a lot like changing complicated clothes with Velcro and zippers; there was always some noise in the process. Maybe he could snap at the Were, and between us we could contain him. No way were we going to take him down. Not alone.

But the thumps and crashes in the other room indicated Bran wasn't going to be free for a while.

The Were stood, arrogance riding his stance. He was a good foot taller than me, wide across the shoulders, and a good thirty pounds heavier if his shadow was anything to go by.

Double crap.

Stone had better be right about what he'd taught us so far about Krav Maga.

I hopped back as if on the defense before shifting direction and springing toward the Were, one foot extended to hit him in the family jewels followed by a quick elbow jab as he doubled over and grunted.

Linking both hands together as a battering ram I followed with a hard chop to the back of his neck. But even as he fell he lashed out at my knees and gave them a solid thwack.

I crumpled. Now we were eye to eye, or more my eyes reached his shoulders but I was close enough I could smell his fetid breath and hear his growls.

Only a quick feint to the right saved my shoulder from his next swing and off balanced him. Now he was toppling forward, across the top of me.

My twist was useless as he used his weight to bench press me into the cement floor, one arm across my windpipe, choking me.

Couldn't. Breathe.

Where was François? Even a doggy lick would help!

Time to get down and dirty, Noziak style.

My arms were free so I snapped them up, using thumbs to gouge his eyes. He rocked back with a howl of rage, which allowed air to rush into my lungs. Thank the Great Spirits.

But I was only getting started.

Pulling myself forward as if doing a crunch I curled my hands into fists and pounded his eardrums. When he pulled his hands from his face to cover his ears I used the old palm of the hand as a battering ram to his nose.

Blood geysered over me. I wanted to gag but there was no time.

He was off balance enough for me to rock back and forth, dislodging him enough for me to crabwalk backwards.

Were's were strong fighters but they relied too much on their size and power. They also relied on turning from human to animal form. Which meant when remaining human if they didn't take out an opponent right away, they started flagging.

Plus I was quick. To survive in the Noziak household agility and speed were ingrained into me.

I wasn't sure why the Were hadn't changed into his animal self. Once he did I was toast and getting a Were pissed was a sure fire way to make him morph.

I rolled to my knees, looking for the next attack when I heard a low growl rumble beside me.

Not another.

Bracing I reared to my feet and scrambled backwards, away from both bulky shadows until my back and shoulders hit a wall. Not pleasant but at least there was one avenue of attack cut off.

The growls increased but all I could see was a huge animal, at least as tall as my waist, casting greater darkness as it moved between me and the Were.

Wiping the sweat stinging my eyes I froze in a standing position. Not that it was going to save me, but between the instinctual response of freeze, flight or fight, the last two seemed like really bad options.

The animal wasn't charging me. Instead the Were beyond the growl was suddenly scampering backwards.

Bad idea. I could have told it that running only ratcheted up the aggression of an enraged animal. But I was chugging too much air to have any left over to save someone who just tried to kill me.

Hands braced against my knees, I watched as the growl shifted into a mastiff, the biggest damned dog I'd ever seen in my life.

A quick look around didn't show me François, but no way was this animal the MI-6 agent. He'd been a poodle last I'd seen him and shifters couldn't shift into more than one animal. Could they?

Not that I'd ever heard of and I grew up with a shifter father and four shifter brothers.

Maybe the dog just wanted to take out the biggest threat before finishing me off as dessert. Or Bran could have conjured it, though the sounds from the other room made that less likely.

Either way, silently cheering on Fido, I slowly shuffled toward the door, trying not to bring attention to my movement. But it seemed like the Were had other ideas.

He started changing, too. His high-pitched scream stopped me in my tracks. He sounded like a cougar.

One of the bad things about Weres is that their animal forms are not normal-sized, they are super-sized, as if big, scary, bad ass Weres need any extra fighting mojo.

The mastiff stood at least three feet at its shoulders and weighed maybe a hundred and fifty, two hundred pounds. His growl echoed down my spine one low octave at a time.

Now this was officially a dog and cat fight.

I swallowed but my throat was too dry, and too clenched to help.

What now?

CHAPTER 26

Jeb listened to the rise and fall of voices in the next room as he rested his hands flat on his knees. They looked at ease to the police officer who was sitting across from him with an expressionless face, but Jeb knew better.

What did Pádraig know about Alex? The question ate away at Jeb's stomach lining as he waited to be interrogated. And he had no doubt it would be an interrogation too, in spite of the formality and low-key approach of the officials so far.

What had Alex done? Did it involve Van? Which was the only reason Jeb could think why she might be in Paris. And why couldn't he reach out to Van? The last was the most worrisome issue as Jeb had always been able to reach his sons across distances, to see them and make sure they were all right. But not since Van had disappeared. He refused to accept that his son might be dead. If he was, Jeb could have found Van in the spirit realm.

But Jeb had never been able to track Alex in either the spirit world or distance viewing her in the physical realm, though they both carried shamanistic abilities.

That was his fault. Not her abilities but her lack of experience using them. After Aideen had left him, and the way she'd left him, created a hole so large within him it was all he could do to get through each day. For the first year or so he was the walking dead. Then he threw himself into his farm and raising his sons. As shifters he understood them and he knew as a shifter himself, how much training they needed to keep their animal selves and enhanced human abilities hidden from too observant human eyes.

He hadn't realized till later that he'd left Alex to fend for herself. What did he know about pigtails and dresses, not that she wore either. As for her magical abilities, what he understood about witchcraft he feared. Better to have her with no understanding of magic than to follow down the path Aideen had travelled.

At least he felt that way until Alex had been twelve or thirteen, coming into her abilities in a willy-nilly fashion that posed a danger to herself and anyone who crossed her temper. Another trait she'd inherited from him.

So he'd found Siobhán MacAuliffe, the closest witch he could track down and she was half a day away in Montana. He hadn't liked the idea of his daughter being trained by an Irish witch but Alex had needed someone to mentor her. Not that Alex had agreed. By the Spirits she'd put up a row. But he'd made up his mind, so off they'd gone to Missoula.

He almost turned right around when he discovered MacAuliffe wasn't Irish at all. She was Chinese. He'd understood her need to hide in plain sight but a witch was a witch. Or so he thought.

Alex lasted three months before MacAuliffe discovered Alex's secret abilities and called for Jeb to come fetch his daughter. It was a long, silent ride home.

He'd failed his daughter then. He wasn't about to fail her again.

If he could only figure out where she was, what she was up to, and how he could help.

CHAPTER 27

Before I had a chance to do anything the Were cougar threw itself at the mastiff and fur began to fly.

I pressed myself harder against the wall as if to become invisible, but that was only going to last until one or the other of the animals survived. Then I was the next target.

If only I could cast Bran's freeze spell. But I couldn't. I also didn't have candles, or herbs, or markers to create runes. Talk about so sorry out of luck.

Focus. What did I have?

As if called, the white light of the waxing moon leaked through the doorway, spreading its finger of light in a wedge shape along the floor.

It wasn't a full moon but I had to take what I could get.

So what spells could work via words and intention alone?

The cougar's screams increased. If I didn't stop them soon both fighters would be dead.

I didn't know where the mastiff came from but it had saved me from the Were so far, least I could do was save it back.

As long as I didn't kill us both.

I had it. A modified bully spell. The kind to repel a bothering bully. Sure it was meant for the playground, and a Were was a lot larger than any bully I had ever met but it was easy, quick and I knew the spell by heart. Thanks again to my brothers who, being on the wild side, made their share of enemies. Enemies that tended to come after me as an easier target. Until they ran into this incantation.

I stepped back from the wall, holding my hands straight away from me like an extended cross, palms facing skyward.

Inhaling a deep breath I skipped the closing my eyes part as just too stupid given the situation.

By Moon beam and Star light heed my will.
By three and nine your power I bind.

I angled myself more toward the moonlight inching through the door.

By Air and Night, keep harm from me and mine.
By two and ten, this power thus bend.

A chill breeze brushed from the outdoors and across my arms. I steadied my voice for the last part.

By Rock and Stone, cast you away.
By one and seven, so mote it be!
Bully be gone. Cast from me and mine.
Now and then, then and now.
So mote it be!

I shouted the last line, shutting my eyes in spite of best intentions. Behind my closed eyes I waited, my breath held, hearing no sounds. No cat, no dog, not even the scuffle in the kitchen.
Spirits be did I kill them all? Again?
Afraid to find out the truth I hesitated then snapped my eyes open.
In front of me only the mastiff remained, rolling its massive shoulders and scanning the room as if to find where his opponent was hiding.
But the Were was gone. Where to?
Did I care?
Suddenly I had to blink against a blinding light that came on overhead.
"What did you do?" Bran said from across the room, looking disheveled and sweaty and very put out as he stood silhouetted in the door jam leading into what I assumed was the kitchen area.

I took a deep breath but didn't move. Not with the Fido from hell still way too close for my comfort. "Why do you always assume I'm the one at fault?"

"Because you usually are."

"Tosh."

His brows raised so high they were hidden in locks of his dark hair. "Where did you send them?"

"Don't know." Didn't care. Just damn glad I was alive. For now. I shrugged, twisting my neck to ease the tightness there, wondering how one coaxed a mastiff outside. "Shoo," I said, waving my hands. "Go, fetch."

"Fetch what?" Bran asked, stepping further into the room and closer to the dog.

"I don't care what, I just want him gone."

"Why?"

I pointed at the dog, half expecting Bran to act like the massive beast wasn't there. The dog at least had enough good manners to flop down on the floor and lay its head in its man-sized paws.

Bran started laughing as he walked around the dog to reach and close the still open door. "Are you talking about François?"

"That's not François. He's a poodle."

"He *was* a poodle." the arrogant warlock used a tone no doubt meant to calm children. "Now he's a mastiff."

No way.

"Shifters can't do that." Now that I wasn't afraid for my life I was starting to get pissed and my tone said so.

"He's not exactly a shifter." Bran lifted one shoulder as he returned to the dog and leaned over to scratch François between the ears.

François just growled, which I understood perfectly. When he shifted or morphed back to his human form he'd have a lot of explaining to do but right now I had other questions for Bran.

"What were you fighting in the kitchen?" I asked, moving to a fifties-style couch set dead center in the cavernous room and sinking down on it. My legs no longer felt steady.

"Another Were. No idea what kind." he said, crossing over to sit beside me. He shot me one of his classic focused looks. The kind you want to squirm under. "You hurt?"

"Mostly my pride." No way was I going to admit I felt bruised from one end to the other. Noziaks took their lumps and kept on going. "You?"

"A few scratches."

It was my turn to glance at him, too many questions pushing against me. "Why do you think they didn't immediately attack as Weres? They'd have been a lot deadlier."

"Don't think they wanted corpses."

"What did they want?"

"Hostages? Something other than to kill us that's for sure."

"Did you recognize them?" I asked, bracing for the answer.

He gave me a WTH look then he must have decided not fighting with me was a better idea as he sighed and shook his head. "Never saw them before."

"Did they follow us?"

"Only thing that makes sense. No one knew where we'd be otherwise."

"Were they after all of us?"

"Not likely." He sounded tired, or maybe it was just thoughtful. "If they followed us they would have had to have known we'd been at the museum, which indicates forethought and planning."

"Vaverek?" The name popped out.

"That would be my guess."

"But why?"

"Tell me what happened back at the museum, with Cheverill."

I summarized as succinctly as I could, aware that even with the door closed, I was shaking. Muscle burn? Possibly. Fear was more likely. Fear of the unknown. Someone was pulling strings, playing a game I didn't understand. One with high stakes.

I finished telling Bran everything I knew, except for the dying man's words about the Seekers and the name Jebediah. The first was strictly agency business and the latter was nobody's business but my own.

He remained quiet, which usually worried me because his silences were not the peaceful kind. They were more the all-hell-is-going-to-break-loose once the thought process was finished. But here in this open, strange place I found I liked just sitting next to him. François, if that was indeed who the mastiff was, acted more like a family pet instead of a killer Fido at our feet.

I leaned against the couch back, aware how tired I was. What happened to Jaylene and Mandy? Had they told Ling Mai what had transpired at the museum? Why I'd bombed out of the place? Or was I on my own?

And what was happening with Van? Another day had passed and still no word on my brother.

"When was the last time you ate?" Bran asked, his shoulder brushing mine.

Good question. "I had some pastry while at the café waiting for Fido here to show up."

The dog cocked one ear toward me but otherwise didn't stir.

"You hungry?"

"Nah." I wasn't. I was too tired to be hungry. Was it only this morning that we'd had the rumble outside of Vaverek's apartment? I glanced at Bran, seeing the way the single room light cast shadows across his face, slashing lines that made him more dangerous warlock. It was a good look and I could feel the kick start of my libido responding.

I never did have the sense not to get involved with the bad boys. And Bran was as bad-ass a bad boy as I'd ever crossed paths with, even when dressed like the international businessman he was.

"Why are you being nice to me?" I asked, so wiped out the words escaped before I could corral them.

He turned his head, a lazy smile playing about his lips. I remembered the taste of those lips. Man, did I remember. His words sounded like slow, warm molasses. "Maybe because you look like you were on the losing end of a fight with a Were."

"You charmer you." But there was no heat behind my words. To have sparks you needed energy.

As if he heard my exhaustion, or wondered who was sitting

next to him without taking his head off, he straightened, facing me. "Turn around," he said.

"Why?" Okay, maybe there were a few sparks left.

"I want to give your shoulders a rub. Looks like it might help."

Damn, way to sneak under a woman's defenses. I was so stiff though that it took a while to turn enough to give him access to my back.

By all the Spirits his hands felt good. Strong and sure and perfect. He kneaded muscles like he did everything else, very thorough and intense.

I may have released a small moan as his fingers started loosening knots I didn't know I possessed.

"The only thing holding you together is tension," he murmured in that low, sexy way he had. Sort of a cross between a rumble and a caress.

"Hmmmmmm."

"You keep this up and you won't be any good to anybody."

I had to smile as his words implied I mattered, at least a little. Something he'd never dare to tell me face-to-face. Guess it'd be hard to threaten and compliment in the same sentence.

"You should give up dress designing and become a masseuse," I sighed as the silence stretched between us. Not the usual tautness since Dominique's death, but a calm hush that let my shoulders relax, the misgivings of the day slide away. I leaned forward, wallowing in the warmth of his hands along my neck, down my spine, heating my lower back.

If he kept it up I'd weep. Or turn around and crawl all over him.

"Your tensing up again," he said, stroking my back with long, sure touches. "What are you thinking about?"

"Us."

I didn't realize I'd said the word aloud until I heard his chuckle. I twisted to glance over my shoulder but found I couldn't speak. Not with the way he looked, heat in his eyes, the flare of his nostrils, the tightening of his jaw. I swear I could smell his arousal. Or was it my own.

"Bran . . ."

I didn't know what I wanted other than him. And that was pure stupid.

He said nothing, as if waiting for me to dig both our graves.

I shook my head as if one or both of us had spoken. "Not a good idea."

His lips quirked upwards but no smile reached his eyes.

It took everything I had to move, to pull myself away, and stand up, locking my legs because they quivered. Not exhaustion this time but with a need I wasn't willing to admit. "It's late."

Stupid comment but better than asking where the nearest bedroom was, though that was my implication. Even I knew not to throw kerosene onto a fire.

He nodded toward a door I hadn't noticed yet. The space felt more like it had originally been, a warehouse rather than a home, so it threw me for a few seconds as to what he meant by his gesture.

"Your room," he said at last, his voice raspy and raw, as if he was struggling as much as I was.

Thank the Spirits. I hated being the only puddle of need.

Fido François yawned at my feet, which helped give me enough umph to move. I'd forgotten all about his presence, which only went to show how far gone I was.

I waited until I was across the room, as far from Bran as possible before I turned and trusted my tone enough to say, "Thank you. For the back rub."

It was meant to be light and casual. But all I could see was Bran's look that promised we were not done yet. What smoldered between us was not over. Not by a long shot.

CHAPTER 28

Jeb woke shortly after nine though it'd been after six when he finally returned to his bedroom last night, or better yet, that same morning.

The French police were less aggressive than he expected, or maybe the first go around was only meant as a warm-up. No questions about Alex. Most about his relationship with Philippe. From some of the questions asked Jeb realized his old friend had fingers in far more pies than even Jeb knew about. Business interests. Politics. International connections.

Before he'd closed his eyes, jet lag and grief pummeling him, Jeb had tried a journey to the other side, to see if he could connect with Philippe. No such luck. Not that Jeb held high hopes. One didn't dabble in the spirit world like a quick day trip to the seashore. To really learn anything he needed to treat his gift as the responsibility it was.

Later then, after he asked some more questions of Pádraig. And after he found new lodgings. He didn't feel right being in his old friend's home alone. Not because of fear of a threat against his own life, but Philippe possessed a bounty of possessions and, in spite of the Frenchman's words to the contrary, Jeb didn't trust Pádraig enough yet. All the protégé had to do was point a finger or raise some doubts as to what might be missing in the house and Jeb would suffer. One's reputation, once stained, remained stained.

Stretching and mentally reviewing what needed to be done first, Jeb's eye was caught by a piece of paper slipped beneath the door. The cream color stood out against the silk Isfahan rug of golds and blues.

How did someone get the note get into the house and know which door to slide it under?

Jeb felt the quality of the note as he picked it up. It was handwritten in older fashioned ink, in a style it took a few moments to decipher. When he did his heart stuttered.

Your son is in danger. Your daughter is not safe.
If you wish to see either again:
Noon – Small park behind 72 Rue de Varenne.
Come alone.

The last line felt like a kick. With Philippe dead, Jeb had no one else to come with him. He had no doubt he'd go. As soon as he figured out how to grab a taxi and find the location.

He dressed with a jerky, rough urgency, though he had several hours before he was supposed to arrive at the location noted. But he wanted to get a feel of the place, a sense if this was a trap or worse.

By the time he opened the door he had a rudimentary plan. But he didn't expect to see Pádraig waiting for him in the hallway. Last time he'd seen the young man was exiting his own interrogation last night. By the time Jeb finished with his and showed the police out of the townhouse Pádraig was long gone.

"What are you doing here?" he said, his voice brusquer than he meant as the younger man stepped back.

"I was sent to summon you to a meeting of the Council today." Jeb remembered that Pádraig was involved with Council business in a periphery capacity. Sort of a Sergeant-at-Arms, who had acted as Philippe's right hand. Most of the members, except for Jeb, had an associate. That individual had no say in decisions made but was held to the same level of accountability and secrecy. Right now Pádraig looked as tired and strained as Jeb felt. "At one. Chamber locations."

Good. Whatever was going to happen at the designated park took precedence. Depending on the outcome there, whatever had been set up, Jeb would attend the Council meeting. Since there would only be six present it could not be a formal meeting, and no doubt it'd been convened as a result of

Philippe's death. But the speed of calling all the remaining members told Jeb one thing for sure. The other associates, who represented all seven continents, must be in close enough proximity with such short notice.

"Will all the Council be in attendance?" he asked Pádraig.

"*Oui*. We have been called to discuss the issue of the dress designer and the possibility of drugs that could expose non-humans to the human population."

But Jeb had not officially been summoned. Not yet at least. Interesting. Jeb's tone must have said as much as Pádraig cleared his throat and added, "Five of the members were at the soiree last night. Where . . . where, you know. . ."

"Where Philippe was killed?"

"*Oui*."

Jeb's radar just tilted from interesting to dangerous. Were some factions within the Council banding together against other members? "Was there Council business being held there?"

Pádraig gave an emphatic shake of his head. "Not that I was aware of, though Philippe might have had his own agenda, outside of the Council."

Then why have the Council members near? Unease rode Jeb. Too many coincidences happening. Van's disappearance. Jeb being in Paris at the summons of an old friend. The threats against Alex. What drew the other members here, too?

Something was going down, he just wished the hell he understood what.

Without another word he started toward the door, his duffel bag clenched in his hand.

"You going somewhere?" Pádraig asked, a frown carving a groove between his brows.

"I'll be staying elsewhere." Jeb's tone indicated his mind was on more pressing issues. It was just half past nine but he felt the time pushing at him.

"You seem disturbed. Did something happen after I left last night?"

"No." Jeb looked at the Irishman and reined in his impatience. This was still Philippe's friend, his protégé. He deserved more. "I received some news. About my children. I'm going to look into it now."

Pádraig lifted his brows but said nothing.

"Did you leave a note under my door last night?" Jeb asked.

"No."

The word sounded sincere. But if the young man hadn't done, who had?

"May I help?"

Three of the most powerful words when one needed assistance desperately.

"How well do you know Paris?" Jeb asked, still hesitating.

"I've lived here for over ten years."

That surprised him. Pádraig didn't look older than his mid-thirties, no doubt because he was a druid, masters at illusions. They could give the fae a run for their money.

"I have a vehicle if that will help you." The Irishman's voice not only held assurance, it offered a solution to one of the issues Jeb wrestled with—transportation.

"If you wish me to wait in the car I'll do that," he added. "Besides, it'll give me something to do. This damnable business . . . I need to be doing something. Anything."

Pádraig sounded like Jeb felt, being driven to action to break the stupor of standing around drowning in uselessness. "Come with me, then."

The other man smiled, straightening his shoulders and for the first time since Philippe called, Jeb felt like the fog was lifting.

CHAPTER 29

I woke up feeling like I'd been someone's punching bag and groaned aloud as I rolled over in a strange bed, in an unfamiliar room, trying to orient myself. A slice of sun skimmed a streamlined armoire against a brick wall.

Where? Oh, yeah, warehouse. The dead man. Were attack. Bran.

I reached for my clutch purse that I hadn't lost, or someone had found for me and set on the nightstand, next to a glass water carafe and what looked like two aspirins. Thank the Spirits.

Until I realized Bran must have entered the room while I'd been asleep which, after last night, was too intimate for my stretched nerves.

At least I'd slept in my dress, not comfortable but in hindsight a smarter idea than sleeping in the buff.

An image of Bran sprang to mind, which I ruthlessly tapped down. Last night I'd been way too revealing. Enough of that. If I wanted to get Van free I needed to focus, focus, focus, on him and not a particular warlock.

Grabbing my second, or was it my third glass of water, still feeling parched, I went in search of my dubious roommates.

I had to clear up the business with Philippe Cheverill pronto or dealing with the Council could prevent me from finding Van. I'd already come up with a plan to find the perfect witness who'd vouch that I hadn't killed the Council leader. The doctor who'd already been bending over the dying man when I reached Cheverill's side.

I should have thought of him last night but I'd been slightly distracted by a Were cougar and a sexy warlock.

Today I had no such excuses.

But the moment I walked into the yawning warehouse, looking even barer by daylight than moon shadow, I knew it was empty. I didn't have my nifty Timex watch that I'd had since childhood. François had turned up his nose at even the hint of my wearing it with the Elie Saab dress he wrapped me in. Not that I had a clue who Elie Saab was. In fact I thought he was a she, which François quickly corrected.

Now I wished I hadn't listened because I couldn't tell what time it was.

It took me only a second to smell the tray with croissants, strawberries, and fresh orange juice on it.

How was I going to keep the distance I needed with Bran if he kept being thoughtful as well as too attractive? The warlock did not play fair.

Then I saw the scrawled note beneath the glass plate.

Stay put. We'll be back.

As if. But it did serve to snap some attitude into my backbone.

"Give me one reason to hang around here." I said out loud, mumbling around a sinfully good croissant. The one thing I was definitely going to miss about Paris, if I lived long enough to leave.

It took me less than thirty minutes to scrounge around in the bedroom closets to find a replacement for the dress I wore, that would have made me look like I was doing the walk of shame rather than hunting for a killer. At last I found a guy's white dress shirt that hung long on me but with the cuffs rolled up at least it hid the jeans that I had to double belt to stay up.

By the front door I found my frou-frou sandals that François had carried last night and apparently tossed aside when we'd been attacked. They might look out of place with jeans but I wasn't going to have to traipse around Paris barefoot. Again.

I wasn't being too-stupid-to-live, leaving the warehouse after my own scrawled note: *Gone to find doctor. TTYL.* I was being proactive, especially after I discovered there were no messages from my teammates on my phone, nor did they answer their cells. I left a message for Ling Mai on her phone but didn't bother with the others. Wasn't ignoring them, but biggest hurdle first. And that described Ling Mai to a T.

I really did miss the team backing me, but I'm sure Ling Mai was keeping them busy. Very busy if I knew Ling Mai. So I'd try them again later, once I had more concrete information to share.

I had no idea where Bran and François had gone, but I wasn't waiting for them to save my fanny. My plan was simple. Return to the museum and try a casting spell before the trail grew too cold. If I got lucky it should lead me to the doctor. Once I knew who he was then I'd contact Ling Mai and give her his name while I finished looking for Vaverek.

The way I figured it, Ling Mai was no doubt focused more on finding Vaverek and his drug connections than Van right now. That issue impacted the balance of humans realizing non-humans existed among us.

But I wasn't finished. As long as I knew in my heart that Van lived, I'd hunt for him, regardless of anyone else's agenda. And Ling Mai knew that, so I was still playing within her guidelines here. Besides, she could always track me by my phone.

Since I didn't keep a wad of cash on me, or even a credit card, I would have to walk. I used a map app on my phone to find the museum, which looked a hell of a long ways away.

It took me a little over an hour to arrive at the Nissim de Camondo Museum, which looked more imposing by daylight than it had last night. A cross between a fortress and a statement of wealth and grandeur from a time long gone. Fortunately it was also open, a fact I hadn't thought about until I stood outside the pale beige stone building.

I had just enough funds to get into the museum and waved off the auditory guide that was included with my ticket. The young girl behind the counter, with magenta hair and three lip rings shrugged as if I was being a fool. Maybe I was.

Since the death had happened on the first level I wasn't surprised to see the large parlor blocked off with stanchions and tape. I couldn't read the words on the tape in French but it was no doubt crime scene tape and a clear no-go barrier. As if that had ever kept a Noziak out of anything. It was more like waving a red flag at us.

I paused, looking into my clutch as if I'd lost my soul, because besides my phone there wasn't a whole lot of room in it to stash much else. Maybe I should have grabbed one of the audio guides. I didn't have to turn it on but it'd give me a reason for just standing around, cooling my heels.

What I was doing was waiting for what sounded like a German grandmother and her two fidgety grandsons to leave the area. They were standing in the curl of the stairway that swept to the second floor. It was where I'd been with Bran when the older man had fallen to the floor. There was a nude Greek statue there, a very well-endowed, graphic statue that I'd totally missed last night.

Leave it to Bran to distract me so much I'd missed the art. If that's what it was called.

The two German boys were snickering behind their hands and pointing, while their grandmother memorized the guidebook clutched in her hands.

"Come on, come on," I mumbled beneath my breath. "Don't have all day."

But obviously the grandmother did. One of the boys, the younger one who couldn't have been older than six or seven, which explained why he was probably bored out of his mind, was tugging on the older woman's sweater and repeating, "Groymutter. Groymutter."

Sounded like a dirty word to me, but what did I know?

It seemed like it took forever but the trio finally moved off, once the grandmother caught an eyeful at what had been intriguing her grandsons.

I waited until I heard their footsteps recede upstairs before glancing around. No one in sight.

A quick duck beneath the tape and I was in the room, keeping toward the walls so I couldn't easily be seen from the open doorway.

Last night I thought the space looked crowded because of the people, but even empty it looked overfull, especially if you compared it to the warehouse I'd just left. A different decorating sensibility than I was used to with great floral carpets blanketing the floor, pastoral murals on the walls, massive gold frames, crystal chandeliers, and wall sconces the only light even though it was barely eleven o'clock. The space was making me claustrophobic. Or maybe it was approaching the spot where Cheverill had died.

Fortunately there weren't any bloodstains to make me squirm. Since the room had been blocked off, it might be a smidge easier getting a reading on the doctor. I was hesitant because it was a museum with a lot of people moving in and out of the space, plus it'd been jam packed last night. But if I didn't try, my alternative was to do nothing. I set my purse on the nearest table and prepared to get to work.

The casting spell shouldn't be hard. I wasn't scrying, which involved looking into a translucent object such as a crystal ball, or water, or even smoke for that matter, in an attempt to see or find someone. For one thing I didn't have any tools though a quick glace around reassured me there were enough crystals dangling from the lighting fixtures that if push came to shove I might be able to try that approach. Instead I planned to cast a lost person spell. It tended to be stronger for me and easier to work.

Inhaling a deep breath I stepped toward the area where the doctor, if that's what he'd been, had been kneeling. Just then my purse started doing a little hum and jig on the glossy surface of the mahogany table. I was so focused on what I was about to do it took a few seconds to realize what was happening. My cell phone.

Could it be Ling Mai?

I lunged toward the table and fumbled getting my phone out, only to recognize the number calling as Bran's. Not that I'd memorized it or anything. Perish the thought.

But I didn't need a pissed off warlock reaming me out for leaving the warehouse, or being at the museum, or my plan. How'd I know that's what he wanted? It was Bran.

Flipping off the phone was a tacky and small-minded gesture, I'll admit, as I shoved it back in the purse once I'd turned it off totally. Somehow I knew Ling Mai wouldn't be calling in the time it took me to spell cast and get out of here.

Back to the spot I settled my nerves and focused to bring up an image of the doctor, which was vague. I just hadn't been paying that much attention to him. Not with another man dying in front of me.

As if sorting through pictures on a cell phone, I let my memory scan past the other impressions of the room, the other faces. Bran with his thunder frown. The younger man I'd talked to after Cheverill had collapsed. Cheverill himself, with his head of silver hair and patrician features.

Then, at last, the doctor. Middle-aged. Gray in his hair, but only slightly. Deep grooves in his face, as if troubled or worried a lot. Really pretty nondescript, but hopefully enough to get a bead on.

I slowed my breathing, lowered my shoulders to release tension in my neck and focused.

Keeper of what disappears, I thee seek.
Open and find he who is lost from sight.
By sun, by earth, by air and by water.
I thee implore. What is lost, now shall be found.

Behind my closed lids I saw a glimmer. So faint I found myself leaning forward as if to see it better. Still vague. Green. An imposing stone building. The sound of traffic.

That could be anywhere in Paris.

I tried again. This time focusing more on my impressions of the doctor than simply his looks. Competence. Or was that what I expected to see? Focus, Noziak, and really see, as Bran had made me see the street yesterday morning. Not what I expected to see but what had really been before my eyes.

Fear. That's what jumped out at me. The doctor's? Yes, and others, as if a riptide of emotions circled around Cheverill's body. Greed. A vacuum of need. The need for power, for control.

Impressions so strong they felt like a physical sensation beating against me. And preternaturals. Cheverill for sure, but I didn't know what kind. Whatever he'd been, the younger man had been one too. Not blood bound but species drawn. And others. So many others. Powerful beings.

I remembered realizing there had been a lot of preternaturals at the event, but now it was being brought home in a different way. There was an intention behind their presence last night which I hadn't been aware of then.

I could feel my focus slip toward that issue and pulled it back to finding the doctor. Everything else could wait. I started my chant again. Only different now.

Earth called, find me the path.
Wind spent, blow me the way.
Sun lit, lead me along.
Water born, reveal the depths.
What is lost, must be found.
Seek. Guide. Direct.
Vessel I am. Vessel I shall be.
Show me the way. So mote it be.

And I had my answer, as clear as a street sign looming out of the fog. Now I just had to find the place.

CHAPTER 30

Van had been waiting. Patiently, because he had little choice. Trial? Experiment? Something was going down today and as he watched the dawn's light brighten and fan across the floor he expected his jailors to return.

But they didn't. Not right away. Even the human who brought his food hadn't appeared.

As the cell grew lighter the nerves danced along Van's skin. A good sign because he'd been so drugged, so numbed for days that even pain was a welcome relief.

When he heard the screech of the outer door opening at last, he adjusted his balance until his weight was evenly on both feet. Then he relaxed his muscles as much as possible. The better to pounce the second he saw an opportunity.

The trio who'd come recently had brought reinforcements. A fourth person who smelled different, not like the Were who'd been here before. No talking today, just purposeful strides.

He sagged against his restraints, faking weakness when all his inner wolf wanted to do was rend and tear. But he wouldn't let his beast gain control. Not yet.

"You are awake?" Jean-Claude the doctor asked, sliding up to Van, but not close. From where Van was restrained he could smell the stale sweat of the man's fear. The stench increased when Van raised his head, slowly, to glare at the man with eyes more wolf than human. A trick Van had perfected back in high school when jerks went sniffing around Alex. He knew his eye shape elongated, the color lightened from a dark brown to a golden amber, and the focus intensified, at least that's what the one being viewed saw.

Which is why so many turned tail and ran. The doctor didn't. He froze. A sure sign of being lower on the food chain, far lower.

The human assistant was either braver or too clueless as he stepped close enough to raise a water bag to Van's lips. The liquid tasted tainted but as both human and wolf, Van knew he had to keep his liquids up. Dehydration would weaken him faster than missing his morning meal.

But it was only after he swallowed deeply that he noticed the change in the doctor's position. His shoulders relaxed, as did the lines around the man's eyes.

Of course, the liquid had been drugged.

Just then the doctor stepped forward, not close enough Van could swipe at him, but close enough the Were could raise a small instrument and shoot a dart at Van. One that struck his neck and lodged.

Something fast acting as Van felt it scream through his system, blurring his vision, numbing his reactions. So fast. Too fast.

"What . . ." he slurred, struggling against the freefall.

"Etorphine plus acepromazine." The doctor smiled, a cocky who's-in-charge-now smile. "No need to worry about side effects," he added, stepping closer and poking at Van as if he were a side of beef. "Vets use it all the time on large animals. Fast. Effective. Little side effects."

Van was crashing. He knew it and there wasn't a damn thing he could do about it. Struggling only seemed to make the stuff work faster.

The other two stepped into the room. The one who'd taunted Van before was the one to speak first. "After you shoot him full of the other drug he won't have to worry about side effects."

Other drug?

As if called, the doctor stepped forward, swabbing something cool along Van's arm.

"You're sure the combination won't kill him?" the new visitor asked, his voice not French.

"Non," Jean-Claude murmured, focused on a vial in his hands.

Good news? Or bad?

There wasn't energy to think more as a needle jabbed him.

Then a long, swift fall into darkness.

CHAPTER 31

Jeb looked at the address he clutched in his hand then the massive maroon door before him. "This is the number," he said to Pádraig who'd found a parking place for his Peugeot Sport Coupe and was now standing beside him outside *72 Rue de Varenne*.

The building looked like the seventeenth century residence it once was, broad, imposing, with cool shadows striping the walls of the interior courtyard, a space Jeb couldn't access from where he stood because of the closed and locked door.

This looked like a dead end as a row of white block buildings stretched on either side of him. There wasn't even a tree in sight. How did the French survive in a city where greenery was regulated to spaces manicured and trimmed until even the grass wanted to weep? And how did Philippe, and Pádraig for that matter, live here being druids, beings tuned more than most to the earth? The only earth Jeb could see was buried in flower boxes on lower level windows behind wrought iron fencing.

"Let me see the note," Pádraig offered, though Jeb wanted to wring the young pup's neck for the suggestion. What was he going to read that Jeb had not read a million times already?

He thrust the crumpled paper at the other man, tempted to shift into his other self, his animal self, not his spirit form. As a wolf he could smell better, hear better, and see movement better. Right now all Jeb could smell was the scent of dark roasted coffee from a nearby café, hear the roar of the insistent Parisian traffic and see a limp French flag above the hotel's doorway.

"Doesn't even look like a hotel," he muttered, frustration rampaging through him, a man who valued control.

"It's not a hotel." Pádraig looked at a small plaque on the wall to the left of the closed doorway. "It's the Ministry of Housing and Cities. Which is why it's closed today. A state holiday."

"So where is this park? How do we find it?"

Pádraig shrugged, then glanced at his Patek Philippe watch. "We're early, which is good. I spotted a *le bistrot* around the corner. I can ask a few questions there."

It was solid advice. Which didn't mean Jeb wanted to hear it. More delays. But hadn't he tried to teach his children that the rushed man was a rash man?

Time to take his own advice.

"Lead the way," he said to Pádraig. "But let's make it quick."

He might be listening to reason but his gut was giving him a different message.

Hurry.

CHAPTER 32

I waited till I was outside the museum to return Bran's call. I had tried Ling Mai's number once more but still no response, which meant by the time Bran answered I was primed and loaded for bear.

"Where are you?" he snarled. No hello. No how are you. No kiss my butt.

"Paris." Two could play the snark game.

His inhaled breath was enough to create an airspace vacuum. "Alex."

My dad could get that same tone. The one on the razor edge between I'm-trying-for-patience-here and the belt strap.

"I have no idea where I am. This city looks the same no matter where you are."

"Try harder."

Or I could hit the cancel button.

He must have heard my thoughts as he backpedaled. As much backpedaling as a warlock could do, which was measurable in micro-millimeters. "François and I may have some information for you."

"Oh?" Van? Getting me off a murder rap? Vaverek?

"Best that we don't speak of it over the phone."

I sidestepped a puce-colored Citroen that was trying to park on the curb and reminded myself that I was low on allies. A quick look around and I answered, "I just passed the *Champs Élysées* on my way to the *seventh arrondissement*."

There was a pause on the other end and some muffled words before he came back on. "Where are you heading?"

"I told you." He must have been speaking to François, if he had shifted from his Fido form, but the streetlight had just turned red. Stepping out to cross French traffic took a heck of a lot more concentration than crossing a street in Mud Lake, Idaho. Unless there was a rodeo in town, then all bets were off.

"Let me rephrase." He was using his put-upon tone. "Why are you going there?"

"To find the doctor who was with Cheverill. He'll be able to validate that I had nothing to do with the old man's death."

"You know his name?"

"Not exactly, but I will soon." I swerved to avoid a matron with half a dozen small pug dogs snorting on their leashes. They were cute as all get out but sounded like a miniature train convention.

"Alex? You still there?"

I guess I missed something but I was trying to decide to cut through the green swath of the *Esplanade des Invalides* in front of me that looked like a wide park area between two busy streets, or head toward one of the thoroughfares, the *Rue Fabert*? Which area was creating the stronger tug?

I angled in the direction of the *Rue Fabert* but immediately halted. Using a casting spell might have been easier but it was like following a scent. I had to focus to make sure I didn't get turned around.

"Yes, I'm here, but I'm busy. Can I call you after I track down the doctor?"

"No." The single word felt like a cold splash of water, until he added, "The Rodan Museum is not far from where you are. A few blocks. Could you wait for us on the front stairs? I promise, we'll be there in less than twenty minutes. We might even be there before you are."

When he was sounding helpful I was most wary. It meant he had his own agenda and was placating me long enough to get me to do what he thought was right.

Like that was going to happen. Unless I agreed with him, which hadn't happened that much.

"If you're not there in fifteen minutes I'm leaving." Not much of a gracious concession but I'd already walked across what felt like most of Paris, was hungry and cranky, so Bran had to take what I had to offer and right now it wasn't much.

"We'll be there."

He hung up before I could ask who he meant by we, but figured it included François.

Today was feeling less and less like my lucky day.

CHAPTER 33

I'd found the Rodan Museum but only thanks to a pleasant Spanish gentleman I figured might be a gnome, even if he was out in direct sunlight. Something about his pointy beard, and the sly glint in his eyes. But he could have been a sprite. I wasn't so sure about the nuances yet.

So much to learn about preternaturals. So little time given the IR team had been run ragged dealing with Vaverek and whatever the man, if he was a man, was up to. Which made me wonder if he might be a mage or sorcerer. Like warlocks they were always stirring up trouble.

Which brought me full circle to thinking about Bran as I cooled my heels near the steps leading up to the museum's entry doors. There was a low-level stage set up directly in front of them so I had moved down a crushed rock pathway toward a pond complete with a spraying fountain. It was pretty in a rigid sort of way, but then that seemed to be the style of Parisian landscaping.

Where was he? I glanced at my cell phone and sighed as I stuffed it into my back pocket. I'd ditched the purse I'd been carrying as useless and to keep my hands free. In spite of the soft blue sky and wisps of clouds the day felt foreboding. Or that could be my mindset, waiting for a shoe to drop, or smack me up side the head.

On the other hand I sensed that Van was near.

That's what kept me going. Yes, I needed the doctor, but I needed to quit shilly-shallying along. Van needed my help and I'd spent all morning not doing a thing about it. On the other hand so much was murky. More questions raised than answers found and yet things seemed to be connected. The death of Cheverill. Bran being called before the Council. Vaverek and his machinations. What was connecting them? If anything?

One minute more and I was ditching Bran and whatever he was going to tell me. Standing around wasn't getting me closer to my brother. Or the doctor guy.

I stepped toward one of the hedges bracketing the entrance area when a hand came down on my shoulder.

My response was immediate. Grabbing the wrist I twisted it into a nice lock, spun to the outside of it and jammed the elbow with my other hand. A few seconds more and I'd pop the shoulder.

"Damnit, Alex, enough!"

Just when the fun was starting.

I released Bran, stepping far enough away he couldn't retaliate physically. At least not without bringing security guards from the museum down on us. As it was a few tourists milling about were giving us the stink-eye look that I smiled to deflect. Friends goofing off, that's all.

I guess it looked more like a grimace as several of them hurried away, their footsteps churning the gravel.

"She always greet friends this way?" A strange male voice asked behind me.

I glanced over my shoulder to see Frank in his François persona shaking his head at a broad-shouldered Mediterranean-looking man I'd never seen before. He smelled like a Were though there was no let-me-eat-you-then-meet-you vibe about him. He looked like a charmer. A Hugh Jackman type with an aw-shucks attitude, sun burnished hair a little long and curling over his forehead, and a smile that could slay women. Not me, not right then, and he looked like he knew it, keeping his hands loose at his sides, his head angled down so that even though he was well over six feet he didn't threaten me with his size.

He wanted to disarm my resistance to the attraction he no doubt usually received from women. But why?

A Were who didn't act like a Were. Why?

"Our Alex is a little jumpy at times," François murmured.

"I'm not 'your' Alex and if I jump it's because you scared the bejesus out of me." I glared at Bran to make my point.

Rubbing his wrist he didn't snap at me but nodded his head toward the newcomer. "Alex, this is Willie."

And I cared because? But I had no beef against this stranger, no need to take my pissy mood out on him.

He extended his hand but he shook as if afraid to crush my own. Thoughtful, but strange, as Weres usually were more aggressive. Even shifters had to practice giving human handshakes instead of pulverizing a stranger's hand accidently.

"A pleasure," he said, tipping his head further, but his eyes were wary, as if waiting for something to happen. From me? Like I was going to take out a Were? I could be rash but not too stupid to live.

I glanced over at François to see what was up.

"He's our new consultant," he said, as if I'd spoken aloud.

"Consulting for what?" This time I looked at Bran. When really confused go to the source.

It was the Were who answered though. "All things Were."

Seriously? I raised brows at him, not intentionally because making fun of a Were was suicidal, but he just shrugged and explained, "I'm a recovering Were."

"I didn't know there was such a thing."

"I admit, there are not many of us." He shrugged his shoulders and I bit the inside of my cheek not to say anything that could get me killed. "In fact, I'm the only one I know in Europe."

"Europe's a large place."

"I'm hoping with a little more visability, other Weres will start to hear about We're Not."

"We're not what?" Talking to him was like walking into thick fog. I was getting more and more confused.

"No. We, apostrophe re. Get it? We're Not. As in we're not Weres. Kinda catchy don't you think? I thought it was much better than Weres-R-Us or Recovering Weres twelve step program."

I thought he was crazier than a Road Runner cartoon. "Sorry, William was it?"

"Willie. Less threatening."

He was right about that. Willie the recovering Were. And this is what I'd waited on Bran for?

My look must have screamed as much as Bran stepped closer and said, "The Weres have been deep in the middle of this. And that's before the attack by the two last night."

"That's what gives Weres such a bad reputation," Willie interjected.

A well-deserved reputation I wanted to point out. Who said I couldn't hold my tongue?

François threw an arm across Willie's shoulder. A move that had me cringing and stepping back. Except nothing happened. No blood. No head forcibly removed from the body. Nothing.

Just two heterosexual buddies having a good time.

I must have fallen down a rabbit hole.

Shaking my head to clear it I ignored the Were, recovering or not, and François, who grinned a smile that dared me to say something, and focused on Bran. "I still have to find the doctor. You coming?"

I surprised myself by asking. I think I surprised him too as he nodded at François and Willie before falling in beside me.

We walked in silence for a bit, in spite of the crushed gravel. I was always amazed at how stealthily shifters and Weres could move as I was the only one making noise, but then I was the only one in stilettos.

"What's your new friend going to help with?" I asked, not bothering to keep my voice down. Weres have great hearing, and eyesight, and smell. They are like Shifters that way. The difference is shifters can change at will, whereas Weres are moon driven. They can change outside of a full moon but it is a painful process. Plus they are driven to change based on the phase of the moon. Shifters have a lot more flexibility and can ignore the moon's cycles.

Weres on the other hand could communicate to one another while in their animal form, the most powerful and older ones at least. Only a few very rare shifters could speak once their animal self manifested. My father was one of them, but my brothers could not.

Someday, maybe, but Van wouldn't if we didn't find him and make sure he lived.

I hadn't realized I had started walking faster until Bran put a hand on my arm. "You're worried. Has something happened?"

"Not yet." But that was the problem. I expected something, something bad. And you know what they say, what you focus on you get.

"We here?" he asked a few minutes later as we stood on an empty street. On one side was what looked like an office building, an office building Parisian style with two wings thrusting toward the street and the main wing hunkered low and far from the sidewalk.

But that's not the direction I found myself facing. It was the park area across the street calling to me. A U-shaped area bordered by shrubs and large trees on three sides, a white rock path bracketing a sweep of mowed lawn and deep into the area a bronze statue. Not Rodan's Thinker but something with more mass. Park benches were scattered along the path, several of them occupied with what looked like ordinary office workers. A few strollers hugged the far shadows. It should have looked calm and innocent but something was telling me it wasn't.

"He's over there?" Bran brushed shoulders with me.

It was a sign of how unnerved I felt that I jumped when he spoke. I nodded my head, a slow, methodical movement. "I don't know where, but the spell indicates somewhere in that park."

"Then that's where we need to go." François was all business now.

Were Willie was the one who broke the tension. Or added to it as he said, "There are Weres around. Several powerful ones. A shifter, too. In distress I'd say."

I couldn't see or smell any though I usually could if they were close enough. I guess it could take a Were to recognize a Were.

François glanced at Bran but spoke to me. "We still 'going in' as you Yanks say?"

I didn't bother answering as I stepped into the empty street to cross it. Even the roar of traffic was muted here. A few birds twittered but I didn't see any. A man turned the page of the newspaper he was reading but as I moved deeper into the park with Bran to one side, François and Willie on the other, there was very little sound.

Until the scream erupted.

CHAPTER 34

Jeb heard his son's shout. The cry of a wolf in agony. Wolves are silent hunters, no growls, no snarls, no yips. The fact Van was howling meant something was wrong. Terribly wrong. He started running down a street that seemed far too long, Pádraig nipping at his heels.

The younger man cried out, "That didn't sound good."

"It isn't."

Jeb skidded around a corner and spotted the green space on his right. The park? Here?

The scream came again. Somewhere deeper into the grassy area. A couple of people were running toward the street, away from the sound, looking over their shoulders.

"Van," he shouted. "Van, where are you?"

A man shrieked, the sound cut off suddenly.

Jeb crossed the street, skirting parked cars and ran toward the nearest pathway.

"You sure this is a good idea?" Pádraig panted beside him. "Shouldn't we wait for the police?"

Jeb shook his head, scanning the area, but he couldn't see anything. Three men and a woman were running toward a group against the far edge, near a statue. Four or five men huddled together, but it wasn't clear what they were doing.

"Sir, we really should wait." Pádraig's voice sounded high and winded.

"My son's here. Somewhere."

Jeb stepped onto the grass. Better to get a wider view.

The huddle of men in the back broke open just as the girl who looked like Alex running toward them was tackled by a dark-haired man behind her.

That's when he saw Van. In his wolf form.

CHAPTER 35

"Let me go," I screamed as Bran tackled me, grinding me into the gravel. "He needs me."

"He'll kill you."

Bran pressed against my back, blanketing me. Couldn't he see what was going on? That was Van. I could recognize him in human or wolf form, which he was in now, in spite of this being a public place. The men had Van wrapped in chains. I had to get to him.

I rocked back and forth but Bran was too large, too strong, and wasn't budging an inch.

"Van," I shouted, clawing the ground to break free.

The group of men huddled around Van peeled away, as if a circle opening. In the middle Van was huddled over, his wolf form struggling against chains, desperate to get free. Wolves were silent predators. They didn't make sounds except to warn others off. But Van's cry had been something else. Anguish. Rage. Desperation.

One man's body lay stretched across the path, an arm torn from his torso, his blood too red in the glaring noon light. No wonder Van was frantic. What idiot would wave red meat in front of a wolf?

Van's wolf nature had taken over and he needed calming. But the men were doing just the opposite. One was lashing him with what looked like a whip. Another pulled the chain around his throat tighter. I could smell the scent of singeing fur from here.

"I have to help him," I cried, but it was useless. Bran pinned my arms to my side. When I got free I'd kill him.

"I don't want to hurt you," he growled against my ear. "Hold still."

"You. Don't. Understand." My words came in short gasps. Bran didn't understand. He didn't know wolves. He didn't know Van.

"That's my brother."

"Not now he isn't."

Van was Van though. He always had more control over his wolf than any of my brothers. He needed my help. If I could get those men away from him, I knew I could save him. I was the only one who could.

Then I smelled them. Weres. Several of those encircling Bran were Weres.

You can do this. It was the woman's voice. From yesterday. You have the power. Use it.

Of course, how stupid could I be?

Adeo. Adeo. Agero. Adepto.

Come. Come. Increase. Acquire.

I started the chant. The one I used yesterday morning. The one that sucked power from the others around me. As long as I pulled back, not using it in full force or with Bran's magic too, I could stop the Weres around Van and free him.

"Don't, Alex," Bran whispered, as he had done in the street, only there was a threat behind the words now. "Don't do it."

The woman's voice washed against me. Listen to me. I'm here. You're not alone.

"Mom?"

Van's wolf roared.

I reached for him, willing him to see me, to know I was there for him.

Suscipio. Solvo.

Receive. Break free.

"Alex."

Ignore him. He only seeks to stop you.

I was struggling to do just that when Bran clamped his hand across my mouth.

Noooooooo!

I thrashed and kicked and tried to bite him, but it did no good. Bran's hand smothered me. Tears leaked from my eyes and I didn't care. I was useless.

Van.

Then I heard it. Another sound. Another wolf's growl.

Twisting my head—I couldn't lift it very high but I spied the cinnamon coat I knew so well. A black band of fur striped his tail as he raced past me, sparing me only one quick wolf glance.

Dad? Here?

It couldn't be.

Where I lay, sandwiched between Bran and the gravel biting into my skin, my face, I was powerless but I could listen.

I heard when the attacking wolf reached the group of men.

"*Merde*," Bran swore. I doubted he even knew he'd said the single word aloud.

What was happening? I sagged, using my ears to tell me as I couldn't see. Why wasn't Bran doing something to help Van?

Male shouts in French. Some screamed what sounded like an order. Then the last thing I expected. The snarls and thudding of two wolves attacking one another.

Van would never fight Dad. But was that Dad I saw? Great Goddess what could I do?

A sudden *zzzzzz* whir. A quick animal cry.

Then only Van's growl. A yelp. Then nothing.

Bran eased up a smidge as I stopped fighting him, instead focusing on what was happening deep into the park.

I could finally raise my head. The wolf that had sped past me was on the ground, curled in a fetal position.

"Dad!" I shouted.

They'd killed him.

CHAPTER 36

"He used a binding spell on me!" I shouted, even though François was only a few feet from where I stood, hands clenched, muscles tensed to fight, back in the warehouse space I'd left only hours ago. A space that seemed larger earlier and now couldn't contain the anger pulsing through me. "He bound me and he did nothing to help my brother. Not lift one pinky mage finger to stop what was happening."

I marched over to where François leaned against one of the partition walls, his arms crossed, his face neutral, though I could tell he was holding on to his temper.

Willie was hustling up some food in the kitchen area beyond a counter dividing half-wall. Staying out of the direct line of fire no doubt. Or maybe he was a smart charmer. Or just a smart Were.

Not me. I was livid and looking for a target. But it wasn't François as much as he wished he were anywhere else.

No. I knew who I wanted to throttle.

Back at the park I'd had a quick glimpse of my dad but before I could do anything Bran had cast a spell on me that rendered me speechless and powerless. It was the last part that stuck in my craw. That and his caveman way of yanking me to my feet only to swing me across his shoulder in a fireman's hold as the wail of emergency response vehicles drew closer and closer. Then he jogged over to a car that François had collected and drawn up to the curb.

I might as well been a sack of potatoes. Couldn't move, speak, or help. And how the last part acid etched me from the inside out.

And now Bran had vanished. Not in a conjuring way but in a drop me off on the couch, say something to François and Willie in French, and walk out, knowing it'd be a good twenty minutes before the spell wore off.

But not before he left another larger containment spell wrapping the building. This was a warlock who could bring a person back from the dead, so when he didn't want someone to leave a building, there was no getting out of it. I couldn't even get cell phone reception. Which meant I'd been cut off from my team.

Warlocks could try the patience of a saint and I wasn't a saint by any definition.

So I faced the next most convenient target and stabbed a finger at his chest. "That was my brother. And my dad. And you. . ," I was so angry I couldn't even find the phrases I was scrambling for. Fear drives anger in me and I don't know when I'd been more afraid. Not for me but for my dad and Van.

"You Neanderthals had no right, no right to take me away." The words were jamming in my throat as I pivoted and strode across the room, not trusting that I wouldn't do something irrevocable to François.

My brothers always said never piss off a witch.

But François hadn't grown up in the Noziak family. "You ever think Bran did what he did to protect you?"

I whirled on him like a dervish on speed. "I never asked for his protection. Don't need it. Don't want it."

François' brows slashed upward. "There are bigger issues at stake here than what you want."

I wasn't sure if I was angrier at his calm tone, or his comment as I stormed back across to look him in the eye even as I had to stand on my tippy toes to do so. I growled through gritted teeth. "That's what everyone keeps telling me. But he was there. Doing nothing. Van was right in front of me. Alive. And now?" I threw my hands wide, when what I wanted to do was pound them into the walls. "Where is he now? I don't even know if he's still alive. Or if my dad is. Because of you three."

My gaze included Willie in my condemnation. He had moved to the dining bar but stepped back with a who-me expression on his face as I paced toward him. "You're a Were for cripes sake. You could have stopped those men. But what did you do? Nothing. A big squat nothing."

He opened his mouth but I gave him my no-bullshit glare. "And don't try to tell me you're a recovering Were so were doing the whole non-violence thing."

"Even if I was?" he mumbled around a large bite of a ham sandwich.

"Bullpuckey!" I snarled, pivoting and walking across the room to give myself some breathing space. How could someone even think of eating at a time like this?

He waited until I was as far as I could get before saying, "Did you have any idea of the power of the Weres in that park?"

"Says you."

He glanced at François who gave a what-can-we-do shake of his head.

"And what about you?" I snapped at François. "You're supposed to be here to help me. Why weren't you doing anything back there?"

He stepped away from the wall, his nostrils flaring. "And who said I wasn't?"

"So what did you accomplish? Shoo a few pigeons away?"

"Didn't have to with you wailing like a banshee. No doubt you scared a few birds from Trafalgar Square you were making such a ruckus."

I swear the man was cruising for a bruising. I took a step toward him, fists clenched. "At least I was doing something, Fido. Not cowering in the background."

Willie might be a recovering Were but he was still lightning fast as he appeared in front of François, acting as a barrier between me and the MI-6 agent.

François smashed into Willie's broader chest as the Were pressed the Brit back toward the wall. Both men might look lanky rather than bulky but I could see the strain in François' face as he pushed back.

Just then the front door opened and like a balloon suddenly popped, all of us turned our attention to Bran strolling in before coming to a sudden stop. "What the bloody hell is going on here?" he growled, looking at me.

Oh, that was choice. As if I were the one at fault. He left me with a wus Were and dog who was as helpful as tits on a bull and thought I was the one causing all the problems.

He had no idea what problems I could cause.

Raising to my full height, which wasn't anywhere near as tall as any of them, I still managed to look down my nose at them all. "Look what the dog drug in," I snipped, before glancing at François. "Oh, wait, the dog's already inside."

The British agent gave me a payback-is-going-to-be-hell look before speaking to Bran. "She's all yours and you're welcome to her."

He then stomped out of the room, brushing past Bran, before he could say a word.

"Have your panties in a twist, Alex?" Bran closed the door behind him as he strolled over to where Willie remained frozen, his gaze sling-shotting between Bran and I as if trying to time the explosion.

As if I'd stoop so low.

I crossed to one of three bar stools set near an arched window and shoved myself up on the nearest one, surprised the flimsy wood didn't splinter beneath my grip.

"You want me to leave?" Willie asked Bran.

"Might be safer for you."

Oh, that was ripe. I was the least powerful of anyone in the room, the one who'd been trussed up like a turkey, and had no say in being caged in the warehouse, and now everyone was acting like I was the threat?

But I held my tongue, waiting till the Were scooted out the door, leaving his sandwich behind. That showed how wary he was.

And he should be. Bran had a lot to answer for.

But as I turned my full focus on him I noticed what I'd missed before. He looked drained, the kind of weight-of-the-world-on-your-shoulders spent, with strain bracketing his killer-blue eyes.

This was not the Bran I knew. The take the world on and then some, king of his universe, mover and shaker. This was a man fighting on one too many fronts and bracing himself.

What had he been doing? Where had he gone?

Even his tone sounded different, less in-your-face and more give-it-your-best shot as he picked at the sandwich before looking me in the eye. "Well, Alex, I'm here now. You want a piece of me? Take it."

CHAPTER 37

Jeb lifted the cool washcloth to his head while sitting on the edge of the bathtub in Philippe's black and white tiled bathroom. His cuts had mostly healed now, one of the boons of being a shifter, but the gash along his head had bled for a good long while.

"Feeling better?" Pádraig said from the doorway.

Jeb nodded though he wanted to growl, what do you think? His son had attacked him. Van, his firstborn, lunged at Jeb as if his father was a pesky coyote needing to be taken down.

And Van had damn near done just that. Jeb couldn't seriously fight back, not without harming his boy.

He'd seen the crazed, vacant look in Van's eyes. If he didn't know his son, his scent, the markings of his wolf, Jeb would have said that hadn't been Van. But it was. While at the same time it wasn't.

Raising his head to eye Pádraig who'd dragged Jeb's wolf form away after one of the assailants had tasered him, he knew he owed the young man. "Thank you. For what you did back there."

The Irishman ran a hand through his ruffled hair. "It was close. Another few minutes and the feukeu would have collected you before I could."

"Feukeu?"

Pádraig cantered one shoulder. "Police."

Jeb nodded then wished he hadn't. His head felt like it had in his old rodeo days, after he'd been tossed from a bronc and landed hard.

"Do you know why your son was there?" Pádraig asked.

"No idea."

Jeb hadn't mentioned that Alex had been there, too, but he was going to find out why. He knew who the man was who tackled her. Bran, the dress designer and the man who was supposed to have been brought before the Council less than an hour ago for suspected involvement in a scheme to drug preternaturals against their will. But the meeting had been put off now.

The charges against this Bran were serious, with two of the Council members already agitating for a death penalty based on the man's cousin's involvement in using a similar drug against humans. If the Council had a full body, and hadn't been dealing with the ramifications of a reported shifter attack against humans in broad daylight, the designer might not have been given another forty-eight hours to prove he was not involved in the drug issue.

None of the Council members knew Jeb and Pádraig had been present at the park. Not yet at least. Nor did they know that the shifter who had broken the basic tenet of the last three hundred years; don't show, don't tell and never, under any reason, reveal yourself to a human had been Jeb's son.

The last time the Council had assembled in a full quorum, and even with Philippe's calm guidance, the chamber had been crowded with several Weres agitating for representation on the Council. They'd always been angry that shifters were represented with a Council seat but not Weres.

Jeb had been willing to listen to their complaints, which held some legitimacy. Wei Pei, the shifter who stood for both shifters and Were interests was older, the oldest of the members now that Philippe was gone. And the Chinese man was sometimes lax in his enforcement of balance among his constituents. He tended to favor shifter needs over Were needs, but not enough to bring the other Council members into the agitation between the two species. Until now. Especially with this shifter exposure.

Now finding out why Van had acted as he did took precedence. The Weres held long grudges, and short of abdication of Wei, or allowing a pure-bred Were on the board, they would never be appeased by the elimination of one shifter as a punishment. The Weres could easily feel the shifters deserved to be removed from the board and Weres allowed species representation. As if that would solve what was behind Van's actions.

And even then Jeb knew the Weres would find something else to be unhappy about.

The truth was they really were angry at the whole Council for not giving them what they really wanted—freedom to reveal themselves to the humans—as a more superior and dangerous race.

But that wasn't going to happen. Not and risk all the other preternatural beings.

Pádraig cleared his throat as if searching for the right words. "If the Council finds that your son was the shifter responsible for the incident today, then you'll have to excuse yourself from trying his case."

Jeb glanced up at the Irishman, wondering if Pádraig was being obtuse or politically sensitive. "If that knowledge is revealed, the Council itself will be destabilized with Philippe being gone, Wei Pei's position compromised as having failed his species, both of them— "

"Why both?"

"The Weres currently feel underrepresented. If they receive what they want, which is a solid position on the Council, replacing or in addition to the shifter's position, then the shifters will feel that the Council and Wei Pei in particular used the actions of one shifter to discredit the whole race."

Paraig nodded as Jeb continued. "If the Weres are given a seat over the shifters, there will be even more open animosity."

"And Wei Pei cannot be removed unless he dies."

"Correct. Discrediting Wei Pei publically by having him abdicate his position will mean he, and thus the shifters will lose credibility."

"Which will anger the shifters."

"And if Philippe's seat is given to a Were, meaning both Weres and shifters are represented, then the other beings, including druids who would lose their seat, will be up in arms."

"Right ol' mess isn't it," Pádraig stroked his chin as if finally seeing the whole picture. "So what do we do?"

Jeb stood up, feeling the morning's change into shifter form and back, in the stiffness of his muscles now. "We have forty-eight hours to find a way to downplay the event in the park to the human population."

"You mean the whole "It was a rabid dog" story?"

Jeb nodded. "For the time being, yes. We need to discover why Van shifted in the first place, who those individuals with him were, and why Van didn't stop his attack the moment he discovered I was there."

"You think he knew you?" Pádraig's tone was diffident.

"Of course he did." That's the part that had Jeb worried the most. That and Alex's involvement.

"What if there's another incident?" Pádraig asked eying Jeb.

"We have to make sure there isn't one."

"Because even humans are not likely to believe there are two rabid dogs the size of overgrown wolves running through the streets of Paris."

"Exactly. One attack we can contain. Two attacks and . . ." Jeb couldn't even voice the next words. Two attacks and the Council, and thus all preternaturals, could be at risk.

Pádraig resumed stroking his chin. "And the warlock?"

Jeb caught himself. He'd forgotten, somewhat about the warlock. But not totally. "Leave him to me."

CHAPTER 38

Van came to slowly, as if kicking and crawling up a very deep well. Struggling to orient himself. What day was it? Where was he? Why did he feel as if he'd been pummeled for hours? All of these questions slid away as awareness slammed into him with the sound of a familiar voice.

The power broker screaming, "The experiment failed and I want heads."

"Sir, I beg to disagree." Jean-Claude, the doctor's voice, rumbled somewhere to Van's right. "The drug was effective, as were the autosuggestions."

"He was to have done far more. Only one dead. And his sister still out of our reach. I'd say that was a failure."

The words dripped like vinegar in an open wound, one painful splash at a time. Who was dead? What had happened? And what about Alex? Van lifted his head that felt like it weighed more than his whole body and bit back a groan when he recognized where he was. Back in the cell. Still shackled against the stone wall, only with heavier chain now, more silver. But why? What had happened?

"He's coming around," Jean-Claude murmured. "*Bonne.*" The doctor stepped closer, examining Van as if looking for something. "How do you feel Mister Noziak? Any after effects?"

Van said nothing until the Were stepped close enough and Van lunged. There was no way he could have reached the Were but it damn well felt good to have the other jumping back.

"He's obviously fine," the power broker snarled. "We need him ready for another trial. A bigger one this time. So there will be no doubt that shifters are unpredictable, dangerous creatures."

The doctor glanced toward where the power broker stood, out of Van's line of sight. "But that may kill him," he stuttered.

"Not my problem," the other said, and Van could hear the smug smile in his voice. "He'll have served his purpose."

The doctor made a noise, as if he wanted to say something else but hesitated.

"In the meantime . . ." the power broker said, "someone must pay for the mistakes of this afternoon."

Van could smell the doctor's terror as the Were asked, "But who?"

"Kill the human. He's expendable, too."

CHAPTER 39

"Well Alex," Bran repeated, crossing the warehouse to stand before where I still perched on my stool. "Nothing to say?"

It wasn't that there was nothing I had to say, I had plenty to say, but no way was I going to kick a man when he wasn't in full fighting form. Instead I tilted my head and looked at him, wondering what caused the change from the man I'd seen this morning. Before the whole park crisis. "What's happened?" I asked, then remembered. "The Council?"

"I've received a twenty-four hour stay of execution." His tone meant to be mocking but actually only sounding weary.

"Don't be a fool. They can't execute you without a reason."

He eyed me, then added in a voice less hostile than it had been. "Seems they think I may be the one who set the shifter off on a killing spree this afternoon."

That threw me for a loop. No way. He wouldn't even have been at the park if I hadn't been going there. And that shifter was my brother. I knew Van wasn't on a killing spree. Someone may have died but after seeing what those people were doing to him I had no doubt the death was a result of their actions. It wasn't like Van woke up as a kidnap victim and decided to lope over to the park to kill some innocent bystanders. "Why is the Council thinking that you had anything to do with Van?"

"They don't have all the details yet, so I have a limited amount of time to prove I had nothing to do with Van's actions."

"Do they know Van was the shifter?"

"Not as far as I can tell."

"And my father?"

"No one seems to have tied your father and your brother together as being in the park fighting one another." He ran one hand through his hair, rocking back on his heels. "There's been no report of your father's death."

I held my breath as I spoke one of my fears aloud. "But someone could have taken his body and disposed of it."

"They could have, but I stopped at the park before I returned here and did a quick casting spell. Except for the one Were who died today, there was no indication of any other deaths there recently."

"So dad may be alive?"

He nodded and I felt my heart stutter and restart. One fear allayed, only to be bumped aside from so many other issues crowding me. Why had Van shifted in the middle of a public place? Who were the people holding him? Why had Van and my father fought? Why were there Weres present? And if Willie was to be believed, why such powerful Weres?

Weres were like shifters in that regard; unless there were ties of blood that could impact relationships, they tended to have the strongest dominant as their leader and a group of lesser dominants beneath their hierarchy. If the dominant became weak or incapacitated he was often killed and replaced. Two Were brothers who were dominants were separated to different packs so that they didn't eventually want to kill one another. Shifters did not have to live in packs so often avoided the chance of brother killing brother, though they still respected and followed the strongest dominant around.

Having several dominant Weres in one location at one time usually resulted in bloodshed unless they were in a rigidly controlled environment, such as a Council session or a gathering of the packs. Several dominant shifters could work together without tearing each other's throats out, which is why my family was still intact. My dad and brothers were all dominants, except for Jackson, and he could be dominant, but chose to be Beta in our family structure.

Bran slid onto one of the stools next to me, a silent acknowledgement that if I wasn't going to be his immediate enemy there could be a cessation, even temporarily, of animosity between us. Sort of the ways shifters and Weres communicated. If feeling threated they face one another, the better to register body language attack signals. If friends, they stand side by side, a much less threatening posture, and for them, an easier way to communicate. Just the opposite for women who preferred facing the one they were talking with. But I'd learned growing up with only brothers and a father, that if I really wanted them to listen to me I had to talk to them their way, not mine.

I glanced over at Bran, hesitating to ask him what was pushing at me the most. "Why was Van in his wolf form and attacking?"

He didn't look directly at me as he answered, another male trait. "My best guess is Vaverek."

"What's he got to do with any of this?"

"I don't have the details but if your brother was acting totally out of character— "

"He was."

"Then there has to be a reason."

I saw where he was going with this. "You mean the drug that's supposed to influence preternaturals?"

"Clearly this is similar to the drug that Dominique was involved with, but different. That difference being it could make a shifter, or a Were, or any other preternatural act in spite of their training and basic desires, human or animal."

That was the scary thing about the drug we'd found Dominique using on unsuspecting humans. It was as if combining a date rape with an auto-hypnotic effect. Once administered the victim could be programmed to steal, or kill, or do all sorts of actions they never would have done otherwise, and then have no recall of what they'd done. But using the same kind of drug on an unsuspecting preternatural could easily multiply the fallout. A Were or fae on the rampage was twenty times as deadly as a human.

His words slammed against me as the repercussions sank in. "This wasn't an accident then."

"You know your brother best. "

I did and I knew he would not do what I saw him do a little over an hour ago unless he was being forced to act, which is exactly what that drug we'd discovered Dominique testing accomplished.

"So Vaverek, or someone working for him, used Van as a test?"

He looked at me then, pain bracketing his eyes. "Isn't this exactly what Dominique had been doing? Showing her potential buyers the effectiveness of the drug over a series of incidents?"

"Yes." I'd been playing down the whole involvement of his cousin, after all it was because of what she'd done that she'd ended up in a position where my actions had led to her death. Now here I was doing exactly what Bran had tried, and failed, to do—protect his family member from being a victim. "So you're saying Van might be used again?"

"Him or another like him." Bran turned away from me, which gave me some breathing room to still my nerves. Van turned into a killing shifter had only one possible outcome—his death. And most likely after he'd killed others.

"Wait." Something had been niggling at me from an earlier thought. "We were at that park because I'd tracked the man, the doctor, from the soiree. Was that a coincidence?"

He shook his head. "I wouldn't say so."

"Which means Cheverill's death could be tied into Vaverek and the possibility of Van and this drug?"

A small smile tweaked his lips. Not a happy smile but a watch-out-someone smile. "If these three individuals are tied together it then means we know a fourth one who can lead us to Vaverek."

"The doctor."

"Exactly."

I jumped off my chair, energy surging through me to do something rather than just sit and theorize. "Then let's go."

"Where exactly?" Bran remained stationary and eyed me like a primed bomb.

"It's time you met Ling Mai in person."

"Is she anything like you?"

I shook my head, feeling my own version of a dangerous smile. "Oh no, she makes me look easy to get along with."

CHAPTER 40

Walking into the Hotel Le Meurice with Bran at my side was a whole different experience than when I'd entered with Jaylene and Mandy flanking me. I looked almost the same, though Bran had brought me a change of clothes, including shoes. Leave it to a dress designer to get the sizes right. They were clean and not frou-frou but I still felt like something the cat drug in, but Bran is eye-candy and has that I-own-the-world walk down. There were so many women, and a few men, who were giving Bran the come-hither look I wanted to jump up and down and wave my arms just to see if they noticed me at all. Have I mentioned that restraint is *not* my middle name?

By the time we reached Ling Mai's suite we were more in my territory, not his, and I realized I liked returning to the IR team fold. Not that I'd admit that aloud, and there was still snarky Mandy, but even in the best of families there's always some friction.

I had called Ling Mai earlier, to let her know we were coming and to make sure bringing Bran to her was okay on her end. She knew who he was, based on our last mission, but the two had never formally met. He'd also met Vaughn and Jaylene, but didn't really have a chance to have more than a passing acquaintance with them, if you didn't count the period where he'd just killed a Were, his first one, in front of them, as close bonding.

So when we entered Ling Mai's suite, which still looked spacious in spite of the whole team being there, and did the intros, Bran was the one giving me the what-are-we-doing-here look. That one you get when you're out of your comfort zone.

Which surprised me because I thought Bran could feel at home anywhere. Showed you how little I knew of the man.

I was the one who cleared my throat and gave a quick overview of what had happened over the last twenty-four hours. I stood closest to the door at one end of the long rectangular living room area. Ling Mai was in a chair in front of the fireplace on the west wall, Vaughn, Kelly and Jaylene on the couch which was long enough to hold several more. Mandy and Bran had both taken chairs grouped around a coffee table, Bran facing me and Mandy giving me her back, which did not surprise me in the least.

"And you're sure the shifter was your brother?" Stone pressed, a frown line drawing his brows into a deep vee. He was leaning on the couch arm nearest Vaughn. They made a formidable team and a killer couple.

Shifting my focus back to Stone's question I answered. "Yes. No doubts it was Van."

He glanced at Ling Mai, who'd remained quiet so far. Now she raised her head and spoke to the group. "Word has already spread through the media about a violent dog attack."

"Which wasn't a dog," I clarified in case anyone missed my whole explanation. "And what we're concerned about," I glanced at Bran to make sure I wasn't hanging myself out on this branch all alone. "is that another attack will happen, with the loss of more lives, including Van's, if we don't find a way to stop it."

"Let me get this straight." Vaughn leaned forward, her hands pressed together in her lap, which meant she was still unsure about believing me. "You're saying the Weres have set up this whole scenario to discredit shifters?"

I nodded. "Yup, showing how unpredictable and dangerous shifters can be to humans that they are willing to attack in broad day light, revealing themselves to the human world, as well as thumbing their noses . . ."

"At the Council's authority."

"How so?" Vaughn glanced up at Stone.

"By letting shifters sit on the Council and not Weres, this action, if not an isolated event will show that the Council are cowed by the shifters and that shifters are allowed to freely act with impunity," Stone finished as if piecing a puzzle together.

"Thus if S\shifters can be discredited by Van's very public actions, fueled by the designer drug, the shifters stand to lose their position on the Council. They won't have any choice except to remove them and replace the seat with a Were representative." I looked around to make sure everyone was with me.

"I don't get how Cheverill's death ties into what's happening with Van?" Jaylene asked. She too looked skeptical, not that I blamed her. This was a plan within a plan by someone very devious. And deadly.

"Cheverill's death leaves an opening on the Council governing board."

"But doesn't that position have to be filled by someone of the same species?" Kelly asked, chewing her lower lip. "So was Cheverill a shifter?"

"No." Damn, I hadn't thought of that. "I know there is a shifter on the board but from what Jaylene said in the kitchen the other night Cheverill was a druid."

"Not just a druid, but the big kahuna of druids being an arch one," Jaylene said to Kelly.

That made me realize something else as I speared a quick glance at Jaylene. "How did you know who he was or what he was? The identities of the Council members is not common knowledge."

"I told her," Ling Mai said, her voice calm and neutral.

I wondered how the director learned that information and Ling Mai answered as if I'd spoken aloud. "It's part of my job, Alex, to know who currently sits on the Council and who is in line to take the next opening." She sliced a quick glance at Bran but I had no idea why. He kept his expression very blank as she continued, "Jaylene and Mandy were on an additional mission the night Monsieur Cheverill died, which is why they were privy to who he was and what he was."

That made sense even if it stung a little. I thought a team was supposed to work as a team. Obviously, not all the time or only when it worked for Ling Mai. Talk about another mind that worked at Machiavellian levels.

I brushed the thought away to focus on why I brought Bran here. "Through a spell I cast I tracked the man who was present at Cheverill's death as also being present with Van in the park. He's the one link we have between the death of the Council member, Van's erratic behavior and Vaverek."

I noticed Stone crossing his arms, Vaughn wiggling just a smidge and Mandy's tightening of her back; all classic signs of not being one hundred percent behind my conclusions.

"I know it's not hard and fast evidence," I said, loosening my own shoulders that felt like ready to splinter. "But I'm sure I'm on the right track."

"This coming from a witch who's been known to screw up most of her spells," Mandy pointed out.

I shrugged, focusing on Ling Mai. If I could get her on board with what I thought we should do next, everyone else would come along. "Look we already know Vaverek and the Seekers are tied together."

"But not how," Mandy murmured, turning her head to stare at me. "Or even who the Seekers are."

I ignored her and continued, figuring if we had all the i's dotted and t's crossed we wouldn't need to be here.

"Vaverek is linked to a variation of this designer drug." Before Mandy could speak I glared at her, which shut her right down. "And Vaverek is involved in Van's disappearance."

"We're with you," Vaughn nodded. "So far."

"But we're not one step closer to finding or apprehending him." Even nay-sayer Mandy couldn't disagree with that. I glanced over at Bran who was watching Ling Mai intently. But why?

"The point you wish to make Miss Noziak?" Ling Mai said.

Which wasn't a good sign. When she used my formal name it usually meant I was in trouble. But I hadn't done anything recently. Not that I knew about. "I think we should focus our attention on this other man, the one I think of as the doctor. Find him and we use him to lead us to Vaverek."

Yes, it was a long shot but the only shot we had. Unless Bran had something up his sleeve.

Ling Mai let her gaze sweep to Bran. "And you concur?"

Bran nodded, but didn't say anything. Not a rousing endorsement, but it wouldn't be the first time I was taking a risk based on my gut instincts. "It's not as if continuing to do what we're doing, which is just looking for Vaverek directly, should start paying off when it hasn't yet."

"Are you not ignoring another issue, Miss Noziak?"

What was she talking about? I glanced at my teammates and only Kelly gave me a wobbly smile back. Mandy and Jaylene both avoided looking at me and Vaughn offered a small shake of her head. "What issue?"

"There are rumors circling through the Council members that you yourself may be involved with *Monsieur* Cheverill's death."

"Get real!" Okay, it may not have been the smartest thing I could have said but surely these people didn't think I had anything to do with it. Did they? "I was there, but only after he collapsed. Why should I kill a man I didn't even know?"

"Are you sure you did not know him?" Ling Mai asked, looking at me with narrowed eyes. "You're certain that you are not using this hunt for an unknown man, this doctor, as a means to deflect attention from your involvement in the Council member's death?"

As if all the air in the room had been sucked out I felt suddenly light-headed and put a hand out to touch the back of Mandy's chair to stabilize me. Surely the director didn't believe what she was saying?

A quick look around though let me know that while I'd been absent the team had been discussing me behind my back.

"She's not saying you're a killer," Kelly offered, playing peacekeeper from her perch on the couch.

"I think that's exactly what she's saying," I shot back, not attacking Kelly as much as fighting in the dark. I hadn't seen this coming. Maybe I should have, with the way Mandy and Jaylene had come into the kitchen last night. The fact no one had called me back after I tried to reach them earlier in the day. So much for making sure I played well with the team.

"What she's saying is the Council has concerns." Stone jumped into the silence, earning a quick glare from Ling Mai and just as quick a smile from Vaughn.

"So I'm tried and hanged based on rumors from a Council of strangers to me?"

Ling Mai cocked her head. "There lies the problem, Miss Noziak."

I shook my head, lost all over again. "You mean I have a bigger problem than being called a killer by a group of people I've never met, that work behind closed doors and love to throw their weight around, making decrees that screw up others' lives just because they can do it?"

Okay, I was getting mad, but anger was better than being gobsmacked and gutted. How dare the Council smear my name? Again. Unless I made a convenient scapegoat, already having a murder rap and conveniently being in the right country, at the right party, at the right time.

"You don't know do you?" Stone asked, nabbing my one hundred percent attention for his question and the soft tone it was said in. Stone didn't do soft, it didn't go with his whole killer, bad-ass personality.

"Know what?" I glanced around, this time seeing averted gazes and uncomfortable silence. It was Bran who I ended up staring at, as if he was at the heart of whatever was going on. "What's happening?" I insisted. "What should I know about the Council that I don't?"

Bran canted his head toward Ling Mai who answered, her voice as arid and lethal as dry ice against skin. "You are telling us that you do not know your father is on the Council?"

CHAPTER 41

When I was a child I once went to the park with three of my brothers. Not Van, but Jake, Luke and Simon. There was a swing that looked like it could reach the sky and made me quake in my shoes just thinking about getting on it. Of course having shifter brothers they could scent my fear so ragged and dared me until I marched up to that old, silly swing and with a boost from Jake, plopped down on that rubber belt that was the seat.

I felt like I'd conquered the world. Until Jake started pushing me forward. Higher and higher, my hands sweaty on the chain, my butt slipping and sliding with each rocket thrust into that summer sky, my heart in my throat. But I didn't say anything. If I screamed I knew he'd push harder; shifter brothers were like that. I just closed my eyes and felt the sky rush down to me, the earth recede with each jerky shove.

And then it happened. I clutched too tight, or slid too far, I don't know what I'd done but I knew it was my fault when suddenly the rubber tethering me to earth twisted and I was upside down, my feet above my head, gripping on for dear life.

I didn't make a sound though I could hear my brothers' shouts buzzing in my awareness. The sky and ground flip flopped and I knew, down to the marrow of my bones, that if I remained frozen I could survive. It was my only option.

I felt exactly like that now. My world had tilted and if I just stayed still, so still even my breaths didn't register, soon my world would right again, even as I knew it never would.

You are telling us that you do not know your father is on the Council?

My father couldn't be on the Council. How'd I know that? Because if he was he'd have been present when the Council suppressed information that would have kept me out of prison. My dad would not have done that. He would not have let me face life behind metal bars.

Would he?

He'd lied to me. He'd said he'd always stand by me even as he knew what keeping quiet meant. He said good-bye to me at the prison gates, knowing he helped send me there.

It was Kelly who popped up at my side, her hands on my arms, guiding me to a seat. She made small soothing sounds, the way you would to a terror-struck child. Or a rabid dog.

"I'd say that was a you-didn't-know answer," Stone said, a little louder than he needed to, or maybe I was being hyper aware of noise, of motion, of everything right then.

If my dad had let me be sent to prison for life then my world as I'd known it was based on a lie. I'd always believed he had my back, no matter what. He was the one who'd stayed and raised me when my mom high-tailed it away to greener pastures. The one who tried to find me a witch mentor to help me handle my magic talents. The one who had been by my side the whole terrible trial and sentencing, when people thought I'd killed a man in about as brutal and violent way as possible, instead of stopping a rogue Were who was trying to kill my brother.

That was the *pièce de résistance* that had me sentenced for life. The crime scene photos that showed a man practically torn limb from limb. I was judged as a vicious, cold, and calculating murderess taking the life of an innocent human. When the truth was I'd sucked the Were's own powers from him and turned them on him, just as I'd done in the street fight yesterday. I did to him what he'd been planning on doing to my brother.

And my dad knew that.

But the Council refused to let humans know that piece of information, as that would have revealed too much about preternaturals to the clueless human population.

My father let that happen.

I let that happen.

I wanted to scream, to punch someone, something. Stupid, clueless me and I thought I was doing the right thing. The best thing for the sake of the greater good. Talk about an idiot throwing herself on the sword for beings who didn't care at all about me. Including my father. Especially my father.

"Alex." It was Bran kneeling before me, so close all I could see was him. Dark hair ruffled, Celtic blue eyes very serious, the slashes of his cheekbones prominent as if he was clenching his jaw really tight. He grabbed my hands between his, rubbing them, which alerted me to the fact they were cold. Arctic ice cold. I was chilled all over, suddenly shaking. "Someone get me a brandy or bourbon," he snarled.

I heard movement in the background as I focused on Bran, using him to anchor me in place so I didn't spiral away and then a hand appeared before me with a glass. Jaylene's hand.

He took the crystal and nudged the rim against my lips. "Drink this. Now."

How like Bran. Do this. Do that. Warlock arrogance. But right then he was right. I couldn't think for myself. In a minute maybe, but not right then.

I took a sip, felt the sear to my toes then shook my head. I didn't want anything to make me more numb, I was so numb as it was I might never surface.

Numbness was better than the hurt hiding just beneath it. Not deep beneath but like a sliver wedged just deep enough into your finger that every time you brushed against it your whole body flinched.

Bran pulled me to my feet. I wasn't a rag doll but he seemed to have his own agenda. So like him. And he was angry, so angry I could feel the heat roll off of him. He looked at Ling Mai who was hidden behind him somewhere. "This is how you treat your agents?"

No one answered. Not that I blamed them. With the tone of his voice if he'd been a shifter or Were he'd already be changing into an angry beast.

"Alex is coming with me," he announced.

"And you're going where?" It was Stone who answered that challenge, stepping forward, his chin high, his stance aggressive. Alpha to Alpha. Great, just what I needed, more potential bloodshed. If they tore each other from limb to limb maybe I'd get two life sentences. Or the death penalty. The way the day was unfurling I'd put my money on the latter.

Before I could speak Bran did. "We're looking for the doctor. When we find him we'll let you know."

"And if you don't find him?" Ling Mai's voice washed over me.

"We will," he said, and even I believed him. I who knew that wasn't his real agenda.

"And what about Alex?" Stone was pushing. I'd like to think it was for my sake, that whole team thing that everyone else seemed to conveniently forget when it was not working for them. But then he added, "The Council isn't going to be too happy when they find out she was here but left."

Of course. When would I learn? No one cared if I lived or died, went to prison or remained free, was a part of the team or not, as long as I didn't rock their boats. I wasn't having a pity party as much as a buck-up-baby and get with the program. Maybe if I could tap into the rage bubbling inside me I could speak and move and act mostly human instead of the walking who kept trusting the wrong people; starting with my mother, my father and right up to here.

"Screw the Council," Bran bit back. The minute I got my stuffing back I'd thank him for that, even if I should be able to stand up for myself. Any time now.

"I'm afraid that is not possible," Ling Mai, ever the voice of calm reason cut in. "Miss Noziak is a member of this Agency and her actions, or disappearance, reflect upon the whole team."

"Then you can tell the Council I'll have her in front of them by ten tomorrow."

And here I thought he'd been working on my behalf. Silly witch, how many lessons did I need to get that message through my head? I was on my own. If my mother abandoned me and my father did basically the same thing behind the closed doors of Council business, why should I expect Ling Mai or Bran to watch my back?

I said nothing. No words, no protests, no scathing comments could ease past the chunk of anger choking me.

Stone kept pushing. "We trust you to appear before the Council tomorrow because?"

"Because that's when I'm supposed to report to them myself."

Oh, yeah, I'd actually forgot about that for a few minutes.

Bran pulled me toward the door, one hand wrapped about my arm which kept me upright. "You know how to contact me. How to get ahold of Alex if you need her, but it'd better be because you've found Vaverek, or a way to clear Alex's name."

I shook myself loose of Bran's hold as he opened the suite's door and turned to look at my fellow team members. Kelly was quivering, half visible, half invisible, a sure sign of stress. Jaylene kept her body still, her expression the same as she glanced from me to Ling Mai and back. Mandy's gaze was averted, not that I expected much from her. Stone was holding back Vaughn, which helped give some oomph to my spine. And Ling Mai looked as if everything was business as usual, and she hadn't just blown my world apart.

To think when I'd entered this room I was glad to see my teammates, the women I was coming to think of as friends.

I wouldn't make that mistake again.

CHAPTER 42

Jeb sat beneath the Linden tree in Philippe's garden, the scrap of paper directing him to the park earlier still gripped within his hands, his thumb idly rubbing back and forth, back and forth, as if touching the words would bring clarity.

Pádraig was off executing Council business and Jeb was alone. Waiting. Looking for connections where he could see none. Yet.

Why did Philippe have to die? Who benefitted? And who was behind Van's initial disappearance and now his actions in the park? Actions that stirred the Council into a flurry of communication with one another, but to what end? If the warlock who had been with Alex was truly a threat, or implicated in what had happened to Philippe, or Van, the warlock should not have been allowed a stay from judgment. Unless he had contacts on the Council, which was becoming a stronger and stronger possibility.

What was the warlock's role in events? And how had he involved Alex?

Jeb couldn't ask such questions during the Council session earlier because they were not directly related to the reason this Bran was being examined and later, when Jeb sought the warlock out, he'd already disappeared.

And the most disturbing question: why had Van attacked Jeb earlier? Shifters and Weres could go loco for many reasons; age, grief, the challenges of balancing both human and animal selves. It was why Weres and shifters banded in packs or clans, as mutual self-protection. If a particular shifter or Were looked as if they could no longer walk the tightrope required of their existence the pack leader was responsible for eliminating them.

Jeb knew his Native American ancestors had resorted to a similar response during times of extreme stress for the tribe. If an individual threatened the tribe's existence, if they could not contribute but had or might become a drain on limited resources, it had been deemed the best to expose the individual to the environment. Let them die so others could live. Sacrifice for the larger good.

The larger non-human population could not let dangerous Weres and shifters walk off and die on their own. No, the Pack or Clann leader would either execute the individual himself, or call upon a designated slayer. One death for the salvation of the many.

If turning loco is what had happened to Van, then Jeb was responsible for ending his son's life.

It was their way and they both knew it.

But knowing and accepting were two sides of a honed sword's blade, and this knowledge cut deep.

He heard the footsteps approaching only because as a shifter he possessed acute sensory abilities. The sound was stealthy but not threatening. Not yet.

Jeb turned a fraction so the man could slide into his view. Still he waited.

"You are not surprised," said the voice that held a hint of his Middle Eastern roots, but not the subservience of a butler anymore.

"No."

The man Philippe called Zeid stepped before Jeb, looking taller and thinner than he had when playing the role of Philippe's servant. The last afternoon light reflected off the darkness of his hair, the swarthiness of his skin, making him more sinister than he might be. Jeb hadn't decided yet if the man was friend or foe.

"You are not afraid of me?" Zeid asked, a frown creasing his face as if revaluating Jeb just as Jeb was doing to him.

"Should I be?"

"I am fae," came the neutral response, that could be either threat or reprieve. Fae were among the most populous of the preternaturals and ranged from relatively harmless and beneficial types, the innocui; goat spirits, garden sprites, bee keepers; to the very powerful and dangerous, the pericui; dream masters, spirits of iron and metal, soul stealers.

Jeb waited. When dealing with the fae, any fae, it was best to not provoke them or make rash judgments or actions. They tended to be very nervous beings and easily spooked.

"I see that what I am does not surprise you either," Zeid said, a smile now playing about his thin lips.

"I think you're only half fae." Jeb made sure his tone did not condemn or hold a slur.

"I have clearly underestimated you." Zeid stepped back, crossing his arms and widening his stance as if he'd grown from the ground.

As intrigued as Jeb might be to discover more of Zeid's faeness, there were more pressing needs. He raised the paper in his hand. "You were the one who slipped this beneath my door."

Zeid nodded but said nothing. Jeb had often taken the same approach with his children, letting them come to their own conclusions to see how much they really knew or just thought they knew.

Jeb glanced at the paper. "You warned me but did not give me enough to prevent what happened in the park." It was a statement though enough of Jeb's frustration must have coated the words for the fae to shake his head.

"I am not a nymph to see into the future." Zeid's tone was sword sharp.

"Then you too are wavering in the dark." Jeb inclined his head, hearing what wasn't being said. This fae did not know what was about to happen to Van ahead of time though he did know that Van was going to be at the park. Alex, too. At a different time and place Jeb knew how to approach the fae, with honeyed words and protocol. They were a proud race and once greatly admired and feared. But with worry clawing him, the words would not come. He hoped the fae understood his bluntness. "What is it you want of me?"

"To know if you are stalwart and true."

Riddles. Jeb forced his shoulders to relax, his tone to a calmness he did not feel as he shadow danced with this one who held his own agenda.

"I have been tested by time and by trial," Jeb repeated the old words, the words of legend when one supplicated a liege lord. "I have sacrificed my heart more than once for the benefit of others over myself and those of my heart."

"Your wife?"

Like a knife piercing the skin, Jeb accepted the cold slice of a pain he still felt though twenty years had passed since her betrayal. A blink of an eye to beings that lived for hundreds of years, and some longer.

He nodded his head but kept his gaze on the fae as he added, "And my daughter."

That wound being more recent, dug deeper. But now was not the time for bitterness or regret. Not if he could save his two children.

"And the Council?" Zeid asked, as if the question was of no consequence, which told Jeb it was just the opposite.

"What of the Council? If you know who I am and what I am then you should know what I can and can not reveal to anyone."

There were some lines drawn in sand and some in stone. This was one of the latter.

Zeid seemed to contemplate something as he shook his head and unfolded his hands, sweeping into a half bow. "May I formally introduce myself. My name is Zeid Malatesta Asuar. Do you know the meaning of Asuar?"

"I know only that it is of Egyptian origin. No more."

"Then you are more informed than most of your country men." Zeid crossed over to brush a hand against the Linden tree as if seeing something far far away before he continued,"Asuar is a form of the sacred name of the god Osiris."

Jeb waited but his patience was wearing thin. If Zeid knew something or wanted Jeb's help, then Jeb was willing to bide his time; time that was precious.

Zeid continued, as if lecturing a new student. "Osiris brought civilization and spirituality to his people." Zeid's brow lifted as if to say and what do you think of that? But he continued, not waiting for an answer. "Osiris decreed laws to regulate the conduct of early men, which was desperately needed."

"And as a descendant of Osiris is this what you do now?"

"My kind walks in the footsteps left by Osiris. We are the Dominatui."

"Dominators?"

"The masters of rules."

"Not innocui or pericui?"

"No. We came before the Council, to arbitrate and maintain the balance between fae with differing agendas."

As a Council member of long standing Jeb should have known of this group. Did others on the Council? And did it matter right now?

It might have been the lengthening shadows across the lawn, the trauma of the last two days, but Jeb had not come to Paris for a lesson on Egyptian mythology. No matter how fascinating.

Zeid must have seen the frustration in Jeb's expression as he smiled, a genuine one reaching his eyes. "True, you do not need a genealogy discussion. You need clarity."

"Yes." At last, Jeb might get some answers. He leaned forward, clasping his hands before him. "What are you doing here and what do you know of my children?"

"The latter are peripheral to my assignment here," Zeid said though Jeb didn't think the fae meant to be cruel or callous with his dismissal of Alex and Van. It was the way of the more long-lived and powerful fae. Human lives, so frail and short, were of no consequence. So Jeb bit his tongue and waited.

"I came into the household of Philippe Cheverill seeking a traitor."

Jeb snapped upright. Philippe was the last man Jeb would associate with the word traitor.

"You do justice to your friend," Zeid said, even though Jeb had not uttered a sound. "My people have no such ties of loyalty and obligation."

"Your people? You mean the Dominatui." Jeb wasn't sure he wanted to hear what Zeid seemed compelled to share, but he pushed for at least one answer in particular. "Are they not under the Council's jurisdiction?"

"No." The single word shot like an arrow, true and deadly. "Osiris feared absolute power in the hands of so few."

"Osiris has been gone for thousands of years. And the Council only arose as the balance between human-kind and our kind shifted."

"You mean when the humans covered the earth and forgot their non-human kin."

"Yes." Jeb clenched his hands together. "The Council has been active only a few centuries. Humans are notorious for forgetting their history."

"*Oui.*" Zeid smiled, but this time it was vindictive. "Which is why their greatest peril is from themselves. That is not my assignment, but left to others."

Jeb wanted to press for more answers but also accepted that the fae would only share so much. Better that knowledge be useful to the most immediate problem, saving Alex and Van.

"So you came to seek a traitor. Philippe?" Jeb braced himself for the answer.

"The traitor is not yet clear to us, though we watch the trail of his actions and see him more and more every day."

Jeb released a breath he didn't realize he'd held. Philippe might still be the being these Dominatui sought, but his friend was beyond caring of the outcome of that search. "What does this traitor have to do with my children? With Alex and Van?"

Zeid's brow popped up again. This time in surprise. "They are mere tools to achieve larger ends."

"Being?"

"That is where I require your help."

Ah, now they were getting down to brass tacks. "My help to do what?"

Zeid paused before looking Jeb directly in the eye, always a dangerous move from a fae. Many of them were masters at mind control and manipulation and used direct eye contact as windows to your mind. When he spoke again his voice sounded deeper, more muffled, as though speaking through a dreamscape. "Your children may need to be sacrificed to expose the traitor."

Like hell they would!

Jeb held his tongue though and stifled his thoughts. As a shifter he was as susceptible as the next being to fae persuasion, but as a shaman he could shield himself somewhat. Since he was a Native American shaman, this fae from the old countries, including what was now the Middle East, did not necessarily know the full extent of Jeb's abilities. By the time Zeid learned, it would be too late. Jeb would have already acted.

"You hear my words," Zeid continued, growing taller and broader, his shape becoming more fae and less human looking as he exerted his powers.

Jeb nodded, making sure the movement was slow and precise.

"Your son will be used to manipulate the Council into rash actions."

Another nod. This one as stiff as before but not because Jeb was faking it. Fear welded the muscles of his neck until they felt rock hard.

"Your daughter may be able to save him. But she is the only one who can."

Relief started flowing through Jeb. But the fae was not yet finished.

"But only one of them may live."

CHAPTER 43

I was outside and in Bran's car, which materialized from nowhere, not by magic but by valets, before I found my tongue. "Why are you staying with me?"

Not what I meant to ask, but I blurted the words out before common sense reared its head. Only an idiot gnawed at the hand helping it. And right now Bran's hand was the only one assisting me.

His lips quirked up in a half smile as he steered his vehicle through the crazy Parisian traffic as he did everything else, with assurance and smooth control.

No wonder the two of us could never find common ground. Our worlds were so different, and our personalities were at opposing ends of a spectrum. I was rash, he was rational. He acted with forethought, I ran off emotion. He used magic with deliberation and experience. I used magic as bombs to lob as a last ditch effort and hope I could clean up the mess afterwards.

"You're thinking too much," he murmured beside me, as if he could read my tumbled thoughts.

"I have a lot to think about." I folded my hands in my lap to control the craziness racing through me. Ling Mai. The Council. My dad. Oh, so don't go there. That betrayal cut the deepest in a day of betrayals.

Instead focus on the mundane, putting one foot in front of another. "Where are we going?" I asked, suddenly looking around, watching Paris flash past.

"To feed you."

I glanced at him, surprised my jaw wasn't unhinged it'd dropped so far. "My world is imploding and you want to eat?"

He kept his eyes forward. "When was the last time you had food?"

Who cared? I know I didn't as I realized the last meal I remembered was the croissants and fruit this morning. Also supplied by Bran if I recalled. What was he now, my caretaker? That would be the day.

As if summoned by my thoughts, or some spell Bran was casting, my stomach started rumbling.

"I thought so," he said, all smugness.

Fine. I'd eat, but that didn't mean I'd be happy about it. But leave it to Bran to find the perfect place to fit my mood. A small hole-in-the-wall with three tables outside. We snagged one of them, out of the day-to-day bustle of people going about their lives, unaware of the danger in their midst. Danger such as me.

"Stop frowning," Bran admonished after he ran a spate of French past the older woman taking our orders. I had no idea what we were going to get but I'm sure Bran knew what he was doing. In this at least.

I leaned across the table, my arms wrapped around my waist, not because I was cool as day eased into evening, but because I didn't trust my hands not to beat on his broad chest. "What would you be doing if your world had just imploded?" I snarled, keeping my voice low.

He gave me one of those lord-to-peon looks he no doubt learned in the cradle and said, "I'd be focused on how to fix the problem."

"Which one?" I threw one hand before me. "I'm no closer to helping Van. I don't even know if he's still alive. My . . ." I lowered my voice though it did nothing for the intensity of my tone. "My team has thrown me to the wolves."

"Technically it's to the Weres."

Maybe I should beat him.

"Easy for you to joke." I snapped back in my chair, too aware how fragile my hold on my emotions had become. "It's not your world that's come crashing down."

Like a switch flicked off his shoulders tightened, the banked emotion in his eyes searing through me. "You don't think I know *exactly* how you feel."

By the Great Spirits, he was right. How stupid could I be? His cousin and nearest family, his only family for that matter, barely buried, his business in upheaval as he lost his CEO with her death, the publicity in the world's press that splashed his pain like so much spilled wine across the media. If anyone knew what I was going through he knew. But dwelling on that made him too approachable, too human, and I needed all the distance I could get from him emotionally. But fair was fair.

"You're right. You do know." I scrubbed my hands across my face. "I screwed this up, too."

"Yes."

Fortunately the waitress interrupted before I had to grovel more, though I deserved it. Short-sighted and callous.

He didn't throw my lack of awareness in my face, nor rub my nose in my apology, brief as it was. Instead he grabbed a slice of bread, cheese and some type of sliced thin meat and shoved it toward me. "Eat first. Then we talk."

Twenty minutes later I had to admit he was right. About the needing to eat part. Not that I was going to blurt that out. I'd probably send him into shock with too many admissions in one day.

Besides I think this was the first meal we'd ever shared together that was peaceful. Last meal we sat down to ended up with his freezing the whole room in place and us going our separate ways. Not that good a memory.

"You're looking pensive, now." He crumbled his napkin and tossed it on the table. "But you're no longer so pale."

All I could think was that I can't be pale. I'm Native American.

"What are you thinking about?"

"How a person can never go back for a do-over."

His face tightened, the color of his eyes intensified, as if he knew exactly what I meant. The me and him bit. Not that I wanted to go down that road of what-might-have-been. Not today, and maybe not ever, given neither of us might have more than a day left if the Council had any say in the matter.

I swear he was a mind reader as he relaxed his shoulders, leaned his elbows on the table in a very un-Bran-like casual manner and said, "Ready for business?"

Of course. This was not seductive, sexy Bran, this was dealmaker Bran, ready to conquer the world.

I gave a short, jerky nod. "Now what?"

His lips tilted, distracting me, then his smile deepened as if he caught where I was focusing. Thank the Spirits his voice was all focused as he said, "Now we figure out what to do next."

Like that was going to be easy. Not that a Noziak shied away from hard, but there was challenging, and then there was jumping head first into trouble. I had a whole lot more experience with the latter.

"Why are you helping me?" It was a variation on the question I'd asked him in the car, and I really wanted to know. Yes, I was obstinate but I'd had one too many rugs pulled out from under me today. I couldn't get a handle on where Bran was coming from and why he was sticking his neck out for me. If the Council decided my leaving that hotel room was a sure sign of flight, they'd take me out, and anyone around me that was in the way. No questions, no negotiations, no second thoughts. It's how they did business.

"You still don't trust me." His voice sounded resigned, and chiseled from granite.

I shook my head. "Nope."

For a second I thought I saw something flash in his gaze. Regret? Nah. This was the man who'd threatened to kill me if I didn't help him track down the man directly responsible for getting his cousin involved in testing designer drugs. I knew I was right when he tilted forward just a smidge. "I still need your help."

"To find Vaverek?"

"Yes."

We find him we find Van. But to find Vaverek I needed to find the doctor guy. "We're right where we started this morning only I don't think my scrying spell is going to work now." "Because?"

"You know how magic can be fickle. The spell brought me to the park."

"Where the man was located, or supposedly located."

"He was there." In my bones I knew he had been.

"And you can't cast a new spell because...?"

"In a public park that's had dozens of law enforcement and news teams crossing it to report the incident today? Too much cross-contamination to make scrying possible."

He rubbed his chin, but didn't seem as dismayed as I expected him to be. It was my turn to state the obvious. "You have something up your sleeve."

"Not something but someone."

No idea what he was talking about but I waited until he paid for the meal and pushed his chair back before I asked," Who are you talking about and what are they supposed to do?"

"Willie."

He was kidding, right?

I rose to my feet and double-timed it to keep up with his long-legged stride back to the car. "What's Willie Were-in-Denial got to do with anything?"

Bran unlocked my door and leaned into the car after I slid into the passenger seat. His size very effectively acted as a barrier to anyone overhearing us. Smart, though a small corner of my mind said I should be more wary with a deadly warlock trapping me in the enclosed space.

But I wasn't. Odd. No time to deal with that though, back to business.

"Willie may be a recovering Were but he's still a Were."

The light bulb went off. "You mean he's been tracking the men from the park?"

He nodded, a real smile curving his lips. "He and François."

A dog. Of course. "It'd have been better if François was a bloodhound." I mumbled aloud as he closed my door and walked around the car to slide into the driver's seat. He waited until after he'd started the car and was pulling into traffic to say, "Who says François isn't?"

I didn't know if I wanted to slug him for holding back this information until now or slug him for lying. He didn't need my help if he had two experts at tracking hard on the trail.

So what did he need me for?

CHAPTER 44

Van snarled and pulled at the chains eating into his skin but they didn't give an inch. All they did was make his temper even more tensile thin. That and the smell of the dead man across the cell. His wolf scented meat and wasn't too happy with Van holding him back.

Not that he was doing all that good a job of it. Whatever they had shot him full of earlier was still impacting him now. His thought process felt sluggish and disjointed, as if the dots didn't connect. He didn't trust what might have happened while he'd been under the full thrust of the drugs, or if he was hallucinating. Had he really heard Alex? Or was that wishful thinking? And fighting with his dad? A figment of his imagination? It had to be. He'd never let his wolf attack any member of his family. Never.

"Ah, I see you are more with us," Jean-Claude spoke from somewhere near him.

Van lunged toward the sound of the man's voice but no one was there.

"*Il fait bon vivre,*" the doctor's voice swam against Van. "It is good to be alive, is it not?"

Where was the doctor? Had Van crossed into the spirit realm as his father could? No, not with the stench of the dead man deep in Van's nostrils, the pain of chains rubbing him raw, the scrape of sharp rock against his back. He was very much trapped in the physical plane, so where was the other man?

Van shook his head, trying to dislodge the voice.

"It will do you no good, my friend."

The doctor was no friend of Van's. He was a dead man if Van ever got loose.

"We have one more trial for you, *Monsieur*. One I am sure you'll be able to execute with flying colors."

No! No more drugs.

"You shall have to kill again."

Again?

"And I'm afraid it will be someone close to you, but that will be the only way to see if the drug is truly effective."

Van froze. A nightmare? The voice must be a frightening illusion. That was all.

"I'm afraid this is no illusion, Mister Noziak. I am very much real. And what you must do is very real, too."

A scream tore from Van's throat. "Never."

"Soon, very soon."

Van would kill himself before he allowed them to kill him.

A laugh whipped against him. "*Bon*. After you kill, suicide is a good solution."

CHAPTER 45

We ended up back at the warehouse, which made sense. I hadn't told my team where I'd stayed the night before, only that Bran had arranged it. Not that they really cared at this moment. I cast a quick glance at my phone, wondering if I should chuck it now so no one could trace me on it. Or wait.

For what? For them to decide Bran couldn't or wouldn't be bringing me before the Council tomorrow? Or for me to head out on my own at the first chance?

"You're thinking too much again," Bran said, walking up behind me so quietly I jumped.

"I expected François and Willie to be here." Yes, I changed the subject but Bran was a little too intuitive for me to trust he wouldn't guess my idea about leaving. Why shouldn't I? The Council had messed with me once, there was no reason to meekly show up on their doorstep to be executed because they were too lazy to find out who really killed Philippe Cheverill.

Bran might think he was being all responsible and honorable appearing before them tomorrow, but not me. If I couldn't find Van in the next twelve hours running was a good option. The result would be inevitable, my death, but at least if I ran I stood a chance to still help Van, if he was still alive. No more acting like a sheep from me.

"Did you hear me?" Bran asked, refocusing my attention back on him.

"Hear what?"

He pulled up a hassock to sit on across from where I perched on the couch, my arms wrapped around me. "I said

Willie and François should be here any moment. In the meantime I have some questions."

"About what?" No way was I telling him the train of my thoughts.

He was sitting on the edge of the stool, his hands clasped in front of him, his attention all on me. And when he focused you felt it. At least I did, like an electrical current running beneath my skin. "Explain what you did yesterday morning in the street fight."

The fight? Was that only yesterday? I had to shake myself away from thoughts of Bran to another topic I didn't want to discuss. No point in acting like I didn't know exactly what he was asking about. "What does it matter?"

His laugh sounded bitter. "The type of people we're going up against are not your normal threat. If you hadn't done what you did, you, me and your team would have died."

Finally, someone who saw what I'd done the way I saw it. It wasn't black magic I'd used, at least I didn't think it was. Most black magic involved body parts and death. I'd only channeled power.

"You want me to use that ability against Vaverek?" Is that where he was going with his thought process? "Because it's not a spell I'm sure I can replicate. With any precision especially, sort of like having an AK47 and a bad case of palsy. I'm surprised the spell worked at all."

Plus my dad had warned me against exercising it. He made me swear I'd never use it, once he'd seen me call it as a child. But I had employed it again, to save Jake from that rogue Were. And look where that got me—prison for life. Is that why my dad had abandoned me to the Council? Because he knew I'd broken my word to him? Or because I was some kind of a freak with what I could do?

Bran waved his hand before my face. "Come back," he said, his voice low and if it had been anyone else, I'd have said concerned. But this was Bran.

"Tell me what happened to the non-humans you'd been fighting after I left."

"Why did you leave?"

He actually laughed, but not containing any mirth. "You stole my magic without as much as a by your leave. Did you think it made sense for me to stick around?"

Well, when he phrased it that way. "It's not like I really planned for that to happen. I was just trying to save all of our skins."

"I realized that." He tapped one closed fist against my knee. "Didn't mean I was happy with you at the time, so leaving was the better part of discretion."

Go figure.

I swallowed and let him continue. "I take it you haven't used that kind of magic a lot."

"Are you serious?"

His laugh this time was genuine. "Thought so. Sort of like playing with a nuclear bomb."

So he did understand. Which I wasn't sure I liked. An enemy was better than a frenemy with him, and way better than trusting that we could be anything more. Been there, done that. Still had the broken heart.

"Back to the non-humans," he said.

See? He wasn't getting all off track. He was precision point warlock.

"What about them?"

"Any survivors?"

"You going to bring this up to the Council?"

He sat up straight, as if I'd dashed cold water in his face. "No."

"You swear?"

"By the secrets of the Craft, I thee swear."

Using the old words meant something and I had to respect that. "Okay." I sucked in a breath that did nothing to quiet the increase of my heart rate. "As far as I know no non-human lived."

"Yet you and your teammates did." His face creased in concentration.

"And so did you." He seemed to ignore that point and had turned inward so I pushed. "Why does it matter?"

He glanced at me. "It makes common sense to know the limits of a weapon."

"You mean me?" I jabbed my thumb into my chest. "You're thinking I'm going to go ballistic like that again?"

"Aren't you?"

I opened my mouth to protest then closed it. He was right. It wasn't like the team or I had a lot of amazing super-powered weapons or ninja skills to stop preternaturals who by and large were bigger, stronger, and deadlier than we were. Except for Kelly who could disappear, and even then it wasn't clear that preternaturals with a strong sense of smell couldn't scent her. The rest of us were like sending a squirt gun to take out a howitzer. What had Ling Mai been thinking creating this team and sending us out so ill prepared?

Oh, wait, what was I thinking? This was Ling Mai whom I doubted gave a rat's toenail for any of us. We were feet on the ground. I had no doubts she had a larger plan in mind, so maybe our deaths might serve to kick-start phase two in whatever she had up her sleeve, but none of us were likely to see it.

I raised my eyes to clash with Bran's, patiently waiting for me to arrive at a conclusion he'd already made. "Given the same or a similar situation I'd probably do the same thing."

He gave a slow, measured nod until I asked, "Why?"

"You've forgotten the prophecy?"

Oh crap, not that again? I rose to my feet, needing to pace. Our last mission together he'd mentioned some witch-warlock prophecy, which was a bunch of hooey as far as I was concerned.

As I marched across the room though I could hear his voice warp around me.

"Acies. Acendo. Adamo."

Like summer lightning raising the hair along the skin his words prodded, challenging me, asking something I wasn't touching with a thirty foot anything.

"It's a bunch of mumbo jumbo," I said, the worst words one could lob at something he obviously believed in. I remembered when he first described it as a very old portent, between a powerful warlock and an even more powerful witch.

It was that last bit that stuck in my craw. Yes, I was witch-born but not witch taught, which meant my spells tended to be hit or miss. And if I did hit, they weren't always the right target. So calling me a powerful witch was like saying a kid's scooter and a Harley Davidson were in the same league.

I knew, to the marrow of my bones, of the cost of playing with magic and there was always a cost. An unexpected boomerang effect that lashed back on the practitioner in unexpected, and mostly unwanted ways.

"The prophecy starts the time of change, the time of loss," Bran continued as if he'd heard nothing I'd said. "We've already started it."

"Bull puckey," I wanted to say something stronger, but my throat seemed to swell shut, as if I'd angered magic itself by degrading it.

Is this what my mother had dealt with? She might have been raised among witches but once she chose my father, and his life on a small farm in Idaho, she was isolated, having to hide her abilities. Alone.

Yes!

I froze in my pacing. The woman's voice. Turning slowly, as if tracking the echo of her words, I reached out to feel her, to find her. But there was nothing.

Why did that not surprise me.

"Something spook you?" Bran rose and crossed to where I stood. "What is it?"

"Nothing." I brushed him off as I wished I could brush the cry away. My plate was overfull, no need to bring one more relative, imagined or not, into the mix. I turned toward where Bran stood, his face set in a thoughtful expression. "I'm beginning to think you made up Willie and François." I waved one hand toward the closed door. "What they're doing."

"Pushing away, Alex?" he said, as if I was the one who brought him here under false pretenses. "So sure if someone wants to help there must be an angle? A demand in response?"

I was sure my brows were hiding in my hairline. Where had this come from? I just wanted to know where Fido and Fang were and what was keeping them.

Before I could open my mouth and set Mister High-and-Mighty straight the door belted open and the missing duo emerged, looking like they hadn't tracked through the streets of Paris but were dragged through them.

"What happened?" Bran demanded, stepping toward them.

François used his thumb to point at the Were two steps behind him. "Someone decided they didn't like Willie sniffing after him."

"The doctor?" I asked, my gaze tap dancing between the two of them. "Did you find him?"

"Several times." Willie coughed as if clearing a jam in his throat. "That was the problem."

"What problem?" I crossed to stand in front of them. Didn't they realize this was a time sensitive issue? "What do you know?"

François was the one who looked up, rubbing his shoulder as if it was sore. "I think we found Vaverek."

CHAPTER 46

"What do you mean, you think?" I snapped at François. He cut a quick glance at Bran as if asking what's-up-with-her? If anyone said PMS there was going to be blood and it wasn't going to be mine.

Willie was the one who answered, swiping at what looked like blood on his shirt. "It's not as if these men had their scents labeled."

Bran raised his brows at me as if daring me to contest that point.

I released a sigh. "Fine. Tell it your own way."

"Not much to tell," Willie shrugged at François. "I took after man one and two."

"And I covered three."

This was going to be harder than I realized. I returned to my seat on the couch, hoping a little distance might buy me some patience.

"So?" I prompted as the well of intel already shriveled up.

Willie seemed the most amendable to my tone, which was tell-me-now-or-you-die. "One and two took the shifter with them."

"While number three exited in a different direction," François added. "Is

there anything to drink? I'm parched." "Me, too," Willie piped up. Who knew an adult male Were could look like a puppy begging for treats?

Bran gestured to the kitchen where the other two headed, like frat boys making a beeline for the beer. I held my tongue, but that wasn't going to last long.

Leave it to Bran to notice. "They'll get to the point."

"In this lifetime?"

"That's not fair," Willie said around gurgling Gatorade. "You try sniffing all around Paris all day."

"Poor baby," I murmured, forgetting about how well Weres hear. Or not.

Bran raised his hands. "So you followed two and François tracked the other. What happened next?"

"The shifter didn't smell right," Willie said, oblivious to the impact of his words. That wasn't just any shifter; that was Van.

I slammed to my feet. "Not right in what way?" I asked. Okay, I may have snarled a little. Willie's first response was classic Were. His nostrils tightened, his head lowered, his stance widened. Then he pulled back, sucking in air as if his life depended on it, closed his eyes and started chanting, "Om madre padre om."

"Seriously?" I glanced at Bran. This was his idea and it wasn't getting us anywhere.

"Recovering Were, remember?" François offered with half-a-joke in his tone until he caught my expression. "Right. Your brother. Forgot for a sec." He turned to Willie. "Hey mate, tell her what you mean. Family connection."

Willie's eyes snapped open and he managed to look sheepish, a hard look for a Were to accomplish, recovering or not. "Oh, yeah. So the scent, it had this bite to it. Acrid, a hint of bitter."

I rolled my eyes at Bran as if to say we weren't at a wine tasting and he stepped in. "Do you mean he smelt afraid? Or worried?"

"No. Nothing like that. It wasn't an emotional smell. More like the scent you pick up if someone is really ill. That kind of pungency."

My stomach plummeted. "Could it be because he's been under extreme stress since he was kidnapped?"

Willie tilted his head as if pondering, then shook it in the negative. "No. I've searched for hostages before and while there was that taint, this was something different."

"Could it have been drug induced?" Bran asked.

Of course. Why hadn't I thought of that?

Willie's slow nod helped me inhale a breath. "Yeah, that could account for the acidity factor."

I scooted forward on the edge of the couch cushion as I asked, "Were you able to trace the scent to where he was being kept?"

"No. It was as if they expected to be tracked." He eyed me, trying to be clear and concise even as I was only half listening past his first word. "They kept doubling back, splitting up and then rejoining."

"The two with Van, you get a read on them?" Bran asked.

"As to what they are?"

"Yes."

"One was clearly a Were. Very strong, too. He was the one who left the shifter then came back and left again. The other was human. His scent wasn't very happy either."

Poor man, I wanted to snarl.

"Where did you lose them?" Bran cut me off from jumping in and stopping the flow.

"*Le Métro,*" Willie answered. "The *Invalides* station. All three of them were together there."

"The subway?" I asked, getting a little lost.

"*Oui.*"

This was making no sense. "Why would kidnappers take a wolf there? It's not like Van would be easily mistaken for a dog in broad daylight."

"My guess." Willie had moved on to chewing a hunk of bread and cheese. Weres were notoriously hungry all the time trying to keep up with their metabolism. "I think he'd shifted back into his human form long before the *Métro.*"

"If he was groggy, or still sedated, two men could manage your brother and he wouldn't resist." Bran was obviously trying to calm me down. Not that it was helping much. "But I don't understand the *Métro.* Why not a taxi or private vehicle?"

"They had a private vehicle, which the Were left at one point. When he joined backup with the other two they left the car near the *Invalides* station. It was as if they waited for rush hour traffic to begin. No way to track through the mess of scents there."

"Plus it'd be easier to hide an impaired man in the crush," François added from where he leaned against the wall. Up to this point he'd been so silent I'd almost forgotten about him.

"So all indications are they suspected we'd do exactly what you did." Bran's voice sounded like a low, dangerous rumble as he glanced at François. "And the man you followed?"

"Either he was meant as a decoy or as lost as the most clueless tourist." François' tone told me which of the two theories he thought was most likely. "Interesting thing is that I followed him to the exact same station as Willie tracked his two leads."

"*Invalides* station?" Bran clarified.

Both François and Willie nodded.

"Do you think that station was important?" I asked, "Or could any station have worked?"

"At rush hour the 1, 2, 4, 12, and 13 lines are the busiest," François said as if he rode them on a daily basis, or had anticipated my question and did his research. The RER lines can be more crowded but if they were looking for packed trains they could have taken several closer stations."

"But didn't." Why one station over another?

Bran pulled out his phone and punched some numbers. I ignored him to focus on François, recapping so I understood. "So both sets of men seemed to be leading you on a wild goose chase only to lose you at this particular Subway or Tube stop."

"*Le Métro.*" Bran said not looking up as he continued to punch his phone. I so wanted to flip him off but didn't, mostly because he wouldn't have seen the gesture. When I glanced back at François though I could tell by the cant of his lips he knew exactly what I was thinking.

Bite me, I mouthed.

Instead he blew me a kiss.

That earned him Bran's attention and a frown, which didn't seem to faze the MI-6 agent at all.

"Anything else?" Bran asked, which had François shaking his head. "One thing."

I didn't realize I was circling my hand in a get-on-with-it move until I caught François' grin. At least he took my hint.

"The man I followed, who also happened to be a Were, crossed paths with another man who was at the park." That had both Bran and me sitting up straighter. Fortunately François didn't need a lot of prodding to continue. Either that or he knew exactly how far he could go in making us wait.

"There was the other shifter who attacked the first wolf."

I didn't say anything, but earned a sideways glance from Bran. We were talking about my dad, but I bit my lip, mostly to keep it from trembling.

"That shifter was removed by this unknown additional man. I'd call him the Green man."

"Why?" I blurted out.

"His scent." François seemed to pause. "The one time I smelled something close to him was a woodwose."

Why hadn't I paid more attention to Fraulein Fassbinder's obscure bestiary lectures? "And a woodwose is?"

"Wild man of the woods," Willie called from the kitchen where his head was buried in a cupboard. Probably still looking for more food. "Weres are sometimes mistaken for woodwoses which is plain stupid as far as I'm concerned." He looked over his shoulder. "I mean who would confuse a nature being with a carnivore?"

François jumped in as if he wanted to save his friend from my acerbic comeback. "A woodwose is considered more a fertility or nature spirit like a Green Man, but both harken back to pagan nature rituals."

"What's any of this got to do with this man you followed?" I prodded, thinking I was doing a pretty good job holding in my temper, until I saw Willie rolling his eyes.

"The Green man and woodwose are universal figures," Bran said. "Which doesn't give us much way to pinpoint who this person was."

"Except he was with my dad."

"Whoa, your dad was the other shifter?" Willie asked, earning a hand across the throat gesture from François.

"The point I was making was whether this man is a nature preternatural or not isn't helping us find my brother or Vaverek."

"But it is giving us one lead," Bran said, looking directly at François. "You said this Green Man crossed paths with the Were. Coincidence?"

"No, I wouldn't say so. Both ended up at the same café and the same table. Their scents indicated they stayed there for at least thirty minutes or so, not much longer and it could be less, but I'd say no less than twenty minutes."

Now I was speared by Bran's freeze-me-in-place look. "Which means we have one thread in common."

"My dad," I murmured, my backbone tensing.

Bran was the one who spoke the words I'd been dreading. "Your father and the Council."

CHAPTER 47

Jeb walked the streets of Paris for what seemed like hours, watching night steal the light and warmth of the day, aware of the rage rushing through him. When he'd accepted his position on the Council he never dreamed he'd have put his family in danger. Now he faced losing one or two of his children.

If Zeid's words were to be believed. A traitor on or close to the Council. Seeking what? That's what Zeid needed Jeb's help for, there had only been so much he could discover hiding in the shadows. Now they needed someone who could talk freely, if not easily with the others.

"Why me?" Jeb had asked, struggling with the information Zeid had shared. "Except for Philippe the others and I have only been at odds."

"Because of your daughter?"

"Yes." Jeb had slammed to his feet. He'd made the hard choice a year ago and lived with that decision every day, as did Alex, but the other Council members had painted Jeb as less than trustworthy because his daughter had come so close to that line of exposing preternaturals to humans. Close but never strayed over the line.

He'd contained her actions and lost her to the prison system in the process. Wasn't that enough of a price to pay?

Obviously not, as someone sought to undermine what Jeb sacrificed so much to uphold. But who were they and what did they want?

There had always been factions fighting factions, one group thinking another group was getting more than their fair share, those who never accepted the dominance of humans over non-humans. The list was endless, so why now did someone work behind the scenes to undermine what had made the world a slightly more stable place?

That's what had been squirreling through Jeb's thoughts as he pounded the pavement. The more he walked the more clarity danced just outside his awareness.

By the time he'd returned to Philippe's townhouse, having never found different lodging, Pádraig was waiting for him. "I thought I had lost you," the younger man said as a greeting. "And without a word."

Jeb had no patience for pleasantries as he jumped right in. "Tell me what's been happening at the Council lately?"

Pádraig tightened his mouth, then seemed to change his mind. "You are more involved in the Council than I am."

"But I only rarely interact with day-to-day affairs." Jeb knew he'd pushed the Irishman, but wasn't sure why the other pulled back as if assaulted. As his wife had always told him he had magic in the way of his words, when he chose to use them. A lesson he'd tried to impart to Alex, though telling her and showing her had not always meshed. Time to use a little of that now if he wanted to get what he needed. "I value your insights, your experience," he said, making sure the other heard the sincerity in his tone. "I admit that I've been distracted of late so may not have paid attention as I should."

Two balms to another's sense of value were to acknowledge their strengths and your own weaknesses. Even as he said the words he realized how true they were, especially the last part.

Pádraig's shoulders relaxed, as he tilted his head toward the formal living room off the entryway. "You mean the Were agitation?"

Jeb followed the other man, waving off an offer for a drink. Instead he crossed to one of the chairs near the far window and eased himself into it. No matter how much he wanted to find what the other knew and sooner rather than later. If he pushed too hard, too fast, he'd learn nothing. "Are the Weres creating the most agitation right now?"

Pádraig lifted the glass stopper of one of the decanters and paused with his hand midair. He seemed to ponder for a moment. "No more than usual. In fact I'd say just the opposite.

They've pulled back a few of their petitions. I think Philippe's recent overtures to them have helped steer their more moderate members away from the fringe fanatics."

"What overtures?" Jeb refused to kick himself for not knowing these details. By nature he was usually out of the mainstream of Council politics but he'd preferred it that way. Maybe at too great a cost but what had been done was done.

Pádraig finished pouring his drink, the smell of aged bourbon reaching Jeb as Pádraig took a deep sip then crossed to sit in the padded chair across from Jeb. He didn't speak until he made sure the crease of his linen pants was centered exactly mid-leg. "Philippe made a few staff changes recently at some of the ancillary Council posts. Brought a few more Weres on as advisors, people with more rather than less power."

"Undoing some of the slights Wei Pei has offered over the years?" Jeb asked, seeing the thought process behind his friend's actions. He leaned back in his chair, steepling his fingers before him. "So if the Weres have been appeased, who else might be unhappy with the status quo?"

Pádraig took another sip, watching Jeb over the rim of his glass before he set it down and leaned forward in his chair, his elbows on his knees. "I may be way out of line here, but there is something that's been bothering me."

"About?"

"This warlock who was called up recently."

"The one called Bran?"

Pádraig nodded, looking very druid with the movement.

"What about him?" Jeb warned himself not to jump too fast but to hear what the other had to say and weigh it.

"I can't really put my finger on it." Pádraig flopped back in his chair, releasing a deep sigh. "I know he's suspected of being involved in this new drug that's supposed to make someone act out of their own best interests." Jeb circled one hand. "Go on."

"They say his cousin was testing the drug on humans . . ."

"But was killed, wasn't she?"

"Yes, but what if this warlock had also been testing the drug on preternaturals at the same time only his tests haven't come to light? Yet."

Jeb shook his head. "Explain more if you would."

The Irishman jackknifed forward, running one hand through his hair. "I may be way off base here but what if the warlock has experimented on subjects using small tests. The kind that would fly under the radar and not attract the attention of the Council."

"Until it was too late?"

"Exactly!" Pádraig threw both hands open, nearly knocking over his drink in his enthusiasm. "How would the Council know if some fae somewhere quit his job of twenty years? An action that might have been totally out of character if you knew that particular fae, such as an Adbertos or something."

"You mean one of those who feel sacrifice is the ultimate good so are willing to do the hard jobs others would or could not."

Pádraig jumped to his feet. "So let's say this Adbertos just ups and quits his job and decides to go on the dole instead."

"Acting totally against his base self needs." Jeb could see where the young man was going with his line of thinking.

"The Council would never know of this individual but the one behind the use of the drug would be aware that he, or she, was able to overcome what makes an Adbertos an Adbertos."

"The Adbertos would die though and fairly quickly," Jeb mused aloud. "Because to act so against their nature would be suicide."

A smile lit Pádraig's face as he grabbed his drink and started walking around the room. "A perfect murder. Self-murder. And no one would be the wiser."

"Are you suggesting such a thing has been done?" Jeb asked, leaning forward.

"No." The Irishman punctuated the word with a wave of his glass before pivoting to face Jeb. "But that's the beauty of the situation. We've been thinking that if this mind-altering drug has been used up to this point that the Council would be aware of it. After all, the impact on preternaturals worldwide is enormous."

"And what does this have to do with the warlock?"

"This man travels around the world on a regular basis."

Jeb nodded. "As far as I'm aware, yes."

"So what if he's been trying out the drug on a chambermaid here, a clerk there?"

"Only these were not humans?"

Pádraig shook his head, a wicked gleam in his eyes. "They were nobodys. A kobold here, a sylph there. Beings the Council rarely considers unless they threaten the Council's functions."

"And what did he hope to gain?" Jeb asked, playing devil's advocate.

"Power of course." Pádraig's eyes appeared to flicker as if he could understand so clearly what could drive this dress designer. "He's a warlock. Their reputation presedes them. Their need to possess and control power legendary. Almost equal to their ability to seduce."

Jeb ignored the knotting of his gut as he thought of Alex with this warlock. From what he'd read of this Bran, his daughter was playing with a true power-player. High stakes for a girl from southern Idaho. Could what Pádraig be saying be so simple and so insidious?

But Pádraig was oblivious to the impact of his words as he poured himself another drink and continued, his back turned toward Jeb. "Seduction is all about mastering the bold move, proving yourself, stirring up the taboos and most of all— " He paused, raising his glass as if to salute the absent warlock. "The absolute win is to create the perfect illusion."

"Which is?"

Pádraig glanced over his shoulder. "Why, that this Bran is a victim and not the transgressor. He is not the brains and power behind the design and use of this drug, but has been victimized by it as he claims his cousin was."

"And what is the end goal?" Jeb asked, his mouth dry, his heart sick.

Pádraig turned, slowly, pointing his glass at Jeb. "If I was such a warlock, I'd be seeking a seat on the Council where, with a few more masterful strokes, I'd become Council leader. Then the world would be mine."

Jeb watched the young man, heard the truth in his words even as he wanted to ignore them. "You are forgetting one thing," he said, tumbling the concept around his mind as Pádraig tumbled the drink around his tongue.

"And that is?"

"There is only one Council seat presently given to the magic users, which is what a warlock is."

Pádraig nodded, taking a deep breath. "Shamans, mages, sorcerers, seers, soothsayers, the whole lot."

"My seat. The one that cannot be passed to another unless I die."

Pádraig raised his brow and gave a low, deep chuckle. "And you think this would stop this warlock for long?"

CHAPTER 48

I scooted back on the couch, my muscles clenched so tight I was surprised I could move at all. All things circled back to the Council.

I should just stencil the damn message across my forehead and look in the mirror every five minutes. Instead I shook my head. Bran's hunting for Vaverek led to Bran's being pulled before the Council. How convenient. Van's disappearance being tied to Vaverek, and thus the Council, has led to my hunting for Van. But the closer I got to him, the faster Ling Mai jerked me back. At this point I wouldn't be surprised to learn Ling Mai was a Council member.

With a sharp glance at Bran I asked, "Was there a full quorum at the Council when you were there today?"

"All six remaining members. Yes."

"I don't suppose Ling Mai was there?"

He paused then shook his head.

"You saying no or you can't tell me?"

"What do you think?" His words held a bitter edge. Not that I blamed him. Die if you do or die if you don't. It was one thing to share that he'd even been called and what happened to him directly, but a whole different thing to reveal anything that those on the Council might see as an attack on them or their bloody group. Which meant everything that might reveal a hint about the Council location, its procedures, and most of all its members.

I glanced at François and Willie. "Maybe you guys had better plug your ears since it appears I can't say anything about my dad without bringing the big C into the conversation."

"Too late." François shrugged. "We're in too deep to get off with a slap on the wrist now. Might as well spill the beans so we can clear up this mess before it takes us all out."

I cut a you-too look toward Willie. His nod was his only answer, though I did notice he had paled a little.

It was Bran I spoke to as I asked, "At this point you're under suspicion from the Council for association with the designer drug, but nothing more. You want to leave it at that or move forward?"

He actually impressed me by taking a moment to consider. No jump-in-first-and-cry-foul-later approach. Instead he said, "Of the six Council members present two were women, the other four male, but I had no idea of all of their abilities. And no, your Ling Mai wasn't there."

I hated it when he seemed able to read my mind. It was only a trick, right? Otherwise I was in even deeper do-do.

"Bet I could have sniffed them out," Willie said, puffing out his chest.

"Not from within the glass tube all outsiders are forced to stand in as they come before the Council," came Bran's laconic reply.

"And I bet that tube is reinforced against any number of super-human preternaturals," François said as if already considering how to get out of such a trap.

Bran nodded.

"I bet it's rigged with the means to execute on the spot, too," I added, thinking aloud. Then I looked around at the three others. Talk about the party pooper. Nothing like pointing out that Bran was going to be contained in that very same tube in about eleven hours.

I squared my shoulders and took a different approach. "So let's go worst case scenario."

Bran's brow arched as if asking, hadn't we already done that?

I waved one hand and pulled myself forward to the edge of the couch. "I mean, let's assume the Council, or someone on the Council—" Please not Dad. Anyone except Dad. I sucked in a deep breath and continued, "That the Council is backing this designer preternatural drug. Why?"

François pushed himself off the wall. "To use it against other preternaturals."

"But why?"

"To wipe another species out of existence?" he offered, then looked at Willie.

The Were scratched his chin. "I know that the Weres have been unhappy for decades at their lack of Council representation."

"But there's always some group that wants something," François said. "The fae want distinct subgroups to each have seats. The dragons are being ignored. The— "

That surprised me. "There are really dragons?"

"Not many but they're very long-lived, have outstanding memories, especially of every perceived slight ever offered to them, and once roused are very nasty and hard to kill. They're also mean as hell when they're not roused."

The description sounded like dozens of the species Frau Fassbinder had discussed in bestiary and myth classes. The ones I needed to pay way more attention to in the future. If there was a future.

François gave a chin nod toward Bran. "Even the warlocks have petitioned the Council for more recognition."

I glanced at Bran, "Was that you?"

His look was short and pithy.

"Right. What was I thinking." Bran was a more behind the scenes manipulator. The pickpocket kind of thief, rather than the one who ran in guns blazing. Not that Bran would stoop to picking pockets, too small potatoes for him.

I was missing something. Something important. "Why now? What's changed?"

"Whatja' mean?" Willie asked, eyeing the kitchen, probably wondering if he'd left a drop of food anywhere in it after his last forage and devour.

"We're talking about longstanding gripes. A feud a few centuries in the making might be at the root of this, but it's not like the Montagues and Capulets decided it was a Tuesday so it must be the perfect day to wreak havoc."

Willie shrugged. "They were Italians, they probably did that all the time."

This was the challenge when working with Weres, they tended to be short sighted. Shifters could be the same way. I can't tell you how many times one of my brothers focused on 'getting the new girl' and forgot that the girl's father was the ump at the upcoming state baseball finals, or her cousin's best friend was just dumped to make room for the new relationship.

"You mean it was Romeo going arse over elbow over Juliet that set off the fallout that Willie wrote about," François said. Then shook his head at our Willie's bright look. "Not you, a different Willie."

"Yeah." At least I think I was following François. "Somebody has gone to a lot of manipulation here. Van's kidnapping. Cheverill's murder. Van's exposure in the park. It's as if all these events are leading to one big kaboom."

"Kaboom?" Bran asked, both brows now raised.

"Get off your warlock high-horse. You know exactly what I mean." I was on to something but it was like wrestling with a ghost in a fog bank. I couldn't figure out what I had.

"Let's look at this from a different direction then." François started pacing across the room. "See what might be missing."

"You mean like Cheverill is now missing from the Council?" I offered, grabbing the most obvious. "Which means the Council is down a druid."

"Right." François snapped his fingers. "And what about your brother's kidnapping? That brought you on the scene."

I snorted. "I don't think I'm important enough to anyone for them go to such lengths."

"There you may be wrong," Bran said, starting a flicker of warmth deep inside me. Then he added, "You're a powerful witch, but I doubt many know of that because you barely acknowledge it."

That quick the flame went out. But he wasn't finished.

"Unless someone suspected that you could do what you did in the fight yesterday." He looked at me as if looking to see if I'd grown a second head.

"But nobody would know about that . . ." Suddenly I realized who did, but Bran was there before me.

"Your father knows, doesn't he." He didn't even bother to pose it as a question.

I was shaking my head. There was betrayal and then there was setting up your own flesh and blood. I drew the line there.

"Yes, he knew but so did the Council. They've known since last year."

François and Willie had been exchanging quizzical glances until Willie couldn't stand it any longer and blurted out. "Know what? What happened in the street? Why did the Council know what?"

"Nothing important," I answered, still dealing with all the ramifications. "What is important is that except for my father the Council are the only other ones who understand what a freak I am."

"Alex's word for gifted," Bran interjected, earning him a head nod from Willie.

I ignored both of them. "All roads lead back to the Council," I said aloud this time. Then added, "But we don't know for sure Van was kidnapped to be used as bait. What if he knew something about someone on the Council that would be dangerous if revealed?"

"Or if he was kidnapped because he was a shifter and someone needed to expose a shifter to the general public," Willie said.

I could have hugged him. Sometimes the simplest was the straightest line between two points. Leave it up to a Were to uncomplicate matters. "And if Van is exposed as a shifter, the person who'll be impacted the most is my father."

"Your father on the Council." Willie connected all the dots. "Which means he could be removed."

"Not could but most likely would," Bran said, being the one of us who thought most like a Council member. "Permanently."

François jumped in after a quick look at my face. "Which would free open another Council seat. So two new Council members within a short period of time. That could change the balance of power among the Council."

"To what?" I asked, still grappling with the ramifications of Bran's words.

"From moderate to radical. Radical to conservative. We'd have to know more about who is currently on the Council,"

François shrugged. "And it's not likely we're going to get that intel any time soon."

"There's one piece we're missing here." Bran pulled all gazes to him, including my own.

"What?" Willie asked, his face screwed up in confusion. For such a good-looking guy he was a few crayons short of a whole box, but that was Weres for you.

"The Were and others who have your brother did not leave him to be exposed at the park?"

Oh, no, not another blow. But I couldn't ignore what he was saying, even if I was surprised at his saying it in a gentle tone, as if aware he was dumping a pile of bricks on my head.

Willie looked from one of us to the other. "I still don't get it."

"What he's saying is they didn't let Van go because they plan to do something more with him." My words were so quiet I could barely hear them but a Were could and Bran knew what I was going to say anyway.

"More like what?" Willie asked.

"Like another exhibition of a shifter running amuck," Bran said looking at his phone again, as if it had clues.

"François, the station where you and Willie lost the trails. That was *Invalides*?"

"*Oui*."

We had been discussing my brother being set up to die and Bran was looking at subway information? It took everything I could do not to whack him with a clenched fist.

"Just what I thought," he murmured, tapping his phone over and over.

"You going to share?" Sure my voice was a little testy, okay, a lot testy, but I had a lot of reasons for that. A large one of them sitting right next to me.

"I'll share when I'm certain," he said, still not looking up.

Did that help? No, he made things worse.

I stood, rubbing a headache building along my temples. Thank the Spirits François stepped in to ask what I didn't trust myself to ask, not without a snarl. "When are you going to be certain?"

"We have to do one more thing." He rose himself, jamming his hands in his pockets. "Then all will be clear."

"We?" I asked as Willie said, "Do what?"

"A scrying spell," Bran answered Willie, no doubt because he had no doubt I figured out the 'we' word. Since I was the only witch around, and the only one able to scry with any hope of find something or someone, it looked like I was the we.

"Small problem your Mageness," I bit off every word. "I need something to scry with. You have a piece of Vaverek handy?"

"No." Every muscle of his body was tensed, which gave me a strong hint I wasn't going to like his next words. But he didn't speak. Not until pulling out a small wadded napkin from his pocket. One stained brown.

"I'm not going to like this am I?" I said mostly to myself as Bran shook his head.

"No."

I swallowed, my throat suddenly too dry. "Is that blood?"

"Yes."

Willie stepped forward, his nose twitching. Once a Were always a Were.

"Whose?" François asked.

I didn't need to ask as I raised my gaze to clash with Bran's. His dark and implacable, not giving an inch even though he knew what he was asking of me.

That SOB set me up. He planned to reach this point all along.

"My brother's blood," I answered François but I kept my gaze riveted on Bran, aware my breathing had gone shallow, my muscles ramrod stiff. "You want me to do blood magic, black magic to find Van."

He nodded, aware of what blood magic meant. A slippery slope that might start slow and seemingly easy, but always ended in a bad place—a very, very bad place.

"And if I say no?"

"Then your brother will be used and discarded like so much dead meat." And, in case he hadn't jammed the knife in deep enough and twisted it, he added, "Your choice."

CHAPTER 49

Van was cramped in a fetal curl against the cold cement floor. Old, blood soaked straw stinking in his nostrils, a fever raging through him. But it was more than a fever; sweats, the shakes, teeth chattering, wave upon wave crashing against him. But it was the dreams, the nightmares that hurt the worst. Alex walking toward him, then running, calling his name, but he couldn't reach her. He'd stretch his hand, watch as the skin morphed into fur, the nails into claws and then see her expression. The horror and repulsion that had him skidding to a halt.

But that was wrong. Alex knew what he was. Knew what all the males in his family were. So it made no sense. Unless it wasn't what he was but what he'd done that made her reject him. And that's when he'd look around and see the limbs and blood scattered at his feet. His father's sightless eyes staring up at him though his head was nowhere near his body. And the other pieces were his brothers, Jake and Luke and even Simon, torn apart and savaged.

Had he done that?

Alex's expression told him he had. But sometimes the vision shifted and he was wading through the corpses of children, screaming and retching. He couldn't. No way.

"Yes, you can Mister Noziak, take another sip," the voice urged him. Jean-Claude's voice.

Van cracked open one swollen eye.

The doctor knelt beside him, but the man wasn't alone. Two men stood beyond him, one with a tranq gun pointed at Van. The other though was the more deadly, the power-broker.

"See, Jean-Claude, you have exaggerated the threat to our guest here. He is not a total beast. Not yet."

Jean-Claude shook his head, holding a small vial in front of Van. "You must eat this. It's only soup. Your sodium levels are too high and you need the liquids."

Van's growl through closed lips was his only response. His last element of control. If he was dead they'd use another poor schmuck to do what they intended to do, but it wouldn't be him.

"See what the problem is?" the doctor said, his voice terse. "Shifters require more nutrients than humans but it's the liquid levels I'm most concerned about. His sodium level is already at 164."

"Which means what?" the power-broker sounded bored, more than concerned.

"He only has a few hours to live, if that much."

The power broker leaned forward, kicking Van's shoulder with Italian leather shoes. "We need him for tomorrow. It's too late to find another carrier."

The doctor threw up his hands. "*Oui*! It's been what I have been saying."

"Can't you give him the drug and tell him to drink?"

"We are too close to the time of the experiment. I can't administer the drug, give a suggestion and in less than twelve hours administer more of the drug and a different suggestion. This is not a puppet we are dealing with here."

"A shame."

A tense silence reigned except for the sound of the doctor's heart beating, the power broker inhaling deeply and the gun-holding one grinding his teeth. The broker spoke at last. "You can force water down him via an IV can you not?"

"Yes, but—"

"Then do it."

"To insert a fluid line we must tranquilize him. I can't guarantee that he will not be sluggish for tomorrow."

The broker laughed, a low, humorless sound. "Not a problem. With what we have planned for him he won't have to be fast, just deadly."

Van shook his head, trying to lift it as he did.

"*C'est la vie,*" the doctor murmured, waving his hand behind his head.

"No," Van mouthed, "Don't—"

The dart struck his left shoulder with enough force it spun Van over and flipped him on his back.

The last thing he saw was the doctor leaning over him, whispering, "Forgive me."

CHAPTER 50

François was the one who joined me in the open space where I was marking chalk clockwise on the floor to create my power circle.

"Need any help?" he asked.

I glared at him, knowing it really wasn't him I was angry with.

"He wouldn't have you do this if there was any other way," François murmured, leaning against the nearest wall, his pose meant to look relaxed, the strain in his muscles betraying the opposite.

I ignored his words and leaned back on my knees, deciding to take whatever time I had to figure out something that was bothering me. "What exactly are you?" I asked, no heat to my words.

"I'm surprised you've been able to wait this long to find out."

I raised my hands palm up toward him. "If you're not comfortable sharing, I can understand that. It's your business."

"It's not that." He looked away, his hands thrust deep in his pockets. I actually expected him to tell me to take a flying leap, or the British equivalent, but instead he shrugged. "I'm a didi-shifter."

"A what?"

"We used to be called splitters but we're now politically correct and using the technical jargon for dissociative identity disorder individuals. Get it? Didi-shifters."

I'd heard of splitters but thought they didn't really exist, sort of like the boogeyman. But come to think of it all of us in the warehouse were bogeymen to a lot of humans. Splitters though were the stuff of legends, sort of a cross between a shifter/Were and a chameleon. Because they could assume different animal shapes historically they were very adept as assassins and liquidators. Which tended to make them loners and very wary.

"Repelled?" he asked, and I could hear him bracing for my response.

"You're talking to a shamanistic witch," I laughed. "Who am I to cast stones because you're something rare and unusual."

His shoulders relaxed as he replied. "That's a nice way to put it. Rare and unusual. Not what I usually hear once someone figures out how much of a face-ache I am."

"Face-ache?"

"You know, a freak, screwed, outside the pale."

I gave him a get-real look. "It's not like there's all that many any of us can share what we are with, so I wouldn't waste any more time worrying about it."

He laughed and scratched his head. "Truth is I don't spend much time worried that the shifters will reject me, which they tend to do, or the Weres. That's their problem." He nodded his chin toward the closed door to the room. "He helped with that."

"Willie?" I asked even as I guessed the real answer.

"Nah. Bran was the first git to not bat an eyelash when he found out. He treated me like his mate from the first and hasn't ever changed."

Obviously he knew a different side of Bran than I did. But I bit my tongue. Instead I asked, "So can you shift into other forms than a dog?"

" I have to stay in the canidae family," he said, " But since that includes all canines; wolves, dholes, coyotes, jackals, and foxes, there's enough variety to keep life interesting."

I bet. I knew my shifter brothers were canis lupis, the Grey Wolf, and that they tended to look down on dogs in part because dogs—canis lupus familiaris—were a subspecies of the Grey Wolf. The worst thing you could call a wolf shifter was any variation of the word dog. I learned that early, and often with my brothers. Not that it kept me from using dog-face, or stop me from telling them they were doggin' it. Yeah, I was a glutton for punishment that way.

"So do you choose what you shift into?" I asked.

"Sometimes. Other times I let myself go and what I become is what I become. I've never let myself down."

Speaking of letting someone down, my thoughts boomeranged back to Bran. No surprise there.

I went back to drawing my line, taking a deep breath to calm my emotions. Any spell involved intentions, including one as simple as a scrying spell. But this wasn't a casting like I'd used to find the doctor, this one used blood, which immediately catapulted it into the tread-lightly zone.

As I drew my circle I was drawing my safety zone, separating what was within from what was without. If I brought strong negative emotions with me into the creation of the sacred space, I was calling forth negativity from the world around me. The last thing I needed or wanted.

"Aren't you drawing that in the wrong direction?" François asked, as I scooted forward about a foot at a time to create the nine-foot circle.

"It's drawn clockwise for invocation, counterclockwise for banishing." I released a breath as I sat back on my heels. "Don't want to banish Van but call forth his location."

Not that using the banishing spell might not be perfect for certain others. Speak of the devil, as I heard footsteps join François. I didn't have to look to see who'd come in, I knew in my gut. Though it was funny that I didn't often hear him move.

"We brought the material you wanted," he said, setting a paper bag near me, being sure not to cross the circle. Even though warlocks were kith and kin of witches our magic was different, and often at odds with one another. Which described Bran's and my relationship to a T.

I still didn't acknowledge him. Petty of me, but hey I was the one about to plunge headfirst into a world I vowed never to venture. But then I'd broken other vows. Not to practice magic, period. Then not to ever use the spell to usurp others' abilities. Look where those vows got me.

Right here, on a concrete floor in a cool room as the waxing moon hovered high in the sky outside the room's only window.

With another calming breath I realized that with each breath I inhaled I was holding tight to my anger, but the exhales allowed me to release a little of my frustration, and my fear.

Time to pull on my big girl panties and admit none of this was Bran's fault. It was mine. My choices created this outcome. Not his.

Releasing another sigh that started somewhere near my feet, I knew I was doing this for myself. If selling my soul to the dark side helped me save Van, then so be it.

I reached across the chalk line and pulled the bag closer, reaching inside for the four candles and setting them aside. Who knew they could find four different colors on short notice in the heart of Paris. The mugwort, sage, burdock root and cedar in small plastic baggies I moved within hands' length to my right. The last item was in a fancy container; French sea salt.

I looked up at Willie who smiled and shrugged. "I didn't know what kind of salt you needed. Figured the fancy stuff might help more."

"Thanks." It was a nice gesture and I knew it came from a good place within him. "Can someone get me a small bowl of water?"

Both François and Willie scrambled. I shouted after them, "Preferably a stone or hand potted bowl if you can find one."

There was a mumbled, "Will do," echoing from the kitchen area.

I rose to my feet, brushing chalk dust from my hands against my jeans, only too aware that this was a fairly large room yet with only Bran and I in it seemed too small.

I finally found enough backbone to look at him and wished I hadn't. There were times when Bran would walk into a room or I'd see him after being away from him for a while and I'd get that knee to the solar plexus take-my-breath-away response. Totally unbidden and mostly unwelcome but damn, there it was.

Maybe it was the thickness of his midnight hair, or the slash of his cheekbones, the lean length of him, the breadth of his shoulders, heck, it was a hundred small details that made my legs weak and my stomach tumble over and over.

And I could hate him for that, even as I hated myself more. He was warlock, enemy to witches, and thus enemy to me. But why couldn't I remember that like any sane witch?

He stepped close, too close, sucking all of the air from the room. I'm not sure if he meant the move as threat or something else. I wasn't ready for either. Just as I opened my mouth to growl at him he raised one hand to brush his fingers along my cheek as his other hand slid to my waist. All thought fled.

Instead all I did was feel, the roughness of his fingers taking a slow leisurely path from brow to cheek bone to jaw. When had just a touch sent me headfirst into a freefall? He so did not play fair.

He started to speak, his voice hoarse and guttural, "Alex..."

Damn him. Just when I needed all my wits about me he scattered them like so much dandelion fluff. I cleared my throat and stepped back, desperate to put some space between us. Something to keep me from drowning. Or begging.

We both spoke at once.

"Why'd you..."

"I shouldn't have..."

We both stopped and I waved him on. He looked like he'd prefer to swallow his tongue but he cleared his throat and said, "I know what I'm asking you to do here. I should have been more forthright about this being a possibility when we left the hotel this afternoon."

And that's why he kept turning my world topsy-turvy. Warlocks didn't offer apologies, because they'd have to admit they were in the wrong. Yet that's exactly what he'd just done. How could you fight a concession? More not playing fair. At this rate he could write the handbook on how to mess with a woman's head. And heart.

I angled my head to look at him, really seeing the cost of his words. He was mage-born which meant he understood the price of black magic. Most warlocks and sorcerers not only went down the path of black magic, they raced toward it, arms wide open. White magic was benign and helpful for life's small things, sort of the Band-Aid on the world's dings and bruises. Black magic was the opposite. If you had an owie white magic would make you feel better. If your femoral artery was cut you called on black magic. You'd save your limb but lose your soul in the process.

I glanced away, looking at the circle, stilling the beating of my heart. Bran knew since he'd returned from the Council meeting earlier that we'd end up here. I think that's what bothered me the most. He knew but hadn't been honest enough to say up front, hey, remember how you used me yesterday? Well, payback's a bitch.

But that's not what I really wanted to say. I was afraid. For him, for me; if the Council acted against him. If we couldn't find Vaverek. So many ifs I was swallowed whole by them. The words on the tip of my tongue scared me. Scared me more than what I was about to do.

Thankfully François and Willie returned before I had to come up with a nice lie – one of the kind that started with, *it doesn't really matter.*

"François thought this should be cold water but I figured warm water would be nicer to put your hands into." Willie clutched the bowl in his wide grip. "If that's what you're going to do."

"I am." I smiled at him. A sight he obviously wasn't used to, or maybe because it'd been twice in a row, but he ducked his head as if I'd patted him, or scared the crap out of him, disarming him before I attacked.

Okay, reputation well deserved.

Before I reached out to grab the bowl I erased a portion of the chalk line with the toe of the fancy shoes François had given me only yesterday. They sure didn't look like pricey designer shoes anymore.

I set the bowl in the middle of the circle as I grabbed the candles and thrust them toward François. "Here I need these set in the following directions—To the south, place the red one; North, the brown; West, the blue, and orange in the east."

François handed two to Bran, one to Willie and they all set them out as I re-chalked the line and returned to the middle where the bowl of water and the bloodied napkin rested on the floor. I kept my eyes averted from it but it was like a lighthouse beacon pulsing at me, warning me of danger.

As if I didn't know that already.

"When I say so I want you to light the candles." I took a deep breath before adding, "No matter what happens you must remain absolutely silent and stay outside the circle."

"What's going to happen?" Willie asked.

"If all goes right I find the general area where Van is."

"And if not—ow, I was just asking," he snapped at François.

It was Bran who answered, though. "Let's focus on making sure all goes right."

I bet the guys who took up bomb disposal heard the same comment on their first day of the job. Because that's what it felt like right then. I faced a ten-ton bomb with shaking fingers.

CHAPTER 51

The first part of the ritual was the easiest part, consecrating with salt and water before I cast the scrying spell. I raised my anathema dagger, which I'd placed in the middle of the circle before I drew my chalk boundaries. Yes, I knew most witches called it an athame, but one of the last things I remembered about my mother before she disappeared from my world was her asking me for her dagger and calling hers an anathema. The word has stuck ever since. One of these days I was going to find out that meaning, but not right now. I needed to focus. One hundred percent align my intention and my thoughts.

I touched the tip of my dagger to the water and began the purification chant:

O creature of water, I banish thee.
Cast before me all uncleanliness and impurity of illusion, of ghosts, of spirits who seek harm.

I moved the anathema to the pile of salt I'd poured on the floor and touched it lightly intoning:

Cast forth all malignancy and hindrances be. Break the barriers held against thy good.
Enter herein all aid and assistance. I call thee forth to render support. That though mayest be.

Then I mixed the salt into the water, stirring it with the anathema in easy smooth strokes, using the restraint to calm and center me.

I set the dagger to the side and glanced to the moon's light through the window.

I conjure thee oh orb of light and guidance. Circle of power I call upon thee to guide and protect.
Between the worlds of men and realms of the Mighty Ones you who see all assist in finding that which I seek.
Raise within thee thy power to bless and consecrate this search.

"Light the candles now," I whispered, closing my eyes and trusting my assistants outside of the circle. "First the east. The south, then west, and last, the north."
I listed to the flare of matches struck and called aloud the sacred words.

Yod He Vau He
Adonai
Eheieh
Agla

East to the waxing moon.
South to the heat.
West to the waning light.
North to the warrior spirits.
Cast back the darkness that I may see.
So mote it be.

Only then did I open my eyes and reach for the bloodied napkin. Blood of my brother. Focus of my heart. Let me see you.
I picked up my ritual knife again and sliced a clean line down the palm of my left hand then picked up the napkin and squeezed it tight.
I expected a jolt. I didn't expect a tsunami of magic and pain slamming against me.
A blast of light blinded me as I twirled and twirled through a tunnel of darkness. I gasped for air but there wasn't any, only cold, ice coating my skin, freezing my blood.

This was it. I was going to die. Alone. Lost. Caught in a space between realms.

There wasn't even time to mourn as one last violent spin spat me through a gap where I splatted onto an unforgiving floor.

Where the Great Spirits was I?

CHAPTER 52

Van slowly, inch by inch roused himself, aware he was once again chained to the wall, but for how long he had no idea. Something had roused him from the stupor weighting his body, numbing the pain but only to a low roar.

His mouth cracked it was so dry but that wasn't his first worry. They were going to do something to him, with him. But what? Think.

Nothing would come except the certainty that he was about to die. That wasn't what was bothering him though. It was something else.

A sound stirred his awareness. A rustle.

The doctor coming back? He'd never entered the cell in the dark hours but that could change. Was that what was pushing at him?

"Van?" A voice called to him, a familiar voice, but one that had no reason to be here. Another hallucination, like the others that promised on one hand and made him quake on the other.

"Van, is that really you?" A shuffle of movement against straw and then hands against him.

He screamed at the pain. The hands withdrew.

"By the Goddess, what have they done to you?" It was Alex. Only she used that witch-word around him. But she couldn't be here.

He raised his chin as high as he could and sucked in an oath. "Alex?"

"Of course it is. How many sisters do you have? And how in hells bells are we going to get you out of here?"

He shook his head. It had to be Alex, no one else could scratch and offer help in the same breath.

"Escape," he whispered, aware his lips cracked and bled. "Before they know."

"Who are they?" She was poking and prodding at him, tugging at the silver chains, burning his raw skin.

"Power broker." There was another. Oh, yeah, how could he forget? "The doctor."

"Not helping me," she snarled, releasing him to tug at the wall attachments. He could have told her it'd do no good. If he as a shifter couldn't budge them what was a witch going to accomplish? Even as determined a witch as his sister.

She had to leave. Not only was she making a lot of noise cursing under her breath and straining against the restraints, something niggled his memory. Something about them, what they wanted.

"Well, you've got yourself in a fine pickle," she huffed, stepping back and glaring as she threw her braid over her shoulder in a gesture so familiar it created a whole new pain in him. He didn't think she meant the look for him and he could hear the fear beneath her words but he still gave a rusty laugh.

"Oh sure, yuck it up. Any suggestions about how to release you might be nice."

"How'd you . . ." The thought vanished, too hard to hold on to.

"Get here?" She shook her head. "Stupid spell backfired." Then she added in a smaller voice he doubted she knew he could hear, "At least I think it backfired."

Her words jumpstarted his heart into beating harder, pouring blood through his system, clearing the fogginess for a second. "Can you escape?"

She glanced over her shoulder, chewing her lip. "Don't know." Then she stepped closer, raising one hand to his chin, her touch very gentle and un-Alex like. She was more the smack-you-once then smack-you-again kind of gal.

"I'll kill whoever did this to you."

This time his laugh held more spirit. "You and me both."

She glanced around the cell again and out the small window. "You know where we are?"

"Cell."

"Duh! I mean any idea where in the city are we? If we're still in the Paris."

He shook his head, each move costing.

"Great, so we'll have to do this the hard way," she muttered, stepping closer and placing her hands on one chain.

Nothing happened. Or maybe he blacked out again. Either way when he stirred himself and looked over at her there were tears tracking down her cheeks. Alex never cried. Never.

"What happened?" he growled, his wolf near the surface, willing to fight whoever put the grief he saw in her eyes.

"Nothing," she mouthed more than said the word, shaking her head. "I can't do it. I don't know any magic to break the binds. Nothing that I can do here. Now."

He found himself relaxing, knowing the frustration only too well. "Doesn't matter."

"Of course it matters." There was more power in her words now, her hands clenched as if she wanted to punch someone, just didn't know who. "We've got to get you out of here. Time is running out. I don't know how long the spell will last."

He shook his head. "You've got to go."

She turned away from him, walking the perimeter of the cell as if looking for a weakness. Against the far bars she stumbled across the corpse and started gagging. With her sleeve over her mouth she managed to ask, "What . . . who . . ."

"Jailor." He licked his lips and tried for more. "Power broker got pissed."

She stumbled away from the body, not removing her arm from her face until she drew near to Van again. "I can't believe I didn't smell him earlier." With a shudder, she shook herself and stood close so her words wouldn't carry. "Tell me about the park. Who were you with? Why'd you shift in public?"

Her words hit like body blows. Vague images danced just outside his thoughts. The more he strained to remember, the faster they tangoed. All he had to offer was a stuttered shaking of his head. Then one image slammed against him. "Dad?"

Her expression tightened as if she'd sucked on a lemon.

"Did I . . . did I kill . . ." His thoughts jarred with his questions. No way. No way would he ever fight his father.

"You didn't kill him," she said, each word a nail against his heart.

"Why?"

She knew what he meant. Not why didn't he kill his beloved father but why would he even consider fighting him.

"Long story." She scrubbed a hand over her face, her voice low and tense. "They're drugging you. Making you do things against your will."

"No." He shook his head, the movement becoming stronger and stronger as he fought what she was telling him. "No."

She rested her hands on his shoulders, calming him by touch as she whipped him with each word she uttered, "You have no choice. That's the way the drug works. Then it wipes your memory."

It made no sense. Nothing tracked, not to his human half, not to his wolf self. "Kill me now," he whispered, aware this might be his only chance. If what she said was true, he wouldn't risk more lives.

That's what he'd remember, the pushing thought that had escaped him before. "Again," the word trailed off.

She stepped closer, cupping his chin in as light a touch as possible, one that still burned through him. "They're going to use you again? Is that what you're telling me?"

"Tomorrow." Isn't that what they'd said. With a half turn he looked at the moonlight peeking through the slit in the wall. "Today. Don't know. Soon."

"Oh, Van. I won't let that happen."

Hope flared then died within the same breath. Whoever these people were they would not be stopped just because Alex wanted them to stop.

"Can you give me anything?" she asked, laying her forehead against his chest. "Any hint of who or what they are?"

There was one thing. Not that it'd do her any good. "Were . . ."

"Where is something?"

He shook his head, then heard the sound he'd feared. Adrenaline coursed through him, helping him fight the lethargy, the pain making thought and words so difficult. "Go.

Now." He pulled forward on the chair, masking his words to her with the rattle of his chains. "Were. Find the Were."

She looked at the silver binding him, knowing she couldn't have him shift into his wolf self with so much silver surrounding him. Then she froze, hearing at last what he'd already heard, the squeak and shuffle of the far door opening and some one coming.

She kept her head, but he expected no less from a Noziak. He could scent her fear as she glanced around the small space. Nowhere to hide. No way out.

Inhaling a deep breath, she kissed his cheek then retreated to the far corner, one obscured by shadows. He hated to point out that she was still visible and would be the minute whoever was swinging a flashlight turned the illumination on her as he came down the hall.

He started to growl and rattle his chains, no matter his throat was raked raw, his skin bleeding enough he caught the scent of fresh blood. He hoped to keep the focus of whoever was coming on him, only him.

With his shifter hearing he could hear Alex's whispers above his sounds.

Betwixt and between. Guide and protect.
Betwixt and between. Shield thine in this darkest hour.
Betwixt and between. Command the seen to beunseen.
Enchant those eyes who seek harm.
So mote it be.

This was his sister, who rarely even played with her magic. What the hell did she think she was going to accomplish now?

Whoever was coming was drawing nearer.

Now they'd both die.

CHAPTER 53

Jeb turned off Philippe's computer, rubbing tired eyes as he looked at the stack of printouts next to his monitor. He might be a Rez rat from Idaho but even he knew how to find a wealth of information via the Internet. He'd been searching for the last three hours to compile anything and everything he could on this Bran, the warlock.

Even as exhausted as he was he was still impressed. If he didn't know the dress designer was a warlock, he might have bought into the rags-to-riches story of a kid from wealth, but more as a pawn between the two egos who'd birthed him, who clawed his way to the top of a small but very competitive industry.

But Jeb did know warlocks, knew how they thought and how they loved playing the game, no matter who they screwed over in the process. How Alex got herself involved with this mage was out of Jeb's ken, but he did know that he'd move anything in the physical or spiritual realm to make sure his little girl wasn't going to get hurt.

"Late night," Pádraig spoke from the doorway leading into Philippe's study.

Jeb hadn't even realized the young man was still awake. He was thankful Pádraig had asked to remain at Philippe's home as that gave Jeb permission to remain too. The more he learned about the intrigues swirling around Philippe and the Council the more he suspected there would be answers here, in this place.

"Had a little more research to do," Jeb said, offering Pádraig a tired smile. "You're up late."

"Ever since the Council told me to be prepared for tomorrow my mind has been whirring." The Irishman rubbed a hand along the back of his neck. "Can't sleep."

Jeb knew about the closed Council session before the formally convened meeting tomorrow but didn't have any details about what was going to be discussed among the six remaining members. Getting a bunch of preternaturals sharing information ahead of time wasn't ever going to happen, at least for another few centuries, after old memories faded. It made sense that the conversation would involve a replacement for Philippe's spot but beyond that Jeb didn't have a clue so could offer Pádraig no advice or guidance.

The Irishman was a druid, as Philippe had been, but fairly young and as a result, lacking in experience. There were not many true-born druids and as a race they were old ones, as old as the fae but more haughty. A running joke among non-humans was that the word arrogance, from the Latin word *arrogans,* had been coined to describe druid behavior. But then the druids always maintained the word was created for the warlocks, ancient enemies. And so the feuds continued.

So far, though, Jeb had found that Pádraig was more like Philippe, the exception to the druid haughtier-than-thou reputation. Most likely why the older man had mentored the Irishman. And Pádraig had been nothing but helpful to Jeb, something Jeb would not forget.

"I think we'd both better get some sleep," Jeb offered, turning off the desk lamp and patting the young man on his back as Jeb would have done with one of his sons. Which is how Jeb was beginning to feel about Pádraig, as a fifth son. "I have a feeling tomorrow is going to be a very long and important day."

It would as far as he was concerned. No matter what the Council decided about the warlock, Jeb was planning a little *tête-à-tête* as the French would say with the dress designer. A very private, up close and personal meeting.

CHAPTER 54

It took everything I had to block the fear racing through me, and the rage, to focus on the cloaking spell. Whoever had hurt Van so badly was going to pay. I'd make sure of it.

If I didn't get caught and killed in the next few minutes.

Betwixt and between. Command the seen to be unseen.

I kept my eyes squeezed closed, ignoring the stench as I repeated the chant over and over, listening as footfalls came closer. Step by step.

Betwixt and between. Command the seen to be unseen.

"What has you so agitated, Mister Noziak?" a voice spoke so close I wanted to jump. Instead I squinted into what looked like a spotlight blasting through the cramped cell. Behind the light a shadow stepped closer.

But he weren't paying any attention to me.

Finally, something went right.

The voice sounded familiar but maybe it was because he was speaking in English. But hadn't I heard it before?

I waited for him to point the flashlight down and not directly into Van's, and thus my, eyes. But instead of doing what seemed like a perfectly sensible move the man froze. And so did I.

He started sniffing the air, his head moving back and forth like a tracking beam.

Of course, how could I have been so stupid? Or clueless? He wasn't a man, he was a Were. I could smell him now, even over the eau du cologne of a rotting body near my feet.

By the Great Spirits I might be cloaked but if he followed my scent trail it wouldn't take that long to break through my spell. A cloaking worked only as long as another didn't pass the barrier. If he did it dissipated as so much mist.

Van increased his struggles and it was killing me. I knew how much he was hurting himself trying to protect me by distracting the newcomer.

I swear hours passed as the three of us stood there. Me not breathing, because I didn't dare to and Van howling and thrashing. The Were with the flashlight not moving at all, as if he couldn't trust his senses.

At last the flashlight tilted down and he turned to look closely at Van. That's when I caught a glimpse of his profile and gasped aloud.

Two things happened at once. First the Were turned, waving the flashlight toward the corner where I stood as he shouted, "Who's there?"

The second a tug against me, like the pull that had shot me through the tunnel.

No. Not yet. I hadn't found anything to help Van. They'd kill him if I didn't do something.

I stepped forward, no longer caring if the Were saw me, realizing almost too late that he had keys. He was our way out of here. If I could overcome him.

But whatever traction was stretching me back into the cold airless tunnel was growing stronger. Too strong. As if fighting against quicksand I felt myself lifted and spun.

I tried to scream. To tell Van I'd be back. To say goodbye but there wasn't time.

Over and over, tumbled like a dryer tumbles sneakers, thunk, kerthunk, kerthunk I flew through the cold darkness.

This time I knew I wouldn't die. No matter how easy it'd be to give up and give in.

But that wasn't the Noziak way.

That's what I was screaming as I slammed onto another

floor, still concrete, still harder than Hades, but less stinky, no dead corpse smell. Just three sets of eyes staring at me. Willie and François bending over from high above. And Bran. Bran smothering me in his grip as he shook me as if trying to extract the last ounce of stuffing from me.

"Ow!" I shouted, batting at his hands. "Let me go."

His eyes changed immediately from worried to wary in almost the same way a shifter or Were's eyes could morph.

Which reminded me. I sat upright, or tried to as the room kept spinning around me, pounding through my head, making me want to throw up.

"Careful, you've had a rough landing," François said. "With that hard head of yours you may have dented the floor."

"Very funny, Fido."

"Yup, she's really back." Willie straightened.

If I wasn't so woozy I'd have kicked at his knee. Who was he to talk? But he helped me focus.

"Were," I said, my throat sore as if I'd been screaming for some time. "Gotta find the Were."

"That's what you've been screaming," Bran said as he helped me to my feet, leaving one hand against my back to steady me. I'd die before I told him I appreciated it.

"I found the Were!" I glanced from Celtic blue eyes to François and Willie's brown ones.

Willie threw his hands wide. "Which Were? There seems to be a lot of them around this mess."

"The doctor." I glanced at Bran, willing him to understand as I fought to get the words out. That was one hell of a spell. I leaned over, resting my palms on my thighs. "The doctor who was there when Cheverill died."

Willie whistled.

"Let's get you out of this room and sitting down," François stepped in, guiding me toward the larger room and the lone couch.

"I've got to uncast the circle," I said, glancing over my shoulder. Even novice witches knew you didn't evoke the help of the Great Spirits and not say thank you. They tended to get very pissy about things like that.

"You broke the circle when you returned," Bran said by my side. "When you landed outside it."

Oh, crap, that wasn't good. The circle was for protection and ripping through it could mean all sorts of things. All bad.

"Sit here," François said, like a mother hen. "Willie can you find something strong to drink?"

I heard Willie shuffle off as I eased onto the couch, my legs not too stable. My head felt like it was splintering and my stomach was none too steady. No more scrying spells like that one.

"Tell us what happened?" Bran knelt in front of me, taking up my whole view. François slid to sit next to me.

I must look like I felt by the expressions on their faces.

"I saw Van." I swallowed, fighting to get beyond the image of him hurting so badly. "He's in a small cell, underground. The only light came from a small opening high in a stone wall."

"You saw could see him then?" François asked, incredulity staining his words. "As from afar?"

"No, I was in the cell with him." I unclenched my hands. "I could touch him, talk to him."

François cut a wary glance toward Bran, which I caught and resented.

"Seriously, I was in the cell with him. He's shackled with silver chains." I used my hands to show how thick they were. "And there was a dead man, a human, tossed in one corner. Just left to rot."

Willie, with timing only a Were possessed, thrust a tumbler of liquor under my nose right then and I closed my eyes and pushed it away.

"Not right now Willie," Bran said as I was busy convincing my stomach to stay down. "In a second maybe."

Bran placed a hand on my knee, which helped anchor me, then asked, "Tell us about this doctor."

Good. I could focus on that. "He must have heard us as he came down a long passage with a flashlight."

Oh, please, don't let him have hurt Van.

"And?" Bran cajoled.

I raised my eyes to him, knowing I'd failed and left Van at the mercy of sadists. "Van tried to distract him while I cloaked myself. But he was a Were and could scent me."

"Not good," Willie murmured, clutching the glass he held as if he'd been there. "Did he know you were there?"

"At first no." Then stupid me had to all but shout, look over here. "But at the end he did."

My words must have trailed off as François nudged my shoulder. "Then what happened?"

I shook my head, paying for it even as I tried to recreate the last seconds. "Then I was shot back through the tunnel and ended up here."

Everyone's eyes shifted toward Bran.

"What did you do?"

He stood up, breaking the tentative bond between us. He raked one hand through his hair then straightened his shoulders. "I called you back."

"What?" I jumped to my feet. Anger pounded through me. "What was the point of my looking for Van if you were going to yank me out before I could accomplish anything?"

He turned, towering over me even with my spiked shoes on, his anger bubbling below the surface, his hands clenched. But when he spoke his words were like a dash of ice water. "The shell of your body was going into cardiac arrest here. You wouldn't have done your brother much good dead."

He was right. But so was I. "All I needed was a few more minutes. I could have gotten the keys from the doctor. Freed Van."

He stepped closer, his eyes glacial. "You didn't have a few minutes."

I leaned into him almost nose to nose. Bran the protector warlock had overstepped his bounds. Way overstepped them and now Van could die. "My spell. My call."

He barked a laugh and stepped back. François grabbed my arm as I wanted to close the gap, but the didi-shifter hadn't stopped my mouth. "I used blood magic because you said it was the only way. And you screwed with the spell. Screwed with me."

Bran as a warlock understood loud and clear what I was saying. He couldn't have it both ways. He couldn't tell me I was a powerful witch and then not trust that I could use that power.

"If the tables were turned," I said between gritted teeth, "If I cut off your magic and someone died because of it, you'd feel the exact same way."

He turned then, looked me square in the eye. "You did. The street fight two days ago."

A blow to the head couldn't have been more lethal.

I'd told him why I'd done what I had done. I thought he understood, may not have liked it but at least he knew I hadn't sucked his powers because I didn't trust him. And that's what it always came down to between us. Trust.

François stepped in, trying to douse the emotion crackling between Bran and me. "Alex, did you find out anything about where Van was? The building? A smell, near water or out in the countryside? Something."

I shook my head, frustration zapping the last of my energy. "Nothing." I wanted to kick something, anything, including me. I'd been that close to helping Van but because of macho Alpha warlock I had zip.

A tight smile curved Bran's lips as he stepped toward me.

I braced, expecting the worst, when he leaned forward and slid one hand into my back pocket.

I'd like to say that his being so close, his touching me, meant nothing, but it threw me for such a loop-de-loop I stood there like a ninny with my mouth open until he stepped back, revealing something in his palm.

"What is it?" Willie asked, saving me the trouble as I focused on taking my next breath. I hated that Bran had that effect on me and I hated even more that there didn't seem to be a damn thing I could do about it.

"A passive GPS tracking device," François answered, giving me an appraising look, as if he was assessing my reaction.

I didn't have a reaction because I was swimming through a fog of thoughts. When? How? And the big one, why?

Bran seemed to know what I wanted to ask but couldn't. "As a backup I slipped this into Alex's pocket before she cast her spell. It'll give us a general area where she was."

He'd expected me to fail from the beginning. The coward didn't even have enough courage to ask me to carry the tracker. No, he slipped it into my pants pocket while he distracted me.

Betrayal, just as swift and sharp as when I found out my father was on the Council of Seven, the ones who let me go to prison.

The bastard. The rat bastard.

CHAPTER 55

The only thing still holding Van upright were the chains biting into him. But he no longer cared. Alex was gone. She'd gotten out and was safe. He slumped against the bonds and released a deep breath.

Jean-Claude still didn't know what had happened. After Alex's catch of breath the Were had rushed to the corner, kicking straw right and left. Then he'd punched speed dial on his cell phone, speaking in French.

Van knew enough to catch most of the words even spoken in agitation. With his shifter ability he could hear a male's voice on the other end.

"Someone was here," Jean-Claude's voice resonated with breathlessness and strain.

"Did you stop them?"

"No. I never saw them."

"Explain."

Jean-Claude paced around the cell as he recounted what had happened.

"So you smelled someone?"

"*Oui*," he barked, "But there was nobody in the cell."

"The witch?"

Van stilled. They had to know about Alex if the voice on the other end of the line reached that conclusion so quickly. But why? What did Alex have to do with this mess?

"It might have been." Jean-Claude sounded less sure, as if he was grasping for straws.

"*Bonne*. Then our plan is working. Till tomorrow."

Jean-Claude didn't have a chance to say more as the other hung up.

What plan? How was Alex involved? Van pulled against his chains.

The doctor turned back to look at him, his expression a mixture of pity and greed.

"Why?" Van found himself whispering around lips so dry they cracked and bled. "Why?"

There was a wealth of rage behind that single word. Why had they chosen Van? Why were they doing what they were doing? What was their goal? Why involve his father? And Alex, especially Alex. His childhood spent watching out for her was all for naught. She was in Paris for him, he knew it now and regretted it to the marrow of his bones. It's not what he wanted. Or ever dreamed could happen. Now, if he didn't figure out what was going down, and find a way to stop it, Alex was going to suffer.

"Why?" the doctor repeated, as if chewing on an old bone. "Money." He looked at Van as one would regard a father confessor. "It always comes down to two things. Money and power. They want the power, but for me, it was just the money."

Van rattled his head, grappling with the banality of this man's words. The doctor was willing to sacrifice Van, and Alex, and who knew who else, maybe his father, for money?

"*Oui*, it is trivial is it not, *Monsieur*," Jean-Claude continued as if they were sitting on barstools, shooting the breeze. "I'm a gambler." He coughed a small, bitter laugh. "Alas not a good one. But there is always that next roll of the dice, next turn of the card and I knew." He clenched his hands in a jerky movement. "I knew I'd come out on top."

He looked beyond Van, seeing something not limited by the stone walls and bars surrounding them. "I lost my wife. My two sons. My reputation, but I did not stop."

His weary eyes turned toward Van before glancing at his palms now spread before him. "I'm a healer and yet I could do nothing against this disease." he paused, then continued, "When they found me I was seven-hundred fifty thousand Euros in debt."

Van flinched. This guy wasn't talking chump change. That was close to a million in US dollars. No shylock would continue to lend money to someone that far out on a limb. Even through the haze of his brain Van was listening to what wasn't being said. Somebody had set up the doctor, knowing far in advance how far to string the Were along until he was solidly hooked. Van swallowed around the anger singeing him and finally managed another syllable. "Who?"

Jean-Claude shook his head, stepping closer to open Van's eyelids and check his pulse, the gestures so automatic Van wondered if the doctor even knew he did them. "They have been very careful to hide their identities from you, have they not," he murmured. "Though why it should matter anymore, with what they have planned."

Van could feel his adrenaline kickstart and knew his pulse had jumped. The doctor had to know too, but still Van pushed. He was glad the doctor was so close because Van could barely mutter. "Who?"

"I doubt it matters now. But one should know who executes him should he not?" The doctor looked into Van's eyes. "It is the human thing to do though neither of us can claim humanity."

The doctor lapsed into silence long enough Van thought he had forgotten Van's question. So he pulled at his chains.

The doctor stirred. "*Oui*. It is only right." He stepped back before speaking again. "The man who comes with me. The one with the drug. He is Delmore Vaverek."

That made so much clear. The man Van had been seeking when he'd been taken, all those weeks ago.

"Ah, I see you know the name." The doctor cocked his head. "He is as you Americans say a right old bastard." His voice trailed off as he turned toward the cell door.

Van thought the older man was through but the doctor paused after locking the cell door behind him. He rested both hands on the bars as if he were the one imprisoned and not Van. "Did you know there was one behind *Monsieur* Vaverek?"

Van raised his head. There always was another, but he hadn't expected to learn who it was. Vaverek was a dead man for what he'd done so far, but if there was another, one keeping his hands clean, then he too would pay.

"Oh, *oui*. One who makes that Were seem benign." Jean-Claude uttered a rusty chuckle that held no mirth. "The other. He is *le diable*. The devil incarnate."

He started walking away but Van needed to know. He rumbled his chains, shouting out a weak, "Who?"

"The other?" The doctor paused, but did not turn around. "He's called Byrne. Pádraig Byrne. And if you ever cross paths with him run the other way. Run fast and run far."

CHAPTER 56

I sat on that stupid couch in that stupid room, my arms wrapped around myself as if that could keep me from bleeding from the inside out. How could I have been such a fool to trust Bran? I'd walked wide-eyed into his plan to use black magic, knowing full well how it was the last thing I wanted to do. He wasn't the one paying the consequences as tremors rocked me. All magic exerted a price, and I doubted feeling gut sick and rattled was going to be the price. More like a down payment.

Willie stood over by Bran who was inserting his nifty little tracking device into a laptop computer. The rational part of me said thank the Spirits we ended up with something. The irrational part wanted to scream and howl.

François was once again sitting beside me so close our shoulders were rubbing. He must have guessed at the state I was in when I hadn't told him to find somewhere else in that cavernous room to hunker down. Right now that would take too much energy. Energy I no longer had.

He leaned close to me and whispered. "Sometimes he can be a right blinkered arse."

I turned, close enough I could see the yellow highlights in his golden brown eyes. My expression must have spoken for me as he quirked a brow.

"He might be my mate but that doesn't mean I don't know when he's a wanker."

I couldn't have said it better, if I understood what he was mumbling.

Then he added, "Still we'd be knackered if he hadn't done his sleight of hand."

"Not helping, Fido," I growled, exhaustion making my voice a low throated rumble.

Bran looked up from the computer, a frown marring his expression as he gave François a WTF look.

Great, just great. The warlock tramples all over me and has the gall to get possessive.

"The whole lot of you are hopeless." I rose to my feet, staggering as I walked toward the kitchen, something to put space between me and the lot of them. If I could I'd have left, but then I wouldn't know the location on the device.

"There." Willie leaned further over Bran's shoulder, jabbing a finger toward the computer screen. "Zoom in there."

I admit it I went on alert like a hunting dog scenting fresh game. So I made sure I held myself still right where I was, one elbow leaning on the counter to prop me up. Cool as all get out as my skin dampened and my breath shortened.

François rose and crossed the room and Bran punched the keyboard as if he were a geek. I thought bigwigs who ran multinational companies wouldn't know a flash drive from a flibbertigibbet. Leave it to Bran to surprise me once again.

"What do you have?" François asked as I unclenched my hands one finger at a time.

"What I suspected," Bran muttered, whipping out his phone and playing with it. I swear he was keeping me in the dark intentionally.

"Oh," Willie breathed, "That doesn't make sense."

"It does if you know where the Council of Seven will be meeting tomorrow." Bran didn't even look up.

My stomach dropped. The Council? All roads kept leading back to the bloody Council. Or maybe that was just Bran's fixation with them. I'd be focused one hundred percent on them if in . . . I glanced at the nearest clock and realized how late it was. Criminy, the spell took longer than I expected. The clock was already creeping closer to dawn than midnight.

"Just what I expected." Bran's voice jerked me back to the present, as he stood, agitation rolling off of him. He stalked to the center of the room and pivoted, his gaze zeroing in on mine.

Even hating him I could feel the zing of those too-blue eyes and feel the hum of his focus buzzing through him and from him, to me.

"What?" I didn't mean to say the word aloud but couldn't help it.

"Versailles?" François asked still focused on the computer, his back to the room. "It's brilliant and audacious at the same time."

I swallowed, still not knowing exactly what they were talking about but knowing it didn't bode well for Van.

Willie straightened, looking from Bran to me, looking confused and wary at the same time. "Someone going to explain to me what's happening?"

I could have kissed the Were though I doubted he'd understand why so I remained where I was, daring Bran to lie to me to my face. Oh, wait, he already had.

"Versailles is where the Council of Seven will be meeting tomorrow." Bran said, a twist to his lips as he added, "Actually later today."

"It's also where the RER C metro line ends," François said, rubbing a hand along his chin.

Willie glanced at him. "That was one of the trains passing through the *Porte Invalldes,* was it not?"Bran nodded but said nothing.

"So Versailles was where the Weres were taking . . . " His voice trailed off as he glanced at me.

"Where they were taking my brother," I finished for him. Then asked Bran, "So is the Council behind Van's kidnapping? And Vaverek?"

"I don't believe so." He spoke as if afraid to rattle me. Too little too late. "I have a gut instinct that Versailles is where Vaverek plans to stage another test of his drug. It's what I'd do."

"In front of the Council?"

I could hear Willie's gulp from where I stood. I knew how he felt. If I had any spit in my mouth I'd be doing the same thing. But I couldn't. Not while I was frozen in place, running through the ramifications of Bran's words.

A test? A shifter drugged to go rugaru, which ironically was a very old word from the French to mean crazy-assed wild and cannibalistic. To become rugaru in front of the Council and any humans in the area was shifter suicide. Then the true despicable genius of the plan hit me and I staggered.

Bran jerked, reaching a hand forward but François was at my side before I could blink. Obviously didi-shifters possessed the speed of their plain shifter cousins.

"What?" Willie demanded. "What'd I miss?"

"*Sacre bleu*, Willie." François whistled through clenched teeth as he made sure I was propped against one of the kitchen stools before he explained. "Think! What does Versailles have that makes it the perfect place to prove the shifters are dangerous and a threat to both humanity and the Council?"

Willie looked like he was mentally calculating then a smile wreathed his face. "Ah, I get it. Lots of people around. If the shifter kills some of them . . .oh, shit."

Weres could be masters of understatement.

"Yeah, humans. Tourists from all over the word. School groups." François scrubbed his hands over his face. "What better place to make a statement."

"Where is the Council meeting tomorrow?" I asked Bran, pleased my voice didn't wobble. "If we know where we could get there first. Spot Van and stop him."

Bran shook his head as if I was being way too naïve. It wasn't naivety driving me, it was desperation. "No one is given the final coordinates of the Council location until just before one's meant to appear."

"So you're supposed to just wait in Versailles? Until they contact you?" Anger shot the words from my mouth like bullets.

"Yes."

I stepped away from the stool, fear giving me a backbone. "So what?" I asked myself as well as the rest in the room. "We do nothing? We just wait for Vaverek to win? Let Van get shot down—" I choked, then straightened my shoulders. "Wait for Van to be gunned down as a rabid wolf?"

All eyes turned to Bran.

"I have a plan," he said. "And you're all involved."

CHAPTER 57

I thought I'd done a damn good job of biting my lip until it bled while Bran outlined his plan. Short, succinct and to the point, it was worthy of a master tactician. There was only one problem. I didn't believe a word he said.

Oh I believed his plan, but I didn't believe that Van was going to come out of it alive.

That didn't set too well with me. I'd made my mistakes by trusting him, but Bran's solution was going to place Bran's wellbeing first and foremost. That piece I was a hundred percent sure of.

Even as Bran's words faded into the tense silence of the warehouse Willie and François' gazes shifted in my direction, waiting for my agreement.

Well this witch had been kicked in the teeth one too many times lately to roll over and say *yes, massah* to this particular warlock now.

I stood straight, locked my legs so I wouldn't crumble and announced, "I'm going to bed."

"What?" Willie did the tennis tournament back and forth, tracking between me and Bran who didn't bat an eyelash and François who was shaking his head. "What's that mean? Are you in or not?"

I marched right past Bran. Let him figure it out.

"You coming to Versailles?" he demanded as I stepped into my bed room.

"Oh, I'll be there." With my own plan.

"That's good then, isn't it?" he was speaking to the other two as I closed my door, not waiting for the answer.

As I stood before the bed, knowing there was no way I was going to get much sleep, I was too wired, I felt my phone buzz in my pocket.

No one knew this number, except for the IR team. My fingers shook as I pulled out the phone and read the text.

Beware the sign of the cross.

That's all it said.

With a small laugh I sank to the edge of the bed. Leave it to Jaylene to change my focus. No doubt this was one of her crazy premonitions, her gift of second sight being as useful as a match in a snowstorm. Most times what she saw was gloom and doom, so I guess her message could have been worse. And the very fact she sent the text meant I wasn't so desperately alone. Someone, even just one person, was thinking about me.

I typed in a response.

Thanks. Versailles tomorrow. Ten a.m.

Then hit send. I don't know why I shared that much. Maybe so someone would know where to come looking for my body. Or if I didn't show up they'd know where to tell my father where I'd disappeared.

If he cared.

I sank my head into my hands. A week ago if someone had said I'd no longer trust my father I'd have laughed in their face. But in spite of Bran's glib words I wasn't counting the Council as blameless in whatever was about to go down. It made sense that Vaverek would set up Van to go rugaru in front of the group to prove something about the shifters. That tracked. But the whole why behind the action is where I differed from Bran's interpretation.

I didn't know the why but my gut told me it was bigger, and badder than Vaverek proving a point. He could stage the rugaru experiment anywhere, but he wasn't. He was using the Council or the Council was using him. One or the other.

And what was I going to do about it?

I had no idea but between now and tomorrow morning I had better think of something.

CHAPTER 58

I heard the footsteps round the end of the warehouse where I huddled on an old stone bench. It felt like it too. As unyielding as a certain warlock I knew.

"You mind some company?" François asked, drawing near, his voice still undercover English with a French accent. Good agents never, ever forgot their assignments and always stayed in role.

I so was not a good agent. I was barely a passable one and there were doubts about that.

Easing my shoulders down, I scooted over on the slab of rock. "Sure. Grab a seat but don't complain if your bum goes numb."

He actually laughed. A sound I don't know if I ever heard before. I tucked that away into my packet of regrets, a packet getting bigger all the time. Then I realized something I'd almost forgotten. Shifters could walk with such a silent tread that most humans never heard them.

"You checking up on me?" I asked, no heat to my words as I angled my head to look at him.

"No." He kept his face in profile to mine, staring out into the darkness as the moon slipped behind some clouds. "I always like to catch a quiet breather before a mission. Helps settle the nerves."

Somewhere far away sounds ebbed and flowed, like the sea in the distance. Probably Parisian traffic but I liked the image of the ocean better. Not like me, grabbing on to the fantasy instead of reality but lately reality had sucked, big time.

I found myself looking in the same direction as François as I asked, "You ever doubt an assignment?"

"All the time," he snorted, which made me feel tons better.

"Yet you go anyway?"

He hesitated, bracing his elbows on his knees before saying, "Sometimes there are no good choices. There's only the best choice you can make at that time. I make my peace with that and move forward."

Not exactly what I'd asked, but then we played in a world of shadows. It only made sense that there would be no black and white choices.

"You second guessing going tomorrow?" he asked, his voice low and non-judgmental.

"No." I shook my head, sure of this piece. "Without me my brother stands no chance."

"Then what's eating at you?"

It was such an American phrase coming from this man that it stopped me for a second. But only enough to take a deep breath. "Motivation."

"As in yours or Vaverek's or the Council's?"

Or Bran's. But I didn't say that. Instead I wrapped my tongue around what I'd been wrestling with out here in the cool night air. "There's always going to be a Vaverek," I said. "Or someone like him. Same with the Council. Ultimate power corrupting the players."

Including my father, I wanted to shout, but bit my tongue.

"So you're debating your motivation?" François had the grace not to laugh at me, which I took as a win.

"My goal is to save Van. Always has been."

"But?"

I turned on the seat, looking directly at François until he couldn't ignore me. "But is it enough?" My voice was tight and low. My emotions bubbling beneath the surface. "Is my wanting my brother safe enough reason to embroil others in fighting Vaverek or fighting the Council or . . ." I waved my hand before me. "Seems damn selfish to me right now."

"That's one way to look at it." François knitted his hands together. "But you're forgetting the family that was killed by the earlier shifter. The one most likely driven by Vaverek."

"But . . ." I hadn't forgotten the family, especially the little girl. "Maybe I'm being stupid but I have to make sure I'm doing the right thing for the right reason."

"That you're not fighting just for your brother?"

"Yes." I leaned forward, mimicking François' pose. "I'm asking you and Willie and . . ."

"And Bran."

"Yes." I bit off the word. "To risk your lives for my brother." I paused then added, "If I'd seen Vaverek torture hundreds, or there was a threat to the city, or the world was at war, then I'd have no doubts. But right now I feel like I'm starting a war rather than ending one."

"If we did not go with you tomorrow would you go alone?"

"Of course."

"Why?"

Now it was my time to snort. "Because Van is my brother."

"Any other reason?"

I twisted my hands together. "Because it's not right. What's been done to him. He's a good man."

He tilted his head as if considering my words. When he spoke there was none of the witty, urbanite Franco I once knew, or the suave and controlled François I knew now, but a man who'd faced his own demons. "Thus in silence in dreams' projections, Returning, resuming, I thread my way through the hospitals; the hurt and wounded I pacify with soothing hand, I sit by the restless all dark night—some are so young; some suffer so much . . ."

"Poetry?"

"Walt Whitman, wrestling with the same issues. Seeing the individual soldiers who fought your country's Civil War, row upon row in hospital beds."

"What does a dead white guy's poetry have to do with my brother?"

"When light faces off against dark then light must win or the world as we know it is destroyed." He paused, then added, "It's the small battles that are most hard won and matter the most. You're not fighting for your brother, you're fighting to stop those who imprisoned your brother. To rebalance right and justice and goodness."

He rose and looked down at me. "The small battles are just as important as the large ones. Because if the Vavereks of the world are allowed to continue next time it won't be one shifter kidnapped or one family murdered. Then it'll be a small community, then a larger one and on it goes."

I listened to his steps receding as I mulled over his words. My dad told me once that every choice has a consequence. I'd made my choice. Could I live with the consequences?

Guess I'd find out tomorrow.

CHAPTER 59

I'd given up looking at the clock to see time ticking past when I decided what I could do. I punched in Vaughn's number on my cell phone, surprised that the phone still held a charge, a week one but enough to get a ring. I wasn't surprised when she sounded half asleep.

"Vaughn here."

"I need a favor." There, nothing like jumping right in and asking for help, persona non grata or not.

"Alex?" She sounded like she'd sat up and was scrubbing her hand across her face.

"Who is it?" A male voice mumbled next to her. M.T. Stone.

Should have calculated that potential speed bump. It was one thing asking my fellow team member, another to run my idea past the Agency instructor. Damn.

"You still there?" Vaughn asked me then spoke to Stone loud enough that I could hear. "Go back to sleep. Nothing to do with you."

Yet.

"Yeah, I'm here," I mumbled into the phone, wondering and not for the first time, if this was a bad idea. "I don't want to put you in the middle of something."

Vaughn laughed. "Part of the territory. What's up?"

And there it was. That unconditional support, no questions asked, just an implied I've-got-your-back. I never expected it. Never looked for it, especially from a group of strangers and a group of women.

I released a sigh I didn't even realize I'd been holding and gave her a quick overview of everything, or as much of everything as I could share. The whole Were agitation, potential involvement of the Council, suspicion of how and where my brother was going to be used to destabilize the whole human versus non-human status. When I finished there was silence.

"Damn, you've been busy."

If she'd been closer I'd have given her a big hug and I wasn't a huggy- feely kind of person.

"So what now?" she asked, all awake.

I sucked in a deep breath. "I was hoping you and the team might be in the vicinity tomorrow. As backup."

Vaughn's voice lowered. "You know who probably won't like it."

"Our director?" I whispered though there was no one on my end listening in.

"Yup."

"Yeah, I kind of figured that." I rushed through the next part. "Which is why this is all unofficial and under the table. If the team, or as many members of the team who are okay with the plan, just happen to be at the palace at Versailles tomorrow around ten, and if they see some bad shit going down, and jump in, then I can ask for forgiveness later."

"As opposed to permission beforehand?"

"Yeah. Something like that."

She paused as I heard my heart beat hard within my chest. Please, please, please, say yes.

"Funny thing," she said as if chatting girl-to-girl anywhere. "Just happen to want to see Versailles. One of my favorite spots from when I was here as a girl."

My shoulders dropped from around my ears and my hand unclenched from the phone. "Vaverek will be there, so this could get ugly." No could about it. Vaverek was a nasty piece of putrid meat and he was willing to do whatever he needed to do to accomplish his agenda. Tough, so was I.

"No worries," came Vaughn's casual reply. Damn, I adored her.

"Ten a.m.," I repeated. "I'll call you when I have exact location details."

"We'll be there." She made it sound as if we were all meeting for a coffee clutch.

I'd just about hit the disconnect button when I added a rushed, "Thanks, Vaughn. You're the best."

"I agree," Stone mumbled into the phone then the line went dead.

Great. How much had he heard? All of it if he was anything like Bran. Control issues and no sense of playing fair.

Okay, maybe I'd just screwed up Vaughn's position on the team. Mine was toast already but saving Van's life was worth it.

I only hoped Ling Mai would agree when Stone told her.

CHAPTER 60

Jeb stood in the liquid sunshine of an early spring morning in one of the side chambers of the *Petit Trianon in* the palace of Versailles, waiting for the initial formal meeting in the salon. He looked without really seeing the designed pastoral feel of the grounds, a world apart from his idea of a rural landscape. His gaze lighted on the infamous *saut-de-loup*, or wolf jump, a ten-foot drop used to give the illusion of accessibility to the French people who wished to see their king and queen, but in reality kept the masses away from the royal court.

Jeb knew how those masses felt, frustrated to be kept just out of reach of what was truly happening. Both his shaman self and his shifter wolf could feel the tension among the Council members and their entourages, including Pádraig. Like the lull before a late summer lightning storm, an edgy restlessness skating the razor edge between euphoric and manic, without any clear reason for either. Not as far as Jeb could see.

He'd tried again last night to reach Philippe on the astral plane but failed. It was as if his friend danced just outside Jeb's reach, always present but at the same time aggravatingly absent. Even this location where Jeb stood had the touch of Philippe in its arrangement, or so it felt as they reached the ornate Palace of Versailles.

Leave it to Philippe to requisition several of the rooms of *le Petit Trianon*, a building designed for the mistresses of one king and given by another king as a retreat for the young Marie Antoinette. Philippe no doubt had to pull a few strings to have the rooms available but also would have enjoyed the irony of holding a Council meeting in a location known for its illusions.

And that's what Jeb was battling—a series of illusions, where nothing seemed quite as it was in reality. Zeid, the Dominatui who posed as a butler, was an illusion. So was this warlock who was involved with his daughter. And the traitor? The one Zeid spoke about? Within the Council or close enough to be perceived as belonging. He, or she felt very, very real, though still hidden. Illusion within illusions.

Jeb considered himself a simple man, which is why he'd avoided Council politics. But that same aversion was biting him on the ass now.

"Are you ready?" Pádraig had entered the room from the far door though Jeb had not heard him. Another sign of his distraction.

"Are they prepared for the full Council?" he asked, touching the medallion within his pocket, the only overt sign of rank and power. Others had asked for robes, one even requested a crown, to show his position as one of the privileged Council members. Jeb had helped shoot down both ideas. By this stage all present should know who and what they were. Since few outsiders were invited to Council meetings, unless to face a judgment or place a petition that had been vetted by lesser circles of power, there should be no need to flaunt who they were to one another.

But times changed.

Pádraig nodded his head. "We're meeting in the red salon."

Jeb followed the younger man's lead, noticing as he did how Pádraig walked on the balls of his feet as he moved into the room that drew its name from the ostentatious mirrored walls and watermelon red satin chairs. He was sure they had a different name for the color but they reminded him of the late summer fruit that grew so well in the long hot weather of Mud Lake.

He also realized he was no longer focusing on Pádraig so almost ran into the young man's back as he came to a sudden halt.

With a quick shuffle Jeb side-stepped the Irishman to see what was happening.

A large, formal table that fit the room had been dragged to the center, with six formal chairs pulled up to it. On the back of each one draped a dark purple robe.

Obviously things were changing faster than Jeb expected.

Cristobal Íñigo de Mendoza, the Council's vampire representative who was even older than the room they stood in, waited at the head of the table, his smile shark-sharp. Beside him aligned the witches and demons. Talk about an unholy triumvirate. That left Wei Pei isolated against the far wall, his eyes nervous, his fingers tap dancing along the cloak he'd already donned. Tintilla, the fae representative had not yet appeared, which was normal. She loved to stage a dramatic entrance. He wondered where she would stand in the divisions already shaping the Council. Philippe would have been dismayed. His funeral not even over and the alliances he'd carefully crafted over the years torn asunder.

It wasn't looking good for the shifters.

Pádraig cleared his throat, which reminded Jeb of the young man's presence. He was the only one not of the presiding group.

Before Jeb could assimilate the meaning of that Cristobal waved one hand toward two empty seats. "Pádraig, if you will stand here." He pointed to his right. "And Jebediah, you opposite if you would be so kind. Next to Wei Pei."

So that was where the old one saw Jeb. Not on the winning side. Not verbally aligned otherwise, but of no import or consequence.

Pádraig stood behind one of the chairs, his smile looking strained, but still in place. So how did the young man fit into the machinations already in play?

Cristobal called them to order, even without Tintilla's presence. "If you will all don your cloaks."

Jeb felt like Alex when she used to play dress up, but said nothing, betrayed nothing. Now was not the time.

"Ah, Tintilla, my precious. It is good of you to join us." Cristobal's words said one thing, his tone another, but then the man had learned statecraft sparring with Henry the Eighth of England. Or was it the Seventh?

Tintilla sauntered in as was her wont, casting Jeb a quick glance that spoke volumes. The fae queen did not like surprises and this appeared to have disturbed her sense of equilibrium.

"Are we to have a theatrical event?" she asked in her high, clear voice as she swept the cloak off her chair, one to the right of Cristobal. "If I'd known I'd have brought my own costume. One of silk."

The vampire ignored her question as he glanced away and stated to all, "We've waited long enough for you Tintilla, now act your age and don the cloak."

Even Pádraig heard the undertones beneath the order as well as catching the tightening of Tintilla's patrician features. No one knew her age exactly but if they'd promoted the senior member of the Council by age alone she would now be standing in Cristobal's place.

Which raised the question: Why was the vampire being so presumptuous?

As if Jeb had asked the question aloud Cristobal waved one elegant hand. "I know I am not our dearly lost brother, Philippe, but I'm sure he, as well as all of you know of the need for a smooth and quick transition. We do not wish the Council to be perceived as weak or indecisive in this time of change."

"And that time would be what?" Wei Pei piped up. Jeb was glad the shifter had asked the question but wished he'd been able to do so with less shakiness to his voice.

"All in good time my dear, Wei Pei. First things first. Pádraig, if you would be so kind as to stand beside me here."

Pádraig raised his chin and moved next to the vampire, close enough that Cristobal was able to drape one skinny arm across the young man's shoulders.

So that was the way of things? Jeb kept his gaze somewhere between the two of them, kicking himself for not seeing the handwriting sooner.

"I'm sure we have all known of Pádraig's devotion to not only his mentor Philippe but to the Council's business, especially in this past year."

While Jeb buried his head in the sand and grieved the loss of

Alex and his failure as a father.

"I find no need to extol his virtues to those of us who take an active part in our Council duties."

A sharp and not-so-subtle jab at Jeb and probably Wei Pei and Tintilla as well. Jeb heard Wei Pei's quick intake of air and Tintilla's face was looking sharper and sharper by the moment.

"I hereby recommend Pádraig Byrne to assume the seat recently vacated by Philippe Cheverill."

Cristobal made it sound as if Philippe had stepped outside as opposed to having been murdered and Jeb found the tightness in his jaw increasing. Fortunately the clapping of the Zinzin, the Kuoura Demon and Breena McShay, the Celtic witch kept the attention on everyone front and center.

"And the vote?" Jeb hadn't realized he'd spoken the question aloud. He looked at Pádraig's raised brow expression as he titled his head and added, "It's tradition." A quick glance at Cristobal who was not pleased. "You do not wish any rumors of improper procedures being raised at a later date. That could put Pádraig's position in jeopardy." *And yours too,* remained unstated.

Maybe he should not have raised the issue. But the last thing Philippe would have wanted was whatever turmoil gripped the Council to spill over to the larger world of preternaturals. Their existence was challenging enough.

And Philippe believed in his protégé, even if Jeb still harbored some doubts. Especially now, at the rapidity of the druid stepping into a position of power with less vetting than one hired a clerk at a convenience store.

"Our shaman member does have a valid point," Tintilla conceded, fluttering one hand though she was not usually given to such gestures. "Propriety matters in such times."

By throwing the vampire's words back at him the fae deepened the rift between her kind and the nightwalker's kind, not that there was any chance they'd see eye-to-eye.

"So shall it be." Cristobal's words sounded like chewed glass. "Pádraig, if you will leave us for a moment." He did not wait for the druid to leave before he added, "And you too Jebediah."

All gazes snapped to Jeb who focused on the vampire. Even Pádraig hesitated at the door leading to the other room.

Jeb asked, "Because?"

The smile wreathing Cristobal's face was obscene in its smugness. "Why, I would have thought that was obvious, Jebediah." He spread his palms to include the rest of the table. "Since your daughter is accused of involvement in Philippe's murder it would not be right for you to have any say in Council business."

How neatly Jeb had been maneuvered and hog-tied. He'd never seen it coming.

He rose without a word. No protesting Alex's innocence. No justification. And no need to tell Cristobal he would rue the day he uttered those words.

Following Pádraig's path Jeb joined the young man but Cristobal wasn't finished yet.

"Oh, Jebediah," He said. Jeb did not turn around but did pause. "You really must do something about those spawn of yours before they cost you your position on the Council."

He did not reply but closed the door softly behind him. The vampire had overstretched himself and Jeb would be pleased to make sure he paid for his smugness.

CHAPTER 61

Bran drove the luxury car through the outskirts of Paris, navigating the morning traffic with the ease and competence with which he did everything. In the silence of the car I wanted to scream. Couldn't he at least act like a fallible human at times?

Willie had been talking nonstop, an obvious nervous habit and a vast contrast to my own silence. I hadn't slept a wink last night, or what had been left of the early morning and now, being trapped in a vehicle with a loquacious Were, a quiet didi-shifter and a tense warlock wasn't doing anything for my nerves.

François had said the trip should take less than an hour, depending on commuter traffic, that we should be there soon but with each kilometer the strain was increasing. And here I thought it'd started at an impossible level. Silly me.

Willie had just launched into a description of the architecture and historical trivia behind the building of Versailles when François spoke at last. "Willie!"

"What?"

"Shut up."

I actually felt sorry for the Were. At least he was trying. I was looking for something to ease François's bitch slap when Bran's phone rang.

He answered with a curt, "Bran. Yes. Yes. I'll be there." Then he hung up.

My stomach tumbled and I was glad I hadn't had anything more than a small cup of coffee for breakfast. Right now even that seemed iffy.

Bran, being Bran and a close-mouthed bastard right then, said nothing more.

I flexed my hands against my jeans. "Well?"

He glanced my way. "It's all set."

Since I was not going to grovel for information I bit my tongue and waited until he navigated the car into a parking area that looked like stadium parking with a tournament in progress. As I stepped out of the car into a wash of early morning air holding a bite I suddenly realized what we were up against. "There are so many cars."

And buses, tour buses and school-type buses and enough cars to knock the breath from me. By the Great Spirits how could there be so many people at Versailles? How were we going to find Van and stop him with these crowds? "Isn't there anything else to do in France except visit here?" I asked, stunned by the enormity of the task.

Bran gave me a suck-it-up look. Leave it to a warlock to be all warm and fuzzy while I was falling apart.

François stepped in to snap me back to reality. "Bran, exactly where is the meeting set?"

"*Le Petit Trianonat*," came the short reply, like a name meant anything.

François again came to my rescue, snagging my arm and tugging me along. "Not to worry. We're still in low season which means *Le Petit Trianonat* will not open to the crowds until noon."

"And *Le Petit Trianonat* is what exactly?"

"The chateau built for Marie Antoinette. As an escape."

That last part sounded perfect about then, but Noziaks were not lightweights. I gave François a wobbly smile and double-timed it to keep up with Bran's long-legged stride until he stopped in the lee of a three-story building.

"Is that it?" I whispered though there was no need to. It was as if I didn't want to disturb the old spirits that floated through the area. Mandy as a Spirit Walker would be driven crazy here, so many unhappy ghosts wandering I'm surprised there was any room for humans.

But there they were, walking around with cameras, paper

guide books and attached earphones leading them from garden spot to garden spot.

"I'll head in, a little early, " Bran said as if to himself.

"Probably better than late with those guys," Willie said, then threw me a quick glance. "Sorry, Alex. Not your father of course."

Of course.

I didn't bother with a response as King Bran was busy dictating. "Everyone knows what they're supposed to do and where they're supposed to be?" François and Willie nodded. When I didn't fall into line he added, "Alex?"

"I know what you want me to do." There, it was as close as I could come to not outright telling him where he could take his plan and stuff it.

According to the Almighty Warlock I was to go with Willie; as a recovering Were he'd be staying far away from any fighting but he could handle babysitting. Me being the one who needed caretaking. François was going to shift into one of his dog personas and literally sniff around for Van. When he found my brother he'd alert Bran. Not me, because I would be too busy twiddling my thumbs waiting until I was given the all-clear signal.

As if.

Bran nodded at François who headed in one direction as Willie stepped away. He really did have an aversion to fireworks.

Me not so much. I held my ground even as Bran stepped closer, having the audacity to put his hands on my shoulders as if I needed to be restrained.

And here I thought I was doing well, only giving him a what-the-hell glance instead of ripping his arms off.

"We went over this in detail last night," Bran said, impatience straining his voice and darkening his eyes until they almost looked black. It was a sexy look for him, but then all Bran's looks were sexy. Focus, Alex, back to the issue at hand.

"No!" I wagged one finger at him. "You went over this last night as if I was a toddler who needed you to tell me what to do."

His hands tightened. Not enough to hurt me, which surprised me because I could read the restraint he was exerting in the tension of his jaw. If he were a shifter he'd be revealing fur already.

"The plan is solid," he said.

"Your plan is solid for your agenda," I bit off each word.

"Meaning?"

"You're using my brother to draw out Vaverek. And your plan does just that. Wait until Van is exposed, assume—" I inhaled a deep breath to repeat that last word. "Assume that Vaverek will be nearby so you or Fido François can jump him."

"What's wrong with that? Your people want Vaverek as much as I do."

"Not quite." I stepped back. No longer able to stay still. I was standing in one of the world's biggest parks and I couldn't draw a breath of air. "You want Vaverek more than anything else. Including my brother's life." This time my finger stabbed his chest as I stepped forward and blinked to keep my eyes clear. "Maybe you're thinking if Van dies that will make up for Dominique's death some way. Tit for tat. But let me tell you, buster." My finger hit with each word. "I. Will. Not. Let. Van. Die."

He glared at me and I was surprised I didn't incinerate right there. "Have you ever considered I'm trying to keep you alive here?" his voice a low growl, his nostrils flared. "That I might actually have *your* interests at heart?"

"In your dreams." Emotions bubbled so close to the surface I kept expecting to spew fire. "If you did you would not have been so quick to suggest black magic as the 'only' way to find Van." I used my fingers for air quotes and to keep my hands from balling and beating against him.

"It was the only way," he snapped each word. "Of all the stupid, stubborn, pig-headed women I had to get involved with I got you."

"Me? This isn't about us. There is no us." He so did not fight fair. Men weren't supposed to throw things from the past into a fight. But obviously holier-than-thou Bran did not get the male-memo book. "There never was an us because you couldn't trust me a micro-inch. Still can't. Which is why you are shunting me off with Willie so the 'big boys' can handle the business."

He towered over me like a predator ready to strike. "Fine. Do it your way, but if you think for a minute I'm going to let Vaverek dance away while you're playing Sabrina the inept witch, think again."

"Oh." Now he'd really done it. I lowered my voice, which my brother could have told him meant hurricane gale force winds about to blow. "If I'm such a poor witch how come we're standing here right now?"

"Because I was told to be here and you were guaranteed to come along."

Okay, he did have a point, but that's not what I meant. I wasn't happy about his logic either. I got us here by breaking my rules and finding Van last night. Sure I might be a screw-up as a powerful witch, and we needed the GPS he'd saddled me with, but I had pulled a few spells out of my ass and they'd worked. Could I repeat the process? Who knew? But I was still willing to do whatever I had to in order to save Van. If we caught Vaverek, that was a bonus.

I took a page from his playbook and switched tactics. "Fine, your Mage Majesty. You do what you need to do and I'll do what I need to do."

"And if you get killed?" He said it in such a flat of-course tone I was surprised I didn't haul off and hit him.

"That will save you the effort." I stood toe-to-toe with him and it took Willie clearing his throat several times for both of us to spin on him.

"What?"

"What now?"

He flared his hands then pointed behind us. "Sorry, but I think they're coming for you."

Bran and I both pivoted to see a delegation of three tall, thin individuals walking down the white gravel path toward us. Only they looked more like they were hovering just above the ground.

"Fae?" I whispered aloud.

"Simin fae," Bran said, all emotion leached from his voice.

Oh crap. I'd heard of them. Think of the most benign looking of individuals, with lightning fast speed and tongues that made a whip look like a yarn tassel. Before most creatures could even think of taking flight one simin fae could have them lassoed and giftwrapped tighter than a crazy aunt's holiday package. But three?

Not that Bran was thinking of running. A quick glance out of the corner of my eye reassured me that he wasn't, which allowed me to start breathing again.

And that's when I realized what drove a lot of my anger. Not fear of him as much as fear for him.

This was a heck of a time to discover that.

Especially as I looked beyond the fae and saw Vaverek.

CHAPTER 62

Jeb waited in the side room, releasing his anger with every breath he took because he knew anger could cloud his judgment and reason. Wheels within wheels were moving. He glanced at Pádraig with his shaman vision, not looking at the physical being but the spirit.

He hadn't expected to see much but what he did see was revealing. Or more specifically what he didn't see. Pádraig was a druid so knew how to cloak his spirit self. The old ones learned the ability to protect themselves when mages and black witches walked the world more freely. It was like covering a beacon with a cloth to not attract attention, or tamping down one's power until needed.

But there should be no need for Pádraig to cloak himself today. But he was, emitting only a small silver aura. Jeb could feel the hum from him, as if banking power and waiting. But why?

That was the piece Jeb struggled with. There was too much unknown.

When the door swung open to allow Jeb and Pádraig to re-enter the red salon Pádraig went first then paused as if realizing his presumption, his assumption that now he and Jeb were equals.

Jeb said nothing but waved the young man ahead. He assumed what had happened and was not surprised when Cristobal announced in sonorous tones as if speaking to a large assembly hall that Pádraig was accepted as the newest member of the Council.

Once again Jeb noticed what wasn't said so asked, "What was the vote tally?"

Cristobal flinched as if struck then tilted his head and shared, "Four for, one against."

Jeb didn't need to look at Tintilla but he sent a high-five thought in her direction. Wei Pei must have felt that a yay vote would earn him some allies but Jeb could have told him not to bother. There would be no reprieve from this group. It'd only be a matter of time before they found a way to replace Wei Pei or he met an untimely accident.

At least one question was answered for Jeb. This is why Philippe had to die. He was standing in the way of plans already in motion. Philippe had always been about building consensus and the need to act for the greater good. Jeb had agreed which is why his daughter was imprisoned. Saving her meant exposing too much to the humans.

But now? What did Cristobal want? Did he plan to use the less experienced Pádraig? Step into the role of a mentor as Philippe had been, not as a guide but as a manipulator. If Pádraig threw in his weight with the vampire, demon, and witch, no telling what trouble a block of four could brew. Wei Pei was like the bamboo stalk that would blow whichever way the wind demanded. Which left Tintilla and himself as the sole voices of reason.

This shift of power was accomplished so smoothly, so easily, it was clear it had been planned for a long time. Jeb's gut told him what had just transpired was the beginning of something larger, but he didn't know what.

CHAPTER 63

"Eleven o'clock," I whispered to Bran, not sure what the hearing range of a simin fae was.

He looked at me as if I'd flipped. "It's not yet ten."

Men!

"Behind the fae. Eleven o'clock. Could be Vaverek."

He followed my directions and I could hear him suck in his breath as I also heard Willie move up behind us.

"Can you smell Were?" I mumbled, not turning around but acting like my attention was one hundred percent on the first threat approaching, the fae.

"Yes," Willie responded after a few good sniffs. Then he added, "At least six or seven. A couple of fae, other than the simins, and . . ." he sniffed again. "One shifter, who's very agitated."

Van. It had to be Van but the man I was thinking could be Vaverek was alone. He looked like a common thug, about as tall as Bran with wide shoulders and a figure that leaned toward thickening in the middle, disguised well by the very pricey suit he wore. Who wore a suit when visiting a tourist attraction? Plus his body language was all wrong. He was rocking back and forth on the balls of his feet, his shoulders thrust forward, his focus on where Bran, Willie and I stood. Sort of a pudgy attack Doberman on alert.

Could I be wrong about who he was?

With a quick glance around I caught what Willie had just indicated. There were a number of individuals, male and female, that didn't seem to be focused on the gardens or the three-story building directly in front of us.

"Freeze the fae," I mumbled to Bran.

"Why?"

"Something's going down. Now. The fae take you and you're a sitting target."

"I don't go with them now and an execute order will be applied."

I glanced at him. "Not if they're frozen and can't do anything. Blame it on me."

"No, I –"

"Do it." We had no choice. His was stronger magic with the containment spell. I could do one but needed a circle and blood.

In a few seconds we might get blood if he didn't do anything.

They were ten feet away.

He straightened and lifted the fingers of his right hand.

"Continere."

Not good enough. "More."

Six feet away.

"Continere."

Three feet away. So close I could see the neon green of their slitted eyes.

"By the power of three," I mumbled. Did he want to be trapped by them?

He uttered the final and last words needed, *"Continere lam."*

A pulse of magic wafted forward, catching the three with their feet planted flat on the ground.

Thank the Spirits they stopped. Close enough they looked like they were just pausing, maybe chatting us up, doing anything except being frozen in place. From the location of the Were that I thought was Vaverek stood all he'd see was the trio in front of us, doing nothing.

"Now?" Bran asked, a bite to his voice.

"Now we stop the bad guys."

"And they are?"

Okay, he was getting downright snarky, even if he was right. There were non-humans and humans spread across the broad rectangle of grass about the size of a football field. White gravel walkways outlined the grass area with the three-story *Petit Trianon* hunkered down on the end closest to where we stood. Rows and rows of sculpted shrubs acted as a visual break between this residence and the rest of the gardens and buildings.

"More Weres arriving," Willie whispered into my ear, looking to the left of us. Four individuals, two male, two female stepped from the shrubs bracketing that side of the grassy field.

"How many is that?" I asked, keeping my attention on Vaverek.

"Twelve by my count," Bran said, his focus on holding the fae still. That was the problem with the stronger containment spells. They weren't static but needed the intention of the caster to remain strong. If they were three humans a simpler spell could have been cast, even one I could manage without a problem. But fae could counter magic and he couldn't risk the spell failing.

"You know where François is?" I asked.

"Circling the back of the *Petit Trianon*," came Bran's reply.

Great. Our only asset was out of sight and out of striking distance.

I could practically feel Willie vibrate behind me. "I can't—I really can't . . ."

"I know." No sight of the IR members. Maybe Stone and Ling Mai stopped them already. Down to Bran and I and if Bran released his focus on the spell we'd have three simin fae ready to attack.

One problem at a time.

"Keep the fae in place," I whispered to Bran.

"What are you—"

"Look for reactions," I mumbled.

"What—"

No time to explain. We were running out of time. I'd already thrown back my shoulders, plastered a wide-eyed expression on my face and was running past the fae and toward Vaverek.

"Help. Oh, help!" I screamed like every Slasher movie I'd ever seen and with four brothers I'd seen a lot, regardless of what we'd told my dad. "A bomb. There's a madman with a bomb."

CHAPTER 64

Jeb's shifter hearing caught the scream of a woman shouting beyond the salon's windows before the others did.

Alex?

He half rose from his seat, earning a glare from Cristobal. "What are you— "

"Listen," he snarled, pushing his chair back.

"I hear a woman," Tintilla said, glancing toward the windows. "What is she saying?"

"Bomb." Jeb's voice was back under control, as were his emotions. It couldn't be Alex. Not here.

Still he hurried as he crossed to the window, looking out at the formal gardens stretched in front of the *Petit Trianon*. A lot of people ebbed and flowed over the grass, too many given the chateau itself wouldn't be open to the general public for over two hours.

"What's happening?" Pádraig pulled near him, leaning toward the window.

Jeb looked around, his heart locking as he sighted what he'd hoped not to see. Alex was running away from a trio of simin fae, the ones sent to escort the warlock into the meeting and two males behind them. She was shouting about a bomb. Others were starting to react, looking around, some groups already fleeing the area. The rest glancing wildly around.

But what Jeb noticed more was the lack of movement from several of the small groups. As if they too remained as frozen in place as the fae. Frozen or they knew more about what was really happening.

"The warlock?" Pádraig said as Cristobal joined them. "The fae are there." He pointed to the trio. "The warlock looks like he's just beyond them. A ploy to escape them?"

"He knows the consequences," Cristobal snarled, sounding shocked that anyone would be so stupid as to even dare disobey a summons to the Council.

From all the research Jeb had done regarding the warlock, stupid was not a word he'd apply to the dress designer. Calculating, focused, determined, yes, but not stupid, especially not to execute such an action within full view of the Council.

"What is transpiring?" Tintilla said, arriving at the next window over, Wei Pei by her side. "Are we under attack?"

"Not us." Jeb said, watching the individuals remaining in the grassy area begin to converge. In twos and threes they moved toward where Alex was arguing with a single gentleman. She was waving her hands, shouting, acting hysterical. Which was not her way. Not at all.

So what was she doing?"That woman appears to be pointing toward something," the Koura demon said from one of the windows. "She keeps shouting about a bomb."

"Then why doesn't she run?" Tintilla said, shaking her head. "Unless . . ." Her words petered off.

Wei Pie murmured quietly, "Careful with others is a must have."

"What?" Cristobal turned to focus a lasered look at him. "Speak up."

Wei Pei stepped back, shoving his hands into the sleeves of his cloak, which effectively hid them from too watchful eyes. Faces could lie, but hands often revealed too much. "I said be cautious of people who may hurt you intentionally."

Tintilla fluttered her hand before the window, "What does that mean? Is she a threat or not?"

The Chinese shifter was correct. If Alex truly feared a bomb, she wouldn't be standing there arguing with a stranger. She'd cold cock him, drag him out of harm's way and deal with the consequences later.

But she wasn't. So what . . . and that's when Jeb saw three men move from between the cone-shaped shrubs behind where the fae and the warlock stood. Three men and a wolf.

Van. Leashed with silver, snarling with rage, primed to attack.

That's what Alex was trying to do. Protect her brother.

Jeb was turned toward the door as he answered, "She is a threat but right now she's being threated more."

"By who?" Tintilla demanded.

"That's what I'll find out," Jeb shouted as he dashed through the salon door, prepping to shift as soon as he knew he could get outside of the building.

CHAPTER 65

If I'd had any doubts about this individual being Vaverek they vanished as I drew closer, playing the crazy tourist to the hilt.

He barely blinked. Instead he waited, a smug twist to his lips as I drew closer and closer.

Others were scurrying away.

Thank the Great Spirits. The innocents might be safe, for a few minutes, though I doubted it'd last for long. Vaverek would find a way.

"Alex Noziak," he said, as if we were meeting under normal circumstances. "Very quick thinking. Though I expected no less from you."

So he knew who I was? Or at least recognized me, which made my skin crawl.

I lowered my hands, saving my breath for whatever I'd need to do next. "Vaverek, I presume?"

He inclined his head, not enough to break eye contact. I felt the same way, not trusting him more than I could throw him. Since he was a Were I knew it wouldn't be far.

"I did expect you to come a little better prepared," he murmured. "Very shortsighted."

I gave him a smile meant to singe him, which seemed to work very well as his brows beetled. "I see your arrogance is well earned," I taunted.

He was right. Bran was busy. Willie was as useless as donkey tits and François was MIA. But I still had my tongue, which, if my brothers were to be believed, was as lethal as any weapon they'd ever faced.

Vaverek took a moment to look around. He must not have been too worried as he turned back to me, shaking his head. "Tsk, tsk, tsk. You are playing way out of your league, Miss Noziak. A common enough error for Noziaks, it appears. Just ask your brother."

Vaverek one, me zero.

Except the rage building within me from his words helped. Then he nodded his chin toward someone behind me and I heard it. A growl. A wolf's cry of pain and frenzy.

Van.

Vaverek two, me still batting a big fat zero. Unless I could stop him. Now!

I sent a silent plea to Manlike Woman, a Kootenai woman of power who was believed by my people to be supernatural because of her ability to don male roles despite her "delicate frame". And if anyone needed to man up here, it was me when facing this Were.

I quietly started my chant.

Oh Mighty Manlike
Bring to justice the one before me.

Vaverek looked at me, a snarl darkening his face.

Make him writhe in pain and feel the harm
that he has caused tenfold.

He started morphing. His height growing larger, broader, and very furry. I chanted louder.

May the pain, the anguish, the fear he created return
Twenty times ten to him.

A Werebison suddenly stood before me. *Bison bonasus*, one of the largest animals in the world and most deadly. But I thought they'd been slaughtered to extinction. Maybe the true animal ones had been but obviously Vaverek hadn't gotten the memo.

Vaverek stood at least twelve feet high at the shoulder, his Were genes expanding the normal width and breadth of a bison, and that wasn't counting his horns. At almost a ton in weight, able to jump six feet vertically, and outrace a human running, I was facing hell on hooves.

By the Great Spirits what had I done?

He was pawing the ground as I stepped back, my throat so dry I could barely utter the final words of the Retribution Spell.

Oh Mighty Manlike
Let his punishment fit his crimes
I call on thee, so mote it be!

Nothing happened.

CHAPTER 66

When in doubt, run like hell. A new Noziak motto as I turned and scrambled away from Vaverek.

Not that he was standing still. With a bellow that shook the ground he roared after me.

Nothing that big should move that fast.

I dove through the nearest row of trees placed wide enough for me to weave among them but close enough that Vaverek's wide shoulders weren't going to easily glide through. They wouldn't stop him but they might slow him down. I had agility and that was about it.

How had the spell failed?

Backlash from using blood magic last night? Could be. Magic was a fickle bitch.

Like one of the cartoon characters my brothers and I watched growing up I threaded in and out of the trees like a roadrunner on crack. My breath was chugging, my leg muscles burning. Every time Vaverek smashed through tree trunks I gained a few seconds as I heard the thud of muscles snapping timber and the rip of roots being pulled out of the ground. At this rate I hoped to reach the simin fae before he did.

"Bran," I screamed, using precious oxygen as I bobbed in and out from one side of the wall of green, seeing Bran and Willie on one side, the parking lot on the other. I waited till I was on Bran's side before shouting again. "Bran!"

Parking lot side.

"What?"

Grass side.

"Release the spell."

Parking lot.

My plan was born of desperation.

"When?" Willie shouted, which told me Bran was either resisting or using everything he had to contain the spell.

Grass side.

"When I say."

Parking lot.

Why couldn't the French have planted thick-limbed trees instead of wimpy ones? Vaverek was tearing through the twenty-foot trees like a St. Bernard puppy through petunias.

Grass side.

"Ready?" I called, so close I could see Bran's strain from holding the limbs of the simin fae rigid, and Bran could probably hear my chugging breath. I mentally asked the faes forgiveness for what I was about to do.

One more round between shrubs. Grass side. Parking lot. Grass.

"Now! Run. Everyone run!" I raced toward Bran, grabbing his arm to catapult him out of the way and break the spell. But he'd already released it.

I could hear the high pitch of the fae screaming in their natural tongues.

"Run!" I screamed again, waving my arm at them to get them to move, but they wouldn't listen.

In the blink of an eye Vaverek was on them, mowing them down like bowling pins. One threat gone. Now they couldn't imprison Bran.

Bran and I flew to the left, Willie to the right.

Vaverek stumbled, his forelegs bending but not stopping.

I scrambled to my feet, clutching at Bran. "Go. Go. Go."

He didn't need the encouragement. Willie was on his own, but he had a Were's speed so was better able to escape.

"Where to?" Bran shouted next to me.

"The building." The only place we might form a defense against Vaverek. I glanced over my shoulder to see where he was and groaned. He was already wheeling around and pawing the ground for a new charge. The building was the only option but it was a good forty feet away. And I had no idea if we could even get in.

One thing at a time.

That's when I heard the cry. A howl of pain. A wolf's roar. Van?

I skidded to a stop, Bran whipping past me, shouting, "Come on."

"It's Van." But where was he?

I looked around, noticing the others. Must be Weres, not humans, as they had been racing toward where Bran had been. And Vaverek still was, which had everyone double-timing backwards.

Vaverek was in such a rage he didn't seem to care who he was took out as he gored the nearest Weres, several in the process of shifting.

Bran ran back to me, grabbed my arm, and tried dragging me along, but I was digging my feet in.

"There!" I spied Van, in wolf form, chained between the doctor man and another, straining against the silver chains binding him. But silver against a shifter meant it was pointless. Vaverek and a dozen Weres were between him and us.

CHAPTER 67

I was Van's only chance. The only one who might be able to stop him. "I've got to go back," I shouted at Bran, still playing protective caveman warlock as he wrapped his arms around me, dragging me toward the building.

"He'll kill you."

"He'll die without me."

And that's what it was coming down to. I knew Vaverek had Van drugged. I knew Van had been programmed. I knew my brother was out of his mind.

But if I didn't try to reach him, there was no hope.

I twisted toward Bran, for once not wanting to slug him as much as make him understand. At least he'd stopped, which gave me hope. "Can you cast a containment spell?"

"To stop a raging Werebison?"

"No. I'll handle him. You keep my brother from harming anyone."

He looked past me, indecision written all over his face. "Please," I said. "Help me."

His face tightened, as if at war with himself, then he released me. His

voice a low growl. The sound of a pissed off warlock. "If you can't stop Vaverek you get out. Understand?"

I nodded, too choked up to do anything else. Bran released me and started running at an angle to intercept Van. It also meant he was moving toward the other Weres. My goal was clear then. Get Vaverek to attack me. Get the Weres to do the same. Give Bran the space he needed.

One thing at a time.

I stood in the middle of the grassy lawn and started jumping up and down, waving my arms. "Here, fur-butt," I called to Vaverek. "I'm over here you big dumb cow!"

Since bison were not bovines, I figured the insult would work. And it did. A little too well as he dug in those powerful front hooves churning up the grass as he rocketed my way.

No material for a banishing spell. My reverse punishment spell had sizzled. What was left?

Not time, that was for sure.

The building behind me? That was a copout and left Bran exposed. What was the Noziak motto? Do the unexpected. Which was a given considering we were all pigheaded and not because my dad was a pig farmer.

Mind made up I started running toward Vaverek. Closer. Closer. Closer. Until I could smell his furry stench, see the foam around his nostrils, the hatred in his eyes. Damn, he was huge!

But I kept running straight toward him, my heart in my throat, my skin iced with fear, until I was within a few feet and then I hurled myself to the side.

He raced past so close the wind of his passage slapped against me.

I landed with a tumble and roll, the earth rattling my bones. But I was still alive.

For now.

As I staggered to my feet I heard a familiar voice call from the tree line. "Alex? Over here!"

I turned to see Kelly waving at me, backed by Jaylene, Mandy and Vaughn. No Stone, not that I expected him.

They'd come. My team was here.

But what could they do except get killed? I wanted to shout run, hide, protect yourselves, but instead I pointed to where the Weres were circling Van.

"Get them."

Vaughn nodded and that's all I needed.

I turned back to Vaverek who'd sprinted past me with so much force and speed he was now a good twenty feet away. That's what I needed. Some maneuverability.

Seeing Kelly had given me an idea. It was a long shot and a spell I'd only tried once before, but I didn't have a lot of options.

I planted my feet wide, said a quick prayer to the Great Spirit to protect my back while I focused one hundred percent on the threat in front of me and started my chant. Out of the corner of my eye I could see two Weres racing toward me from the side furthest from my team.

Ignore them. Focus. I swallowed deep.

Defluo modo.
I call the chameleon to me now.

Vaverek shook his mangy head, slobber raining every direction. The Weres were shooting closer.

Recedo nunc.
He shifts, he changes, he blends

The Werebison lowered his massive head and shoulders. Another ten feet and the Weres would beat him to me.

Defluo modo
I change as he, to fit my need.

Hooves to ground he started pounding. A mass of muscle, speed and menace tearing toward me. I licked my lips and sucked in a deep breath to say the last lines, holding one hand out as if it'd stop the Weres almost on top of me.

Recedo iam
My corporeal self you can not see.
I thee will it, so mote it be!

Magic washed against me, staggering me back hard enough I stumbled and fell, landing on my backside.

Thank whoever watched out for fools and inept witches, my less-than-graceful tumble meant the Weres raced right past where I'd been.

The damn Invisibility spell worked.

I was so busy giving myself a mental yippie-kayee I almost forgot about the one-ton monster barreling down on me.

Almost.

With a choking cry I rolled away from Vaverek's hooves, so close I could feel the clods of earth pelting me as he chewed past.

Too near.

But we weren't done fighting yet.

I looked over to where Bran stood, hands stretched toward Van, freezing my brother and the two handlers with him. Good.

Jaylene, Mandy and Vaughn were not having as easy a time of it as they danced in and out of a pack of Weres attacking them. The Weres had not morphed, probably because they'd be too visible to any Council members looking out from within the building. A quick glance in that direction and I could see shadows at the second floor window.

Yup, my hunch was right. Van's drugged state was to look like a shifter run amuk and attacking humans. Which made it necessary that the Weres didn't reveal themselves. Except Vaverek already had. How was the Council going to ignore a raging bison?

Their problem. Mine was still stopping him. Now. He might no longer see me but that didn't mean he wasn't still lethal as hell and looking for a new target.

Which meant Bran and my brother, or my team.

I ignored my body screaming in protest as I lurched to my feet. That's when I noticed the bullet of black-banded fur race past me.

"Dad?" The cry escaped me before I realized he couldn't see me.

The wolf paused a heartbeat, shook his head then continued to bullet toward Vaverek. Of course, wolves used to be one of the few threats against bison, but that had been when wolves hunted in packs and they attacked a young calf or ill animal for food.

Dad had already reached Vaverek, launching himself to latch onto the bison's nostrils. Shifter wolves were larger than their pure wolf brethren, which meant Dad was a good two hundred pounds of snarling, ferocious killing machine, using his forty-two teeth to exert over two thousand pounds of pressure to tear into Vaverek.

Made me want to be a shifter myself just so I could have done the same.

But right now I needed to get to my team.

Staggering across the grass I was glad I was still invisible. That way I wouldn't have to live it down that I basically limped into the fray. But I was there and I'd do what I could.

Thank Stone for teaching me enough Krav Maga. A key thrust here, sideways kick there, and a few sweeps of my invisible legs to an attacking Were here and there. It didn't take long for them to start turning on one another.

Punch. Smack. Kick, Thrust.

I felt the reverberations up every bone of my body but at least they weren't getting powerful return hits on me. Weres at the best of times are a wary lot, fighting something they couldn't see just messed with their Were-sized brains.

With a jerk of his thick neck one Were, who must have been the most Alpha one fighting, growled, "Retreat."

Yes!

Not one of the other Weres hesitated. And it couldn't have happened a minute sooner. Vaughn was curled on the ground but alive. Jaylene and Mandy were leaning against one another, blood streaming from one's nose, the other cradling her still healing arm.

My hard-pressed team assumed Kelly had been at work since she wasn't visible anywhere. Which made me wonder where she'd disappeared to.

I didn't have time to say anything as I heard the sharp crack of a rifle shot.

As if in slow motion I pivoted and watched Bran as his arms were flung out before him. Then he toppled forward, red blooming along his side.

I was running before I realized it, racing to his side, pressing my hand to staunch his blood flow, to make sure he was still alive.

He was. Barely. But his eyes were open, his lips moving. I leaned forward, reassuring him, "Don't worry. I'll get you out of here."

I didn't know how. But I'd do it.

He shook his head. Even here he didn't trust me. Then I made out the word he kept repeating over and over. "Van."

Too late I looked up to see my brother less than five feet away, his wolf lips pulled back in a silent snarl, his fur bristling, his body crouched and ready to attack.

CHAPTER 68

I raised my hands before me, using my voice to try and reach my brother's human part, if he had any left. "It's me, Van. Alex. I won't hurt you."

He maintained his crouch, his yellow eyes narrowed, focusing. Good news; he hadn't immediately attacked. Maybe I could connect with him.

"I want to help you. Protect you from the people who did this to you."

The same people I'd seen scampering off the second Bran's containment spell broke. One of them, the doctor who'd been with Philippe Cheverill the night he'd died, paused long enough to shake his head before he disappeared through the shrubbery toward the parking lot.

Cowards the lot of them.

Behind me I could hear my father still attacking Vaverek. Another sound reached me. A barking dog.

François? Finally. If I ever got out of here Fido and I were going to have a few words and not of the hey-how're-you-doing kind.

But right now I had to keep my brother from going ballistic.

"It's me Van," I repeated, my voice not betraying the terror racing through me. Bran needed help. Now. "We can all walk away if you just go easy, Van."

Usually not a problem, of my brothers, Van was the calmest, the most controlled in wolf form or human. But I couldn't see an ounce of humanity in the raging-yellow eyes staring at me.

Not at me. At my bloodied hands in front of me. Talk about stupid with a capital S. The invisibility spell had held, except for where my hands had touched Bran's blood. So here I was, speaking in the voice of his sister but not looking like her, holding bloodied hands in front of a rabid wolf as if I were a hunk of raw meat.

I had to turn visible.

Now.

My lips were so dry I croaked as I started the reversal chant.

Animadverto, percipio, specto.
See and be seen. I thee seek.
As I was, so make me be.
Intellego aspicio sentio.

The magic flowed around me, strong enough to fluff the hair along Van's back and there I was, hands beneath the blood, arms attached to the hands, attached to me.

At last, something went right.

Until I realized popping back into visibility solved one problem only to create another. A more lethal one.

I'd surprised Van and the last thing you wanted to do to an angry wolf was startle it.

He made no sound as he sprang forward, all hundred and ninety pounds of him slamming me to the ground, his teeth piercing my shoulder.

CHAPTER 69

Bran rolled to his good side, sucking in a deep breath as the pain from near his ribs spiraled through him. But he had to do something.

A voice shouted. He had to move.

Bracing one hand against the ground, the sounds whirling around him became more distinct as clarity returned to his sight.

But what . . .

Alex was tumbling across the grass not far from him, her arms locked around the throat of a wolf, its muzzle covered in blood.

If he cast another containment spell now he'd freeze both together in a death struggle. If he didn't act, she'd die.

A bellows nearby echoed across the lawn. Van paused in his attack, both Noziak siblings glancing in the direction of the cry.

Bran didn't have to twist to see a large dark-haired wolf rip into the side of Vaverek, savaging the bison, pulling entrails until the large animal's legs gave out and it shuddered to the ground.

Alex used her brother's distraction and thrust her knees to her chest, wedging her feet against the belly of the wolf and catapulting him toward Bran.

Brilliant.

Before Bran could rise to his feet he stretched one hand toward Van and uttered the chant, feeling the magic pull from within him, channel down his arms and through his fingers.

The wolf froze in mid-leap. Alex curled into a fetal position and Bran sank to the ground, crawling toward Van.

If he could save Van he'd save Alex.

Using elbows and knees he pulled himself until he was almost on top of the wolf, who lashed out at him.

Too weak to hold the spell solid, he had given Van just enough juice to lunge toward him. Now Bran was the one fighting for his life, rolling over and over through the grass and gravel.

CHAPTER 70

I sank to the dirt, burning pain ripping through my shoulder where Van had savaged me. Blood streamed from between my fingers, the ones I pressed to stop the flow.

Useless. As useless as trying to save him in the first place. The beast that attacked me was not my brother. Not even human.

Screams and shouts echoed around me. My back was against the crushed gravel of a walkway, the soft blue of a French sky overhead. I could lose myself in that sky, let it waft me away on one of those big puffy clouds.

That's when I noticed the contrails intersecting the expanse. The form of a cross. Well I'll be damned, Jaylene had been right. Beware the sign of the cross.

If it didn't take so much energy I'd have laughed.

But it hurt too much. Way too much. It was easier to just lie there. Feel my life seep away, my breathing become shallow, my heartbeat slowing.

Fight. Don't give in.

The voice slashed against me. I ignored it.

In a minute I'd move . . . figure out what to do, help the others.

But I couldn't do anything right then. Too cold. Too empty. Sounds around me grew softer and softer.

A face suddenly loomed over me, blocking the sky with its shadow. A small Were by its smell, breathing heavily, and dripping moisture from his half-morphed mouth. A part-man, part something else. A meerkat?

Stubby in size, yellowish-brown fur. Sort of like an elongated rat or woodchuck. Not as dangerous as the other Weres rampaging through the park grounds.

Weren't meerkats supposed to protect villagers from the mood devil; another name for Weres? Frau Fassbinder would love the irony.

Thoughts flitted here and there. Memories. Regrets. The might-have-beens. I struggled up through the fog growing thicker around me.

The Were looked over his shoulder. "She's still alive."

Not for long, rat face. I'd show him.

"Good." Another voice rolled over me, deep timbered and unfamiliar. "He wants her in one piece.

He?

The meerkat's chuckle rasped along my nerve endings. "Not sure she'll stay in one piece with a shifter's bite. Probably die."

"She could turn."

"Nah, most females don't make the transition."

I wanted to shout, I'm here. I can hear everything you idiots are saying. But no words came.

Just as well. My brothers always told me my mouth was my biggest weapon, one that backfired more than helped.

Van? What happened? And Bran?

As if I'd spoken aloud the meerkat glanced to the near distance beyond where I lay. The last direction from where I'd seen Van. "You see that wolf shifter? Brown and black pelt?"

"Yeah." A harsh chuckled was followed by, "He ain't moving now."

They couldn't mean Van.

The meercat shook his head. "Doesn't look good."

"Dead?"

Noooooo.

"*Oui*. Other one's not in much better condition. What was he? Mage?"

"Warlock. He wasn't supposed to survive. Only her."

The meerkat glanced back at me. "Then we best get going with her. She dies and it'll be our heads."

Hands reached beneath me, spiking the pain till I screamed out.

Van was dead. Bran had killed him.
Nothing left.
I welcomed the darkness.

CHAPTER 71

Where the bloody hell was she?

Bran glanced over to where he'd last seen Alex's body, crumpled and bloody, but she was no longer there. Had she only been slightly wounded by Van's attack and managed to get away?

Not likely. Not from what he'd seen. So where was she?

François was still battling Weres over by the *saut-de-loup*, herding them like a sheep dog until they tumbled into the drop. The trench on the other side wasn't going to hold them for long, but they'd be out of sight as soon as the human gendarmes arrived. Which they would. Any moment.

Alex's team had limped away. Humans, even with strong abilities, didn't fair well when matched against Weres and fae in their human forms.

Bran knelt beside Alex's brother, aware the only thing keeping the wolf from killing him was the most recent containment spell Bran had managed to cast. A weak one except it was tainted by the blood coating Bran's side.

If he moved the spell would break, which would unleash Van on anyone in the area. But everything inside him screamed to find Alex. She needed him. Now.

Whether she ever admitted it or not.

Out of the corner of his gaze Bran caught the flash of a cinnamon wolf with black bands racing toward him. Friend? Or enemy drawn by the scent of blood?

Didn't matter as Bran struggled to his knees, the better to brace for an attack.

Something about the black striping the wolf's tail seemed familiar. An earlier attacker? Or . . .

The wolf pulled up short about three meters out, crouched, his eyes golden bright, his lips stretched back into a growl that raised the hackles along Bran's skin.

But while it was Bran being threatened the animal's gaze kept shifting to Van as if trying to figure out why the other wolf wasn't moving, except for his eyes spitting fire.

"You a friend?" Bran asked, using his one free hand to point to Van. "You know Van? Know this wolf?"

Just then a gunshot sounded. A spilt second later Van yelped.

What the—

Van sprang back as if propelled then folded, a puddle of blood pooling around him.

A quick glance around didn't show a threat. Must have been a sniper, targeting Van specifically. The same one who'd hit Bran no doubt.

Bran leapt forward but the other wolf was there first. The growling changed tone, not enough to have Bran trust but enough to give him hope.

The containment spell was broken. When he felt for a pulse on Van's neck, nothing.

"I need help." He nodded toward Van, willing the other wolf to understand. "Now."

The growling stopped.

Bran waited. He didn't have enough left to fight the cinnamon wolf so the ball was in his court.

In the blink of an eye the wolf shifted, leaving an older man, fully clothed and with the dark hair and skin tones of Alex. Bran hadn't associated with a lot of shifters but knew power when he saw it. Plus the ability to transform clothes was very rare.

"What did you do to him?" the other man said, his tone hostile and brutally curt. The wolf form might be gone but not the threat.

"Nothing. Sniper." Bran glanced at Van. Having one Noziak to deal with was a full time job. Now having three was enough to fry anyone, even a warlock. "I can save him but need your help."

"Why would you help him?" the older Noziak demanded, his eyes still looking part wolf.

"For Alex," he said simply. Sometimes the truth was the best option. Then he added, "She's been doing everything in her power to find and save her brother. If I let him die she'll kill me."

The older man seemed to grapple with something.

"I have less than a few seconds to save him."

"Do what you need to do." Noziak came to a decision. "How can I help?"

"Watch for others."

"What others?"

"The gendarmes are coming."

The older wolf glanced around. "Shortest way to a safe exit."

Bran nodded toward a line of cone-shaped shrubs. "I have a car beyond there. Safest and quickest route out."

"So you know who I am?"

"A Noziak."

A curt nod. "Get started."

Bran hesitated, knowing how much energy what he was about to do would take. Alex's father might have two corpses on his hands.

Still he slowed his breath, closed his eyes and laid his hands, blood and all on Van's side. The fact he was still in his wolf form might help. If Bran could pull one part of Van back from the dead, the other would follow.

Anima. Vita. Fiducia.

He tried again, pushing his energy harder.

 Mortifer. Mortifer. Mortifer.
Anima. Vita. Fiducia.
Fiducia. Fiducia. Fiducia.

Beneath his fingers a faint pulse. Van was alive. For now. He'd take what he could.

"Does he live?" the older Noziak demanded.

Bran managed a weighted nod.

"Good. We'll talk more." the other man barked his voice all business. "Where's Alex?"

"I don't know. She was here. Then . . ."

The world grayed slightly then solidified.

The senior Noziak looked like he was going to say something then lifted his head in attention. "They're coming. No time now."

Bran rallied. "Can't trust that he'll survive being moved."

Noziak bit off an oath. "I'm stronger than he is. Let him go. I'll take responsibility to keep him calm."

Bran would be glad to keep Van from killing anyone else, not that it was likely given his condition. With a reluctant nod he eased away from Van.

The older man lifted his son, still in his wolf form, and slung him over his back. "Ready," he grunted.

"Let's get out of here."

Bran took one last look for Alex but couldn't see her among the chaos and dead bodies. If she had died though he'd know. Wouldn't he? Across the field he could see the members of her team limping toward the parking lot, so at least they lived. Still no sign of Alex as he followed her father and brother to his own car.

Where the hell was she?

One step at a time. Save her brother, or at least get him stabilized. The second that happened, Bran would turn his attention to Alex. He'd find her. No matter how many people he had to expose and destroy to do so.

CHAPTER 72

Ling Mai picked up her phone by the second ring, recognizing the numbers she had memorized. The male voice on the other end sounded smug, which wasn't unexpected.

"We have her," he said.

Ling Mai nodded though no one could see her. "Any complications?"

"No."

"Her brother?"

"He has escaped."

"That could cause both of us problems."

"Not to worry. I shall see to him personally."

"Then my part is done. I'll expect payment as agreed."

"I understand."

She hung up the phone, cast a half glance at the folder on her desk and sighed. A shame. But one must be willing to sacrifice when needed.

Her fingers rested on the file for a moment then removed it to the credenza behind her before buzzing M.T. Stone.

He answered so quickly it was easy to believe he had been waiting for the news.

"Alex Noziak is dead," she said.

"Verified?"

"Yes."

He hung up.

Phase two was about to start.

THE END

FROM THE AUTHOR

Thank you for reading about Alex Noziak in this novel and I hope you enjoyed her story! I'd appreciate your sharing your feedback via Amazon, Goodreads, or with fellow readers. Books are discovered by the willingness of great readers to share with others.

I also love hearing from readers! Find me on Goodreads or Facebook or Twitter!

WANT TO READ MORE ABOUT ALEX NOZIAK AND THE INVISIBLE RECRUIT TEAM?
CHECK OUT:

INVISIBLE PRISON (novella) http://www.invisiblerecruits.com/books.html#prison Discover how Alex Noziak became an Invisible Recruit team member and at what cost to herself, and those around her.

INVISIBLE MAGIC (full length novel)
http://www.invisiblerecruits.com/books.html#magic On her first official mission for the Invisible Recruit Agency Alex Noziak discovers that to save the innocent she must call upon her untested abilities. But at what cost? She has nothing to lose, except her life.

INVISIBLE DUTY (novella)
http://www.invisiblerecruits.com/books.html#duty On her first official mission for the Invisible Recruit Agency Alex Noziak discovers that to save the innocent she must call upon her untested abilities. But at what cost? She has nothing to lose, except her life.

INVISIBLE FATE (full-length novel) (coming Fall 2013)
http://www.invisiblerecruits.com/books.html#fate Alex Noziak will find out who her friends and who her enemies are. Nothing is clear as she faces a powerful Druid who is using her magical powers to release a three-thousand year-old demon on the world.

ABOUT THE AUTHOR

Mary Buckham is the author of WRITING ACTIVE SETTING: Book 1 and Book 2; http://www.marybuckham.com/nonfiction_books.html the best selling book in a three-book series on the craft of writing; co-author of BREAK INTO FICTION™: 11 Steps to Building a Story That Sells, and now the amazingly well-received INVISIBLE RECRUIT Urban Fantasy series.

When not conjuring preternatural beings, and figuring out how to eliminate them, she lives in Washington State with her husband, and is hard at work on more stories of the Invisible Recruits.

www.MaryBuckham.com
www.InvisibleRecruits.com